The Adventurer's Guide to Dragons
(and Why They Keep Biting Me)

WADE ALBERT WHITE

Illustrations by **MARIANO EPELBAUM**

LITTLE, BROWN AND COMPANY

NEW YORK BOSTON

Text copyright © 2017 by Wade Albert White
Illustrations copyright © 2017 by Mariano Epelbaum
Excerpt from *The Adventurer's Guide to Treasure (and How to Steal It)*
copyright © 2018 by Wade Albert White
Illustration from *The Adventurer's Guide to Treasure (and How to Steal It)*
copyright © 2018 by Mariano Epelbaum

Cover art copyright © 2017 by Mariano Epelbaum. Cover design by Karina Granda.
Cover copyright © 2017 by Hachette Book Group, Inc.

Little, Brown and Company
Hachette Book Group
1290 Avenue of the Americas, New York, NY 10104
Visit us at LBYR.com

Originally published in hardcover and ebook by Little, Brown and Company
in September 2017
First Trade Paperback Edition: August 2018

Little, Brown and Company is a division of Hachette Book Group, Inc.
The Little, Brown name and logo are trademarks of Hachette Book Group, Inc.

The publisher is not responsible for websites (or their content) that are
not owned by the publisher.

The Library of Congress has cataloged the hardcover edition as follows:
Names: White, Wade Albert, author. | Epelbaum, Mariano, 1975– illustrator.
Title: The adventurer's guide to dragons (and why they keep biting me) /
Wade Albert White ; illustrations by Mariano Epelbaum.
Description: First edition. | New York : Little, Brown and Company, 2017. |
Sequel to: The adventurer's guide to successful escapes. | Summary: Anne and
her best friends Penelope and Hiro are tasked with an unwanted quest that
could start a war between the Hierarchy and the dragon clan, and so to avoid
disaster and save the world, the three friends must face dragon trials,
defeat robots, and circumvent bureaucracy.
Identifiers: LCCN 2016051848| ISBN 9780316305310 (hardcover) |
ISBN 9780316305297 (ebook) | ISBN 9780316311526 (library edition ebook)
Subjects: | CYAC: Dragons—Fiction. | Robots—Fiction. | Magic—Fiction. |
Adventure and adventurers—Fiction. | Humorous stories. | Fantasy.
Classification: LCC PZ7.1.W448 Add 2017 | DDC [Fic]—dc23
LC record available at https://lccn.loc.gov/2016051848

ISBNs: 978-0-316-30532-7 (pbk.), 978-0-316-30529-7 (ebook)

Printed in the United States of America

LSC-C

10 9 8 7 6 5 4 3 2 1

This book is dedicated to
the third person on your left.
Please let them know.

· CONTENTS ·

Definitely a Prologue

At Saint Lupin's Quest Academy for Consistently Dangerous and Absolutely Terrifying Adventures, every student is treated with the same amount of care and consideration. They are each provided with eight brand-new sets of pants and tunic (one for each day of the week plus a formal set for special occasions), two pairs of well-made shoes, and a yellow cloak with CAUTION: STUDENT ADVENTURER printed in large letters on the back. Each is fed a well-balanced diet and required to bathe every day—always just before heading off to bed for a good night's sleep. This treatment, incidentally, is consistent with the advice given in the popular do-it-yourself guide *How to Train Students for Adventure (and Their Inevitable Untimely Deaths)*.

Understandably, potential recruits count the days until they can apply. And in that spirit, it is widely recognized that there are three ways to enroll at Saint Lupin's:

1. Submit an application form, filled out in triplicate and certified by a squirrel.

2. Sneak in by swimming the moat. (Tip: Beware the zombie sharks.)

3. Obtain an official questing gauntlet and become a Keeper of the Sparrow, illegally activate a Rightful Heir quest, get chased by iron knights and fireballed by a dragon, destroy your quest academy, cause widespread mayhem and destruction, successfully complete the quest, become heir to your very own kingdom, and offer the academy use of the aforementioned kingdom as its new campus. (Please note: Thus far only one student has gained admittance using this method, and she doesn't recommend it.)

Once accepted, of course, there are only two ways to leave:

Pass or fail.

The Sapphire Palace

Anne was leaving Saint Lupin's.

The annual Quest Academy Awards were being held that evening in the Hierarchy's capital, and Anne and the other members of her adventuring group had learned they were nominated in the category of Best Illegal Quest That Nearly Destroyed the Entire World. The category wasn't as prestigious as Longest Duel with a Rabid Pumpernickel, but it was certainly preferable to Most Spectacular Protagonist Death, since you actually had to die in order to be eligible—meaning they buried the award with you (or whatever was left of you). Award nominees enjoyed a fancy lunch at the royal palace, got front-row seats to the awards ceremony, and were invited to a host of after-parties where people sat around on uncomfortable chairs, held drinks decorated with little umbrellas, and pretended to like one another. It was quite an honor.

There was only one problem: Anne didn't want to go.

Or more accurately, she didn't want to go if it meant wearing her new formal academy dress uniform.

Anne winced as a needle jabbed into her thumb.

"My apologies, dear," said the woman standing next to her. Her name was Jocelyn, and she was for all intents and purposes the headmistress of Saint Lupin's Quest Academy (if you overlooked the fact that, according to the official paperwork, the actual headmistress was an orange-and-white cat named Her Royal Highness Princess Fluffington Whiskers of the Mousetrapper Clan, who was currently sleeping atop a cushion on the desk next to them). Jocelyn had dark brown skin, a head of voluminous, meticulously styled black hair, and twinkling brown eyes.

Anne always noticed people's eyes, mostly in hopes of someday finding others with yellow eyes just like her own.

They were in the academy's main office, an octagonal

room lined with wall-to-wall shelves and three large stained-glass windows. Anne was standing on a stool, trying to remain as still as possible, while Jocelyn fussed and fidgeted with her new formal uniform, which had only arrived that morning. Anne watched as a tiny bead of red formed on her dark brown skin where Jocelyn had poked her. She pressed a finger over it to stop the bleeding. Apparently, a quest academy could be a dangerous place even if you were just getting dressed.

Jocelyn regathered the loose material of Anne's cloak and continued jabbing at it with her needle. "I cannot believe they got your size wrong," Jocelyn said for the umpteenth time. "I sent them everyone's exact measurements. All the others fit just fine."

Given that the uniforms had arrived in a box marked HORRIBLE HENRY'S TERRIBLE UNIFORM SHOP: THE PLACE TO BUY YOUR UNIFORM WHEN YOUR BIG DAY HAS ARRIVED AND ALL OTHER OPTIONS HAVE RUN OUT, Anne was surprised anyone's had fit properly. But they had, and so her best friends, Penelope Shatterblade and Hiro Darkflame—who were the only other students at the academy besides Anne—had gone ahead to the capital while she remained behind getting hers altered.

After a few more swipes of the needle, Jocelyn tied

off a final knot and stood back. She smoothed out the wrinkles of her own bright yellow jacket, which had pearl buttons down the front and coordinated well with her light brown pants and dark red leather riding boots. As always, Jocelyn looked every bit the professional adventurer, albeit one who spent more time in the library doing research or in a well-padded gymnasium practicing her sword fighting than going on actual adventures where one might come into contact with dirt or grime or unpleasantness of any kind.

Jocelyn studied her handiwork. "I never claimed to be much of a seamstress, so hopefully that will suffice."

Anne looked down. The cloak was a sickly green and featured a wide, floppy collar and three oversized pockets. It was also several inches too long. The material bunched at her sides, and multiple threads crisscrossed one another in a haphazard pattern. The rest of the uniform consisted of a pair of stark white pants that attracted dirt like a magnet, a blinding orange tunic, and a pair of stiff leather boots that were already causing Anne's feet to blister. In addition, she also wore her most prized possession: a single brown leather glove covered in strips of overlapping metal, with a circular inset on the underside of the wide extended cuff. This was her questing gauntlet.

"So," said Jocelyn, "what do you think?"

"Er," said Anne.

"Still too loose?"

"No, that's not the problem."

Jocelyn picked up a wide-brimmed hat that featured a black veil and a large peacock feather sticking out of the top. "Shall we try the headpiece?"

Anne grimaced.

Jocelyn caught her expression. "Did I forget one of the pins?"

"No," said Anne. "It's just…"

"Yes, dear?"

"It's just…the uniform…it's…"

Jocelyn nodded encouragingly. "Yes?"

Anne sighed. "It's ugly."

At first Anne thought Jocelyn would scold her for being ungrateful. Instead, Jocelyn burst into laughter. "Oh, my dear, you're absolutely right. The whole thing is a disaster, in every way possible. The design is an affront to fashion, and the colors are giving me a headache. And even Dog would do a better job with the alterations." At the mention of his name, Dog, the small black fire lizard napping in a basket in the corner of the room, briefly raised his head. Seeing nothing of interest, he dropped immediately back to sleep.

Jocelyn tossed the hat back on the desk. "Headgear is optional. Unfortunately, there's nothing to be done about the rest. And anyway, this ridiculous outfit is not what's important. It's you, the newly minted Rightful Heir of Saint Lupin's. That's who people will be eager to meet."

"Does that mean I can wear one of my regular outfits instead?" asked Anne.

"No," said Jocelyn.

"But you just said—"

"Dress uniforms are required at such functions. Anything else would go against proper etiquette."

"Do we always have to follow proper etiquette?"

Jocelyn raised an eyebrow, and Anne sighed inwardly. Jocelyn would give up breathing air before she would give up proper etiquette.

A distant chime sounded from elsewhere in the building, and Jocelyn looked out the window. "My goodness, is it noon already?" she said. "We need to be on our way." Jocelyn belted a rapier around her waist.

Anne walked over to an eight-foot-tall suit of armor

near the door—an iron knight, one of three that belonged to the academy, or rather to Anne, since she had inherited them along with the rest of Saint Lupin's upon the completion of her first quest. They obeyed her commands, provided she was wearing the gauntlet. Curiously, they each also had a small white stone in the middle of their helmets that glowed red whenever they grew agitated. The knight by the door held a plain wooden box.

Anne paused.

"Is something wrong?" asked Jocelyn.

"Are we sure it's safe?" asked Anne. "For me to travel around wearing the gauntlet, I mean."

"Why wouldn't it be?"

Anne shifted uncomfortably. "Because the last time I put it on, it activated a Level Thirteen quest that nearly killed me and my friends and the entire world along with it."

"Hence your award nomination," said Jocelyn with a note of pride. She placed an arm around Anne and gave her shoulder a reassuring squeeze. "That gauntlet marks you for what you are, my dear: You're Anvil of Saint Lupin's, Keeper of the Sparrow."

Anne cringed at the mention of her real name. She'd been an orphan from birth, and she had always assumed whoever had named her hadn't given it much thought. All of that had changed two months ago when she discovered that beneath the academy grounds were the remains of an Old World laboratory, and inside that lab were the remains of a chamber that was inscribed with the phrase PROJECT A.N.V.I.L. Exactly what the project was and what it had to do with Anne was still a mystery, not the least because the lab had been completely destroyed in a fire, leaving no clues. In fact, pretty much everything about Anne was a mystery.

"Besides," Jocelyn continued, "it will be in its box most of the time, and in any case you've been wearing it here for the past hour surrounded by all of these." She gestured to the thousands of medallions lining the shelves of the office. Each medallion sat on a piece of padded felt underneath its own glass dome, and each contained within it a quest that could be activated by inserting the medallion into the slot of a questing gauntlet. Anne remembered only too well what had happened two months previous, when she had put on that gauntlet in this very office, only to have a tiny silver medallion fly through the air and attach itself to the slot—an unheard-of occurrence, according to Jocelyn. Typically, medallions did not insert themselves.

Anne smiled. "Thanks. I definitely want to wear it. It's just…"

Jocelyn smiled back. "Perfectly understandable, dear."

Anne gestured to the iron knight, and it followed her and Jocelyn down the long hallway, through the main lobby, and out the front doors. The grounds were empty. Although anyone could go on a quest, the academy typically accepted only students aged thirteen or older. Any orphans younger than that who had lived there while it was still an orphanage (which aside from Anne and Penelope were all of them) had been found suitable homes. The trio proceeded over the drawbridge (which spanned the moat filled with zombie sharks) and up the hill to a small observatory.

As they walked along, Anne spotted several massive islands floating in the distant sky. These were known as tiers, and the entire world, including Saint Lupin's, was made up of them. The tiers orbited a giant sphere known as the Big Glowing Field of Magick, or BGFM, and together they formed what was known as the Hierarchy.

Next to the observatory was a circle of flat stones, and lying in the grass next to the circle was a twenty-foot-long dragon with black scales, tiny wings, and a spiked tail.

At the sound of approaching footsteps, the dragon opened a single emerald-green eye.

"Hi, Nana," said Anne.

"Took you long enough," Nana replied in her low, rumbling growl.

"Anne's uniform required a few last-minute adjustments," Jocelyn explained.

Nana studied the cloak. "Are you sure it doesn't require a few more?"

"Now, now. That'll be quite enough of that," said Jocelyn. "Just transport us to the capital, if you please. We're late enough as it is. And make sure you follow along immediately. Showing up without a dragon would make us the laughingstock of the entire ceremony."

"Am I getting paid overtime for this?" asked Nana.

"The honor of being nominated is payment enough."

Nana snorted. "That's what I figured."

Anne removed her gauntlet and placed it in the box being carried by the iron knight. She tucked the box under her arm, and then she and Jocelyn walked to the center of the stone circle.

Nana reared back. "Two fireballs to the capital city, coming right up—from one highly intelligent, constantly overworked, and severely underpaid dragon."

Jocelyn opened her mouth, presumably to scold Nana again, but the dragon was faster and spewed out a ball of green flame.

While fireballs might strike some people as a rather unusual form of travel—especially if those people are standing inside a designated fireball landing zone when one arrives—it was the most common form of transportation in the Hierarchy. It was also the most terrifying. Anne had traveled by fireball a few times, but she wasn't sure if she would ever get used to it. A standard fireball took eight hours to reach its destination no matter how far away that destination was from the starting point. Because this was a special occasion, however, Nana had used premium fireballs (typically a very expensive form of travel), which were nearly instantaneous.

In a cloud of smoke and ash, the fireball deposited Anne onto a different circular stone platform. Knowing Jocelyn would be close behind, Anne moved quickly from the landing zone. She had barely stepped aside, however, when a large redheaded girl enveloped her in a bone-crushing hug.

"Hi, Pen," said Anne with a big grin. She and Penelope

had grown up together at the orphanage, and for Anne, the only thing more exciting than winning an award was the prospect of sharing it with her best friend.

"What took you so long?" Penelope asked, stepping back. "They're about to serve lunch."

Anne tugged at her cloak. "My uniform needed a lot of fixing."

"I'm pretty sure the only way to fix these things would be to burn them," said Penelope, and she tugged at the collar of her tunic. Her uniform featured a cape instead of a cloak and looked rather more disheveled. "I'm pretty sure whoever designed these was given explicit instructions to make them as hideous and uncomfortable as possible."

A second fireball landed on the platform, and Jocelyn emerged from the accompanying cloud of smoke. She took one look at Penelope and frowned. "Miss Shatter-blade! What exactly have you been up to? You're all wrinkly!"

Penelope tapped the hilt of the wooden sword hanging from her belt, standard issue for first-year students. "You two were taking so long, I figured I could kill time by training with the royal guards." Penelope was the official fighter of their three-person adventuring group, and she loved training whenever she got the chance.

"But you're sweating," said Jocelyn.

Penelope discreetly tried to smooth a few wrinkles out of her tunic.

"I think it makes her look rugged," said Anne. "Who knows, there might be a handsome prince in the audience. If he's in need of saving, she has to look the part, doesn't she?"

Jocelyn frowned but didn't pursue the matter. Anne suppressed a giggle, and Penelope mouthed her a silent thank-you.

"Where's Hiro?" Jocelyn asked instead.

Penelope's demeanor changed instantly. "He's driving everyone up the wall," she said. "Look, I know you appointed him to be the academy's liaison because he's super good at organization and everything, but he's been ordering everyone around all morning, and pretty soon someone's going to kill him and hide the body, and no one is going to mind. Thankfully, his mom and dad just arrived and told him to knock it off."

"Hiro's family is here?" asked Anne.

"Yes," said Jocelyn. "They were so excited when I sent them word of your nomination."

Anne felt a slight emptiness. Neither she nor Penelope had any living family. Anne had spent her entire life at

Saint Lupin's, and Penelope had arrived there when she was still very young, after her parents died in a quest gone tragically wrong—so wrong, in fact, that it had left a permanent black mark on their family name and had caused every academy Penelope had applied to prior to Saint Lupin's to deny her admission solely on that basis. By contrast, Hiro had attended a highly respected preparatory school before arriving at the quest academy, and Anne knew that his parents worked for the Wizards' Council.

"Isn't Nana coming?" asked Penelope.

"I'm right here," said a voice behind them.

The three of them jumped and turned. Nana was sitting in the stone circle.

"I know dragons can fly at supersonic speeds, but do you have to constantly sneak up on people like that?" asked Jocelyn, straightening her jacket.

"I don't have to, no, but it's definitely one of the perks of the job," said Nana. "Besides, there are other dragons here, and I don't want them getting the impression I've gone soft on humans or anything. I do have a reputation to uphold, you know." Despite her words, she winked at Anne as she sauntered ahead.

"Let us continue onward," said Jocelyn. "Fashionably late is one thing, but we don't want to be rude. First impressions matter, especially since a new student will be joining us today."

"There's a new student coming to Saint Lupin's?" asked Anne.

"Yes. We've received numerous applications, and now that the renovations are finished and we're ready to officially open the doors, I've begun the selection process. As wonderful as you all are, one cannot run an academy with only three students, but I think I've found someone who will be a good fit for your group. He'll be joining us at the awards ceremony and will return to Saint Lupin's with us this evening. I've not met him before, but was told he would be wearing a red cloak, so do keep an eye out."

The three humans followed the dragon across the rope bridge that connected the fireball landing zone to one of the larger main tiers of the capital. The city consisted of hundreds of tiers interconnected by bridges, ropes, ladders, and in some cases giant tree roots. Towers leaned precariously over the edges, sprawling gardens filled every space with tall trees and bright flowers, and hundreds of airships littered the sky. In the center of it all, on the largest tier, stood a castle of glowing blue stone.

"Behold, the Sapphire Palace," said Jocelyn.

It took several minutes to walk to the palace, where

they were met by Rokk, a ten-foot-tall metal man whom Anne and her friends had met during their first quest. He was an Old World creation known as a robot—a person made entirely of metal who could think and act on his own—yet another thing Anne had only learned about two months ago. A third arm protruded from Rokk's right socket, giving him a slightly hunchbacked appearance, and the word PALADIN was inscribed on his back. Rokk was the only other person Anne had met who also had yellow eyes, although his glowed as if there were a tiny fire burning behind each one.

Anne waved. "Hi, Rokk."

"According to my calculations, we are currently thirteen minutes and four seconds behind schedule," said Rokk.

Security was heavy, and they had to stand in line as the royal guards checked everyone before entering. One of the guards located Anne's name on the guest list while another tied one bright orange ribbon around her wrist and another around her gauntlet box.

"It's a matching set," the guard explained. "You can't remove the gauntlet from the premises without both ribbons. Also, your gauntlet is to remain in its box until the time of the awards ceremony. Under no circumstances should it be removed before that or a medallion inserted and activated." Anne saw several other people carrying boxes like hers who were also receiving ribbons.

The guard waved Anne through, and the rest of the party soon followed. Just beyond the security gates, there was an alcove with a large set of double doors. A plaque above the doors read:

MINE ENTRANCE

"Who digs a mine under a palace?" asked Penelope.

"The mines were here first, before it became the capital of the Hierarchy," said Jocelyn. "This whole tier is threaded with tunnels and shafts, and the walls are still embedded with gems and veins of precious metals. I hear there's even one they call the Cave of Marvel."

Instead of going into the mines, Rokk escorted the group down the palace's long central corridor. They passed other doors with plaques, including the SECRETARY OF STRAIGHT LINES AND RIGHT ANGLES, the OFFICE OF TALKING RABBITS WHO WEAR TINY WAISTCOATS, and even one labeled the UNNAMED DEPARTMENT. Eventually they arrived at a spacious dining hall packed with people and dragons. While Nana lumbered off to join a boisterous group of dragons in the corner, everyone else followed Rokk over to a table at the side of the room. Here, a small crowd had gathered around a short woman dressed entirely in black. She had tan skin and shoulder-length gray-black hair, and she was in the middle of telling a story.

"...so I simply hung him out of the window until he confessed," said the woman.

Everyone laughed. Everyone, that is, except for a boy at the table with light beige skin, brown eyes, and long dark hair tied back in a ponytail, who at the moment looked thoroughly disgruntled.

"Mother," said the boy, "your work for the Wizards' Council is classified. You're not supposed to talk about it!"

"Nonsense," said the woman lightly. "What's a harmless story among close friends? Besides, they all know if they share even one word of anything I've said, I could kill them with my pinkie finger." She spoke with a smile, but her eyes held a glint of iron.

After another, slightly more subdued wave of laughter, the group melted away into the larger crowd. The woman seemed not to notice.

Anne and Penelope took seats next to the boy.

"Hi, Hiro," said Anne.

Hiro nodded glumly. He was the wizard of their adventuring group, but he wasn't a big fan of actual adventures.

The places were already set, and the table was piled high with food: thick slices of buttered bread, cut vegetables, stacks of sandwiches, a ceramic pot filled with what smelled to be onion soup, and a purple juice that tasted like grapes when Anne took a sip. There were also chocolate squares and slices of cake and a basket of fresh fruit. Penelope immediately started filling her plate.

Jocelyn walked over and shook the woman's hand. "Good to see you again, Tora."

The woman beamed. "Jocelyn, you look fabulous, as always." Then she clapped her hands together. "And this must be the famous Anvil and Penelope. Or should I say *infamous*?" She winked and shook both their hands as well. "I'm Tora Darkflame, Hiro's mother. How wonderful finally to meet you both. Our agency already has an impressive file on your adventuring group, of course."

Jocelyn and Mrs. Darkflame seated themselves at the table, and Rokk stood next to the wall.

"I hear such wonderful things from Hiro about your academy," Mrs. Darkflame said to Jocelyn. "Thank you again for taking him on such short notice and for giving him such an honored placement. It's a great relief to Raiden and me to know he's in capable hands."

"That's very kind of you," said Jocelyn. "And speaking of your husband, where is he?"

Mrs. Darkflame pointed across the room. "Here he comes now."

The man in question was storming over to their table looking very agitated. He was tall and possessed what most people would refer to as a rather prodigious stomach, emphasized by the fact that the buttons of his bright green dinner jacket seemed to be straining to hold together across the middle. He also wore a ten-foot silver cape that dragged behind him.

"Did you know," Mr. Darkflame began with no preamble or introduction whatsoever, "that Jai Tigerclaw is wearing my exact same outfit, made by the exact same designer?"

Curiously, his dinner jacket had one short sleeve that ended at the elbow, exposing the dark tan skin of his arm, and one sleeve that extended long past his hand, so that every time he waved it, which was frequent in his current state of distress, the sleeve whipped around dangerously.

"I paid a lot of money to wear this 'one-of-a-kind' ensemble," he said.

24

"Don't remind me," said Mrs. Darkflame.

"And it wasn't by accident, either," he continued. "Oh, no. Jai specifically sought out Henry, asked him what I had ordered, and then requested that he make a second one. I mean, the nerve of the man! The sheer and utter gall!" Mr. Darkflame circled the table as he spoke, gesturing emphatically and forcing Anne, Penelope, and Hiro to duck repeatedly as the sleeve tip pinged off the water glasses.

"The general has just as much right to dress like an idiot as you do, my love," said Mrs. Darkflame patiently.

"But this is outrageous!" Mr. Darkflame blustered.

"It most certainly is."

At that moment, another equally agitated man marched over. Anne guessed he must be General Jai Tigerclaw, due primarily to the fact that he was dressed identically to Mr. Darkflame, right down to the long green sleeve that flew around and threatened to put out someone's eye.

"Sir, I cannot allow your insults to go unanswered," the general said. Then he pulled out a white glove and proceeded to slap Mr. Darkflame across the cheek with it. "I therefore challenge you!"

"I accept!" roared Mr. Darkflame, his eyes wild with fury.

Penelope bounced in her chair. "Oh, wow, a duel!"

Hiro merely sighed.

"Choice of weapon?" the general asked stiffly.

Mr. Darkflame snatched two utensils from the table. "Salad forks at ten paces."

"Agreed. And whom do you choose as your second?"

"Hiro can be his dad's second," said Penelope. "I'll be yours, General."

"But I don't want to duel with salad forks," Hiro protested as Penelope yanked him out of his chair. The two men walked to the middle of the room and stood back to back. The crowd eagerly created space for them.

Jocelyn rose from the table. "Gentlemen, please! Think of the children."

"Yeah," said Penelope. "Make sure we have a good view of the fighting before you start. I don't want to miss anything."

Anne was fascinated. She'd never witnessed a duel before, and as the two men counted off paces, she stood on her chair for a better view. Not wanting to hold her gauntlet box, she decided to set it on the table, but as she did so, something sharp jabbed into the back of her hand. The wooden box tumbled from her grasp and clattered to the floor, where it was immediately kicked away as people and dragons scuffled for the best position from which to watch the contest.

Anne dropped to the floor and scrambled on her hands and knees after the box, which had disappeared within the buffeting sea of legs. After ducking and dodging through a multitude of feet, she caught a glimpse of dark wood lying underneath a chair at the next table. She scuttled over, but just as she reached the box, a pair of hands grabbed it—hands that belonged to a boy who looked to be around her own age, with short black hair, light brown skin, and blue eyes, and wearing a deep red cloak.

Anne stood and brushed off her knees. "You must be the new student coming to Saint Lupin's. I'm Anne, the Keeper for our adventuring group. Thanks for rescuing my box, by the way. I was afraid it was going to get damaged."

The boy said nothing. Instead, he turned the box over several times, inspecting it closely.

"I'm sure it's fine." Anne held her hands outstretched. "May I have it back, please?"

Instead of giving it back, though, the boy pulled it to his chest, turned, and dashed away through the crowd.

THE TACTICAL GUIDE TO BASIC TABLE SETTING SAYS THE FOLLOWING ABOUT THE PLACEMENT OF THE SALAD FORK:

The salad fork has long been regarded as the most lethal of the silverware. When salad is a first course, the salad fork is laid to the left of the dinner fork. When salad is served after the main course, the salad fork is placed to the right of the dinner fork. If a duel is expected at any point prior to the salad course, however, the salad fork should be placed wherever it is most accessible.

Supplementary note: The salad fork is especially useful for stabbing people in the back of the hand to make them drop something you want to steal.

The Quest Academy Awards

Anne stood in shock as the boy ran off with her box. The box with the gauntlet.

Her gauntlet.

"Hey! Stop, thief!" she yelled.

Anne plunged into the mass of bodies, elbowing her way through and ignoring all the grunts and protests this caused. She caught a glimpse of red on the other side of a knot of people, but when she reached it, she found only a pot full of bright red flowers. She turned one way and then another, no longer sure which direction the thief had gone.

Penelope rushed over, hauling Hiro behind her.

"What are you doing way over here?" Penelope exclaimed. "You're missing everything! Mr. Darkflame lost his fork, so now he's holding off the general with a soup spoon."

Hiro touched Anne's arm. "Hey, is everything okay?"

Anne shook her head. "Someone just stole my gauntlet."

"What? Who?" said Penelope. She unsheathed her wooden sword and scanned the crowd.

"I think it was the new student," said Anne. "At least, he was wearing a red cloak like Jocelyn described."

Penelope swished her sword back and forth several times. "Just point him out and I'll give him a good thrashing."

"It's too late," said Anne. "I tried to catch him, but he got away."

"Why would anyone want to steal your gauntlet?" Penelope asked.

"Are you kidding?" said Hiro. "Anne achieved the near-impossible when she completed that Level Thirteen quest. I've been here for two days, and it's clear she's become something of a minor legend. I bet there are adventurers who would give their left hand just for a look at that gauntlet."

At the mention of "left hand," Anne glanced at her wrist, tied with an orange ribbon.

"That's it!" she said.

Anne bolted out of the dining hall and sprinted through the mostly empty corridor back to the main entrance.

Penelope and Hiro caught up with Anne as she stopped in front of the security area. The guards were still at their posts.

"What are you doing?" Penelope asked Anne.

Anne held up her wrist with the ribbon around it. "The thief must still be here in the palace somewhere. You can't take a gauntlet beyond the gates without both ribbons."

"That's smart thinking," said Hiro.

Not seeing the thief or anyone suspicious, Anne was unsure where to turn next—when the three of them were nearly run over by a wheelbarrow being pushed by a man so short that the top of his head only reached as high as Anne's shoulders. Yet for all that, he had more weapons hanging off him than all the guards put together.

"Captain Copperhelm!" Anne exclaimed.

The man looked up. "Oh, it's you three," he grumbled. Captain Copperhelm was their professor of combat and also Penelope's supervisor.

Inside the wheelbarrow lay an old, white-haired man wearing long robes. His name was Sassafras, and he was their professor of magick. He was known for nodding off

31

midsentence and had a platypus magickally attached to him instead of a left arm. Sassafras was fast asleep, but the platypus was wide awake and enjoying a tray of hors d'oeuvres.

"What's with the wizard on wheels?" asked Penelope.

Copperhelm shrugged. "He passed out from all the excitement. I was looking for somewhere to park him."

"Why is his platypus eating oyster cream puffs?" asked Hiro.

"It keeps him quiet," said Copperhelm.

The wizard stirred. "What's going on?" he asked. "Did I miss naptime?"

"You *are* napping, you nitwit," said Copperhelm.

"Oh, good," said Sassafras, and he promptly fell back to sleep.

"Captain Copperhelm, we could really use your help," said Anne.

Copperhelm surveyed the group. "Let me guess. You got caught up watching that duel in the dining hall, and while you weren't paying attention, someone stole the gauntlet."

Anne cheeks flushed. "That's not...I wasn't trying... I didn't even get to see the duel."

Copperhelm shook his head and pushed the wheelbarrow against a wall and out of the way of the security gates. "Crazy novices...no common sense...probably blow up the whole city before the day is over...and look at me...distinguished military career...undefeated in single combat...now I'm pushing wizards around in wheelbarrows and looking for lost gauntlets their owners can't manage to keep on their own hands."

Copperhelm marched over to the security gates while the others trailed behind. "There's been a theft," he said to one of the guards. "You lot are going to help us search for the culprit."

The guard looked him over. "Erm, no offense, buddy, but why should we listen to you?"

In response, Copperhelm pulled a small card out of his pocket and handed it to the guard. Anne read it over his shoulder:

EMERGENCY
TAKE-COMMAND CARD

The holder of this card is hereby granted permission to take temporary command of all security personnel, including (but not limited to) guards, soldiers, sentries, watchmen, lookouts, city watch, and border patrol.

CAUTION: NOT RECOMMENDED FOR POWER-HUNGRY MEGALOMANIACS.

When the guard finished reading, he immediately snapped to attention and saluted Copperhelm. "Y-yes, sir! R-right away, sir!" he stammered.

"That's more like it," said Copperhelm.

As the guard showed the card to his companions, Jocelyn, Nana, Rokk, and Mrs. Darkflame came running up the corridor and joined them.

"Where in the world have you been?" Jocelyn asked, sounding exasperated. "We've been looking all over for you. The ceremony is about to begin."

"The new student stole my gauntlet," said Anne.

Jocelyn's demeanor changed instantly. "Are you okay?" She began poking and prodding Anne, checking for any sign of injury.

"I'm fine," said Anne. "He got away, but we think—"

"Did you report the theft?" asked Mrs. Darkflame, cutting her off.

"Not yet, but—"

"This group is with me," said Copperhelm, indicating the security guards. "We're going to check the perimeter." He led the guards through the security gates and out the main entrance.

"Actually," said Anne, "we think he's still—"

"Rokk, will you speak with the Lord Chamberlain?"

said Jocelyn. "He's the master of ceremonies this afternoon and should be informed of what's happened—although I suspect they'll proceed with the ceremony anyway. This sort of thing is not entirely unheard of."

"Affirmative," said Rokk, and he left as instructed.

"But—"

Jocelyn turned to Mrs. Darkflame. "In the meantime, Tora, could you check with your network? No doubt your resources far outstrip those of the palace."

"Consider it done," said Mrs. Darkflame, and she headed off down the corridor.

"I'll inform the other dragons," said Nana, and she too galloped away.

"Well, then, I guess that takes care of that." Jocelyn adjusted her hair and smoothed her vest. "I'll escort you to the ceremony myself," she said. "It's being held in the Royal Library. I'm afraid lunchtime is over, but if we hurry, we should make it there just in time."

Anne's stomach growled. She'd hardly eaten a single bite.

"Adults," whispered Penelope. "What are you going to do with them?"

"What about Professor Sassafras?" asked Hiro, pointing to the sleeping wizard.

Jocelyn glanced into the wheelbarrow. "I'm sure he's

fine here. He'd just sleep through the ceremony anyway. Platypus will keep an eye on him, won't you, platypus?"

The platypus looked at them blankly, crumbs falling from its snout.

"Who is this new student, anyway?" asked Penelope.

"Well," said Jocelyn, "given the current makeup of your group and your chosen professions, I thought it wise to begin our recruitment by filling in the gaps, in order to round out the team."

Anne understood immediately. "He's a thief, right?"

Jocelyn coughed and looked slightly embarrassed.

All adventurers, whether they were Keeper of the Sparrow or not, had to choose a profession from the Bag of Chance. The most common beginning group consisted of a fighter, a wizard, and a thief. Penelope had chosen a fighter token, and Hiro had chosen a wizard, but Anne had pulled a blacksmith token out of the bag, not a thief token.

"Don't worry, dear," Jocelyn said to Anne. "I'm sure your gauntlet will be found in no time."

Anne wasn't sure at all.

After zigzagging along several lengthy corridors, they arrived at the royal library. There was another checkpoint in front of the library entrance, and they filed through the security gates under the watchful eyes of the guards. As they stepped into the library itself, Anne gasped. The vast space was filled with shelves that rose several stories, with the upper levels being reachable only by ornate (and precarious-looking) spiral staircases. Light streamed in through five tall stained-glass windows and a large circular opening on the wall above the windows, through which several dragons flew.

"There must be a million books in here," whispered Penelope as they joined the crowd milling about inside.

"Actually, the collection contains just over two million volumes," said Hiro. "That includes this main area as well as several special collections kept under lock and key." He pointed down an aisle to where several large glass cases stood in an alcove with a few select books and other knickknacks on display.

Penelope scrunched her nose. "Who locks up books?"

"Some of them are quite valuable. Others are ancient and falling apart and in need of protection. You can only see those by special request."

Other doors were visible at various points around the room, but all of them had been chained closed. Someone was taking security very seriously. Beyond a long row of study tables, they turned left down a central aisle leading to an open area where hundreds of chairs had been set up in front of a raised platform that acted as a stage. And on the stage stood—

Anne froze midstep. In a line along the back of the stage were seven iron knights. They were eight feet tall with barrel-shaped torsos and a small white stone in the center of each of their helmets, just like the ones at Saint Lupin's. Unlike the ones at Saint Lupin's, however, these were green and held long staffs in their hands rather than swords. Each knight stood behind an empty chair.

"Whatever is the matter?" asked Jocelyn, coming up behind Anne. "Why is everyone standing about in the middle of the aisle?"

Anne pointed at the stage.

Jocelyn put a hand on her shoulder. "They're absolutely nothing to worry about, my dear. First of all, you're not on a quest, so there's no reason for anyone to come after you. Second of all, those are fakes. They design new ones every year to serve as decoration, in honor of the famous Copper Knights, which explains their coloring. Come now. The ceremony is about to begin."

Anne felt only partially reassured. She knew Jocelyn must be right, but her pulse was racing nevertheless. She was used to the iron knights at Saint Lupin's, but her encounters with unfamiliar knights had taught her to be wary.

They followed Jocelyn down the aisle to the front row of chairs. At the beginning of the row, ten seats contained cards that read: RESERVED FOR SAINT LUPIN'S QUEST ACADEMY. Anne, Penelope, Hiro, and Jocelyn each took a seat, leaving six empty seats reserved for Rokk, Copperhelm, Sassafras, Mr. and Mrs. Darkflame, and no doubt one for the new student. There was a space at the end of the row large enough to accommodate Nana when she arrived as well. As the audience settled into place, three men and three women stepped onto the stage and sat in the chairs, leaving one empty seat at the end.

"That's the awards committee," Jocelyn explained.

One of the committee members, a thin man with pale white skin and only a few wisps of white hair, rose and approached the podium. The room fell silent.

"Good afternoon, citizens of the Hierarchy," he said. "I am Niles Twinkletoes, the Lord Chamberlain of the Sapphire Palace, and I will be your master of ceremonies today. So in a way, I guess you could say that makes me the LC who's an MC."

He paused expectantly but received only a smattering of polite laughter.

"Anyway," he continued, frowning slightly and clearing his throat, "it is my great pleasure to welcome you this afternoon to the seven thousand one hundred and fifty-third Quest Academy Awards."

This received a hearty round of applause, and despite her concerns about her missing gauntlet, Anne couldn't help but feel excited.

"First, committee member Liren Stargazer regretfully could not make it today, as she is currently at home with a severe case of the pixie flu. Hopefully, she recovers soon and returns to her normal size. And with that out of the way, on to business. Our first award of the day is for Shortest Quest. And the nominees are..."

The Lord Chamberlain read out three names, where they were from, and what their quest had been. The winner was an old gray-looking man who had activated a quest to find his spectacles only to discover he was already wearing them. The award was a plaque with a bronze medallion attached to it. The winner accepted the plaque graciously, and everyone applauded.

"The award is a quest medallion?" asked Anne.

"They're not real," said Hiro. "Just copies."

Anne couldn't help but notice that the man proudly

wore a black leather gauntlet, and she felt the loss of hers even more acutely.

The afternoon progressed in the same way through dozens of awards, including Best Imitation Quest, Best Invisible Quest That No One Actually Witnessed, and Loudest Quest Completed by a Mime. All the winners received bronze-coated medallions on a plaque, and they also each wore their gauntlets, some plain-looking and others quite extravagant. At no point in the proceedings, however, did anyone appear on stage to announce that the thief had been caught and to present Anne with the stolen box containing her gauntlet. Anne kept twisting around to see if by chance any of the other adults she knew had shown up, but there was no sign of them.

"Now, our next award is one of the big ones," said the Lord Chamberlain, and a wave of excitement rippled through the audience. "It's for Best Illegal Quest That Nearly Destroyed the Entire World. Typically, hard to pull off, and even harder not to get arrested for."

Anne's pulse raced, and Penelope bounced in her seat. If possible, Hiro sat even straighter than before.

"The first nominee is Max Sheepstone, former owner of the Canine Inn, who attempted to harness the power of small, yappy dogs, bless his heart. If Max wins tonight, he'll be receiving the award posthumously. Who knew poodles could explode like that? The second nominee is Tsunami Quibblebibble, of no fixed address, who accidentally calculated the correct answer to the question, How many angels can dance on the head of a pin? Although legend has it that anyone who solves the riddle will bring about the end of all life, fortunately for us, Ms. Quibblebibble immediately forgot the answer, thereby preventing certain catastrophe. And the final nominees are a trio from Saint Lupin's Quest Academy, led by Anvil, Keeper of the Sparrow, who embarked on a Rightful Heir quest that almost obliterated our space-time continuum. Incidentally, folks, this was the Level Thirteen quest we've been hearing so much about lately, so hats off to those intrepid young adventurers, since you don't see many of those.

"As a side note," the Lord Chamberlain added as he opened the envelope, "our thanks to each of the nominees for not blowing us all sky high."

The audience laughed.

"And the winner is..."

He extracted a tiny piece of paper from the envelope.

"Saint Lupin's Quest Academy!"

The crowd erupted in cheers and whistles. Anne was instantly hugged on three sides by Jocelyn, Penelope, and

Hiro. She scanned the room one last time for any sign of someone returning her gauntlet, but no one appeared.

"It's all right," Jocelyn whispered in her ear. "Just go receive your award."

As they made their way to the stage, the Lord Chamberlain continued. "Anvil is accompanied this evening by her mentor, Lady Jocelyn Abigayle Daisywheel the Third, formerly of the Death Mountain Quest Academy, and her two adventuring companions, Hiro Darkflame and Penelope Shatterblade."

At the mention of Penelope's last name, Anne caught brief snatches of muttering from the crowd. Penelope's expression was unreadable, but Anne gave her arm a quick squeeze of reassurance.

"I would also like to note," said the Lord Chamberlain as he picked up the award plaque, "that this is the first time in over fifty years that an adventuring group led by a thief has won this particular award."

That was a mistake. Anne was a blacksmith. She was about to correct the Lord Chamberlain when a commotion arose on the stage behind them.

It wasn't Jocelyn or any of the committee members.

It was the fake iron knights—the Copper Knights.

They were moving.

THE SCULPTOR'S GUIDE TO SUPERIOR STATUE DESIGN SAYS THE FOLLOWING:

When designing a statue, there are many factors to consider: what materials to use (bacon statues have a questionable shelf life), overall aesthetics (not everyone appreciates a piece covered in foot-long spikes), what purpose it will serve (for example, will it ever be used as a battering ram?), and location (the very best art reflects its environment, meaning there's no point pouring your heart into a piece that's going to spend the rest of its existence stuffed in the back of a closet).

Special Design Tip #42: Don't make statues that come to life and attack at random. People don't like that.

3

Battle in the Royal Library

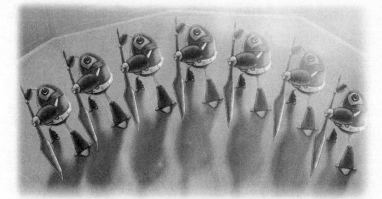

A number of things happened at once.

The Lord Chamberlain turned around and addressed the knights, "Now, see here—"

But this was as far as he got because the nearest knight extended its staff and with a loud *SNAP!* zapped him with what appeared to be a bolt of lightning. The Lord Chamberlain crumpled to the floor, and the award plaque spun out of his hands and clattered up the center aisle.

At the same time, the other knights zapped the five remaining committee members, and *SNAP! SNAP!*

SNAP! SNAP! SNAP! they all toppled on the stage. Jocelyn pulled out her rapier and surged forward, but the seventh and last knight zapped her, too, and she collapsed next to the others.

"No!" yelled Anne.

Yelling turned out to be a really bad idea. Anne instantly drew the attention of all seven knights, who raised their staffs in unison and pointed them at her. Anne gulped. She couldn't dodge them all. As the seven staffs fired as one, a large gray blur appeared in front of her. It was Rokk.

The seven bolts struck Rokk square in the chest and encompassed the robot in a sphere of light. The blast hurled Rokk from the stage and over the audience. He landed with a thunderous boom at the back, crushing several of the study tables and scattering floor tiles in every direction. The force of the blast also knocked Anne, Penelope, and Hiro off the stage. They landed hard and skidded into the front row of chairs. Cries of fear and anger rang out from the crowd, but seeing what had just happened to the committee members and the giant robot, no one seemed eager to rush forward and challenge the knights.

Someone stepped up to the podium. Anne immediately recognized his red cloak. It was the thief who had stolen her gauntlet. In fact, he was wearing her gauntlet on his left hand. Without thinking, Anne jumped to her feet, but Penelope and Hiro grabbed her arms and held her back.

The boy raised his hands. "Quiet, please!"

The room fell silent.

The boy motioned toward the Copper Knights with the gauntlet, and just like the iron knights at Saint Lupin's, they obeyed. They stepped forward to the front of the stage with their staffs held out, blocking anyone from reaching the prone forms of the committee members and Jocelyn. The Copper Knights made no further hostile moves, but the message was clear: Try anything and you will join the victims.

"I'm sorry for the interruption," the boy continued, "but if everyone would cooperate, I promise this will all be over shortly. I'm going to ask you to make your way out of the library. Right now. Single file. You've seen what the knights are capable of, so please don't test them. They will not hesitate to shock anyone who fails to cooperate. The blast isn't lethal, but I assure you it is very, very unpleasant."

A wave of relief washed over Anne. Jocelyn and the others were alive. That was the most important thing, even if it didn't make Anne less angry about what the boy was doing.

The Copper Knights stepped down from the stage and moved toward the crowd. Following the boy's instructions, people moved quickly toward the exit with expressions of grave concern. Anne, Penelope, and Hiro followed everyone in a single line down the center aisle, turning right at Rokk's motionless body and proceeding past the study tables and out of the library. Once everyone was outside and through the checkpoint, the knights closed the metal security gates, backed up several paces, and raised their staffs once again. Seven arcs of lightning hit the spot between the gates, and the bars momentarily glowed white. Then the knights turned and proceeded back through the library doors.

Anne held her hand near the gate, making sure not to touch it. Waves of heat rose from the metal, and she pulled her hand away.

"It's hot," she said.

Penelope gave the gates a kick, but they didn't open. "Welded shut."

As the knights tromped past the study tables, they

halted next to Rokk's prone form, and one of them stepped out of line and knelt beside him. Anne couldn't see clearly, but it looked as though the knight was doing something to the robot's head.

"Hey!" Anne shouted. "That's my friend! You leave him alone!"

The knight ignored her and continued what it was doing. Then it stood and rejoined its companions.

The boy appeared alongside the knights and knelt as well, and at first Anne thought he too was going to do something to Rokk. When he stood, however, he was holding a plaque—the award plaque for Saint Lupin's. As Anne watched, the boy pried the bronze medallion from the plaque and tried to attach it to the gauntlet. The medallion didn't seem to be sticking, however, and the boy grew increasingly frustrated. Finally, he threw the medallion and the plaque to the floor.

Then, one of the Copper Knights did something Anne didn't think knights were capable of: It spoke to the boy. The iron knights at Saint Lupin's had never spoken a single word to anyone, not even the Matron when she had run the orphanage. Anne couldn't hear what the knight said, but it didn't go over well. The boy shook his head vigorously.

"No, it has to be here," he shouted. "Now spread out and find it."

The Copper Knights hesitated, just for a second, but the boy noticed and pointed the gauntlet at them, yelling, "I said, Find it!"

The Copper Knights moved off, disappearing among the library's bookshelves. The boy glared at Anne for a moment, and then he too walked out of sight.

By this point, the audience members had broken off into smaller groups and started arguing about who should take charge of the situation. Several people pulled out cards that they claimed granted them temporary authority, but since there was more than one card, this soon devolved into a shouting match between different factions. The person who had won the award for Most Sneezes During a Quest stepped forward and tried to rally the crowd but soon fell into a sneezing fit and had to be led to the side.

Hiro walked over to one of the groups, chatted briefly with someone, and returned. "They've sent word to the royal guards, but apparently the guards are still spread out all over the city looking for your gauntlet."

Anne frowned. "I bet that's exactly what he was hoping for."

"What *who* was hoping for?" said Penelope.

"The thief. If all he wanted was the gauntlet, he could have waited until we were back at Saint Lupin's to take it when no one was looking. Instead, he stole it here, knowing the theft would keep the guards distracted, all so that he could obtain what he really came for: a specific quest medallion."

"In the middle of the ceremony?" Penelope asked.

"That's the only time they're out in the open," said Hiro. "The rest of the time they're kept under lock and key."

Anne nodded. "Hiro, you said my gauntlet is famous now. The thief probably knew he could use it to control those Copper Knights."

"But why?" asked Penelope. "Isn't the medallion a fake?"

"Yes, but maybe the thief didn't know that till now." Anne turned to Hiro. "You said the awards are copies. What are they copies of?"

"Famous historical quests," said Hiro.

"And where do they store the real ones?"

Hiro shrugged. "They're kept in various collections all over the Hierarchy. Palaces, museums—"

"Libraries?"

"I suppose. But they're all quests that have been completed already. There would be no point in trying to steal one, other than for a souvenir."

Anne looked back at the stage, and a sense of calm settled over her. "I have a plan."

Hiro muttered under his breath. "Please let her plan not involve me casting magick. Please let her plan not involve me casting magick. Please let her plan not involve—"

"Relax, it doesn't involve you casting magick," said Anne. Using magick always cost its user something, and in Hiro's case each spell he cast also had an unintended consequence, usually nothing good. "Or at least not yet, anyway," she continued. "If I can get my gauntlet back, I'll be the one controlling those iron knights, or Copper Knights, or whatever they are. Then we would only have the thief to deal with."

"So what's the plan?" asked Penelope, rubbing her hands together.

Anne pointed to the top of the metal security gate, where the arch of the corridor created a small gap. "I think I can fit through there. I just need a way up."

Penelope studied the gap. "I could try throwing you."

Anne rolled her eyes. "Why does that suggestion not surprise me?"

"If Penelope and I lock arms, we could make a bridge for you to stand on," suggested Hiro.

"Brilliant," said Anne.

After several tries, Penelope and Hiro managed to create a stable platform. They squatted so Anne could climb on. Once she had her feet firmly planted on both sets of arms, they lifted her into the air.

Penelope grunted. "You know, for a small person, you're surprisingly heavy."

"Gee, thanks," said Anne.

Anne stretched her arms as high as she could. Her fingers barely grazed the top of the gate.

"I can't quite reach," said Anne. "I hate to say it, but I think you actually might have to throw me."

"On the count of three, then," said Penelope. "One, two..." and on *three*, she and Hiro launched Anne into the air. Anne grabbed the top of the gate and swung one leg over. From there it was easy to lever her body through the gap and drop down to the other side. The rattle of the gate echoed loudly across the library, but neither the Copper Knights nor the boy came to investigate.

"Wait here," Anne whispered.

Anne crept between the study tables, her eyes scanning continuously and her ears straining for any sound whatsoever that indicated someone was nearby. If only one Copper Knight saw her, they'd all come running and she'd be caught. She moved past Rokk without stopping. As much as she wanted to make sure he was okay, she had to deal first with those knights. She scurried quietly down the center aisle and onto the stage. Strangely, the bodies of the committee members, as well as Jocelyn, had all been moved and neatly placed in a row. Had the knights done that?

At the sound of approaching footsteps, Anne quickly lay down alongside Jocelyn. The boy reappeared from behind a bookshelf and walked onto the stage. He was so focused on examining another award plaque that he failed to notice the extra body.

After he walked past, Anne rose silently, slipping the rapier from Jocelyn's sheath as she did so, and then cleared her throat. The boy whirled around and froze. The rapier was pointed at his chest.

"No talking," Anne said in a low voice.

The boy nodded.

"Good," said Anne. "Now set the gauntlet down and move back."

The boy took off the gauntlet and placed it on the stage. Then he took several steps back. If anything, he looked scared, which surprised Anne. She had expected him to be defiant. Her heart leaping for joy, she stepped forward and picked up the gauntlet.

One of the Copper Knights reappeared.

"Stop her!" the boy yelled.

The knight surged forward. Wasting no time, Anne shoved her left hand into the gauntlet and held it up, willing the knight to stop. To her shock, the knight kept coming. Anne backed away, still holding out the gauntlet. She had been so certain she could gain control of the knights that she hadn't formulated a backup plan.

The knight raised its staff.

"No!" said the boy. "You might damage the gauntlet." He held out his hand to Anne. "Give it back, and I'll order the knights to let you go."

"The gauntlet is mine," Anne said firmly. "But if you explain what you're looking for instead of threatening and scaring people, I might actually be willing to—"

She didn't get to finish the sentence. The gauntlet suddenly jerked her arm around and began pulling her in the other direction. She tried to slide her hand out, but the gauntlet formed itself into a fist so that she couldn't uncurl her fingers. She stumbled off the edge of the stage and fell to the floor. The knight lunged for her, but missed.

The gauntlet dragged Anne along the floor. It turned sharply down an aisle between two rows of bookcases, aiming for one of the glass display cases in the alcove at the other end. Anne noticed the case was vibrating violently. Moreover, an ancient-looking plaque containing an equally ancient-looking medallion was rattling against the front.

The gauntlet didn't slow down, slamming Anne into the glass display case. Despite her small stature, her momentum was strong enough to tip the case over and send it crashing to the floor. The glass shattered into a million tiny pieces, with Anne landing in the midst of it.

Anne remained very still. She was now lying in the shattered remains of the display case, but somehow the broken glass had transformed into small round beads, as if by magick, which explained why she wasn't covered in lacerations. The ancient plaque lay beside her, but its small copper medallion had broken free and lay next to it. Before Anne could register what was happening, the medallion leapt off the floor and clicked into the slot on the gauntlet's cuff.

Anne's arm spasmed, and she rolled to her knees. She tried desperately to pull the gauntlet off, even though she knew it was too late. The medallion glowed and the gauntlet grew hot. She screamed as her entire arm throbbed in pain. She heard footsteps approaching but paid them little mind, focusing all her concentration on not passing out. Gradually, the heat subsided. Anne crawled away from the broken display case and collapsed on the cool tile. When she finally looked up, she saw the boy and the seven Copper Knights standing over her.

"It has begun," said the boy.

Behind him, the Copper Knights struck their chests with their staffs.

"It has begun," they echoed in unison.

"Kill the queen," said the boy.

"Kill the queen," the knights repeated.

One of the knights stepped toward Anne. "Give us the medallion."

Anne instinctively hugged her gauntlet-hand to her chest.

"Leave her alone," said the boy. "It's too late anyway."

The knight ignored him. It reached for Anne—

—only to be knocked backward as a large dark blur dropped from above and slammed it to the ground. Nana had arrived. The knight struggled to rise, but the dragon smacked it again with her tail, driving it into the floor. The force of the impact sent glass beads spraying in all directions, and an odd-shaped one even bounced off Anne's forehead. The knight didn't move again, and Nana perched on top of it and let out a low growl.

The boy turned to the six remaining knights.

"Let's go," he said.

One of the knights hoisted the boy onto its shoulders. Then the knights ran down the aisle and with incredible power leapt through the circular dragon hole high on the wall and disappeared from sight.

As Anne lay on the floor, trying to absorb what had just happened, there was a sudden burst of light and a little rainbow-colored sparrow appeared in the air above the gauntlet.

"Wow, that was quick," said the sparrow. "Is it time for another quest already?"

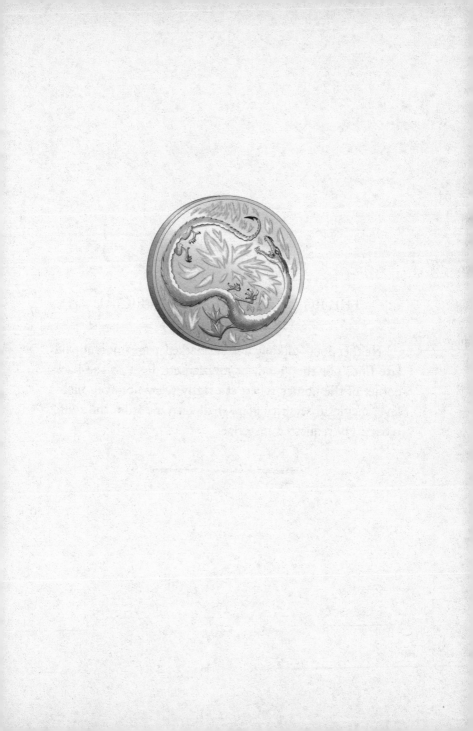

THE ROYAL LIBRARIAN'S OFFICIAL
OATH OF OFFICE:

Neither loud talking nor earmarked pages nor unpaid late fines nor the gloom of low lantern light in the back corner of the library where it's really scary nor even high-level magickal security glass shall keep me from the swift retrieval of requested materials.

The Copper Medallion

The sparrow's name was Jeffery. He was the GPS (that is, General Pathfinder Sparrow) who lived inside the gauntlet and could only appear once a quest had been activated. Usually he had to be activated with the command "Activate GPS," but sometimes he seemed to have a mind of his own. Regardless, his appearance now confirmed the sinking feeling in the pit of Anne's stomach:

The medallion was indeed real.

Which meant she had just activated another quest.

Anne stared at the medallion. The only discernible

differences between this one and the medallion from her first quest were that this one was copper instead of silver and there was no scratch across the surface. Otherwise, each medallion had the same dragon image on its face—the Sign of Zarala.

Nana crouched next to Anne. "Are you injured?"

Anne checked herself over. "I don't think so."

There was a crash of metal, and moments later Penelope came sprinting down the aisle. She fell to her knees beside Anne, scattering glass beads in every direction.

"What's going on?" asked Anne.

"Captain Copperhelm just arrived and broke open the gates," said Penelope. "He sent the royal guards after the knights, but I doubt the guards will catch them. Those knights are superfast." Penelope nudged the knight on the floor with her foot. "How did you defeat this one?"

"Nana stopped it," said Anne. She looked up at the dragon. "Thanks for that, by the way."

Nana grunted. "No one attacks the students from my academy while I'm around."

This warmed Anne's heart. Despite Nana's sometimes gruff personality, Anne knew the dragon was fiercely loyal.

Hiro ran down the aisle and joined them. "Thank goodness you're all right. We tried to figure out a way to get the gate open sooner, but we didn't want to make too much noise and draw any unwanted attention your way."

Penelope snorted. "I told him magick was quiet, but he kept going on about unintended consequences."

Hiro raised his chin. "It's a legitimate concern. Someone could get hurt. And who knows what forms of punishment they have here at the palace for spells gone wrong."

"I suspect we're all about to receive plenty of punishment," said Anne, and she showed them the medallion.

"Uh, does that mean what I think it means?" asked Penelope.

Jeffery landed on Anne's knee and waved. "Hi there."

"What...when...where...why?" stammered Hiro.

"That covers four of the five W questions," said Jeffery. "The one you're missing is *who*, but the answer to that one should be obvious."

Hiro grabbed Anne's arm, nearly wrenching it out of its socket. "Where did you get this medallion?"

Anne yanked her arm back. "Hey, take it easy. The medallion was attached to the plaque in that display case."

Hiro knelt down and examined the plaque. "This one doesn't look like a replica. I think it's authentic."

"I know," Anne said, and her sinking feeling sank even further. How much trouble was she going to be in for activating another quest? "Before he left, that boy said something about killing the queen. We'd better go inform the royal guard."

"Whoa," said Penelope. "Jeffery, what kind of quest is this?"

"It's a Dragon Slayer quest," said Jeffery.

"What?" Anne, Penelope, and Hiro said in unison, while Nana growled, "I beg your pardon?"

"A Dragon Slayer quest," Jeffery repeated. "That is, a quest whereby you slay a dragon. As in kill it. Specifically, in this case, the dragon queen."

Nana pointedly cleared her throat.

Anne felt her cheeks grow warm. "Nana, I had no idea that a quest like this even existed. I mean, I didn't even know the medallion was here. I would never have—"

"It's okay," said Nana. "I know this isn't your fault. Nevertheless, it presents a problem."

"I'm not going to kill the dragon queen or any other dragons, if that's what you're thinking," Anne said with determination. "I'll purposely fail the quest if I have to."

"I'm not worried about you," Nana said, "but you

heard the boy and those Copper Knights. They're going to try to kill the queen, even if you don't. And dead is dead."

"But it's not their quest."

"It might not be that simple. Even if they don't kill her, the simple fact that such a quest has been activated could start a war between the dragons and the Hierarchy. One way or another, I'm afraid this quest is going to cause trouble."

"Truer words were never spoken," said a deep voice behind them.

They turned to find a tall man standing in the aisle. He had white tanned skin, dark hair that was graying at the temples, and a firm square jaw. His charcoal jacket was crisply pressed, and his black leather boots gleamed. A crow perched on his shoulder. With him were the six members of the awards committee and Jocelyn.

Anne and Penelope stood.

"L-Lord Greystone," said Hiro.

"What are you doing here?" asked Penelope.

A brief shadow of annoyance flickered across Greystone's face. "It's the Quest Academy Awards. I'm the Minister of Questing. Where else would I be?"

Jocelyn seemed to be staring off into empty space, and Anne walked over to her. "Are you okay?"

"I'm fine, dear," Jocelyn said absently as she continued gazing at nothing.

Before Anne could inquire further, Hiro interrupted. "We need to send word to the dragons," he said. "To let them know what's happened."

"No one is sending word to anyone," said Greystone. "I've ordered the capital locked down. Nothing in, nothing out, until we catch the culprits responsible for this unprovoked attack."

"But a Dragon Slayer quest has been activated," said Anne.

Greystone smiled. "Which is why I'm also placing the three of you under arrest."

Anne frowned. "Arrest?"

"Dragon slaying is illegal," Hiro explained. "The Hierarchy has a treaty with the dragons, and activating a Dragon Slayer quest is a direct violation of that agreement."

"Oh."

" 'Oh' is right," said Greystone.

"But we need to stop the Copper Knights," said Anne.

She looked pleadingly to Jocelyn, who continued to remain uncharacteristically silent. "Jocelyn, tell him to let us go."

Jocelyn shook her head, as though coming out of a daze, and glared at Anne. "I'll do no such thing. Lord Greystone has every right to impose whatever penalties he sees fit. And keep in mind, any rule breaking or bad behavior on your part will show on your final evaluation."

Anne gasped. "We're still being graded?"

Jocelyn raised an eyebrow. "You're always being graded."

Anne was taken aback by Jocelyn's sudden change in demeanor. The bolt from the knight's staff must have rattled her. This wasn't like Jocelyn at all.

"As soon as the palace is secure, I'm sending you to the dungeons," said Greystone. "Until then, you three will remain in the library under guard." With a swish of his black cape, Lord Greystone turned and walked away. The committee members followed.

Jocelyn turned to go with them, but Anne grasped her hand. "Please, Jocelyn, you have to help us."

Jocelyn pulled away. "My proper title is Professor

Daisywheel, thank you very much. And you can help yourselves by doing as Lord Greystone says and staying out of trouble." She walked away without another word. Anne was flabbergasted. How could so much have gone wrong in so short a time? Her trip to the capital was definitely not turning out as she had expected.

Hiro slumped against a nearby bookshelf. "I really need to think about switching academies."

"What's the actual quest?" asked Nana.

"What?" said Anne.

Nana nodded in Jeffery's direction. "The quest riddle. It might at least help to know what exactly it is we're dealing with."

Jeffery saluted. "No problem." He hopped onto the edge of a nearby bookshelf and sang out in a rather sorrowful tune:

Forge anew the blade of fifteen fingers,
Anoint it with a true heir's final breath,
Kill not the queen of dragons on her throne,
But let wonder bring the harbinger of death.

Jeffery's last note echoed mournfully throughout the library.

" 'The blade of...' what?" said Anne. " 'Anoint it with an heir's...' what?"

"What's a harbinger?" asked Penelope.

"It's like a herald," said Hiro.

"Who's Harold?" asked Penelope.

"Not Harold. A herald."

"You mean like any random guy named Harold?"

"No," said Hiro. "I mean *a herald* as in *a messenger*."

"Oh," said Penelope, nodding. "So it's 'Let wonder bring the *messenger* of death'?"

"Exactly."

"And the messenger's name is Harold."

Hiro placed a hand over his eyes and shook his head.

"Wait a minute," said Anne. "It says *not* to kill the queen. What kind of Dragon Slayer quest tells you not to kill a dragon?"

"Technically, it only says not to kill her on her throne," said Hiro. "That could just mean don't kill her while she's seated."

"That would be very specific," said Anne. "Maybe 'on her throne' simply means 'during her reign.' "

"But if you don't kill her during her reign, then she isn't the queen anymore," said Penelope.

"That is curious," said Nana. "I'm also intrigued by

the last line. There's a saying among dragons: *May the wonders of life carry you to its closing*. It means, 'May you live a long and enjoyable life.'"

"That makes even less sense," said Penelope.

"Jeffery, how much time is there to complete the quest?" asked Anne. They had only been given four days to complete their first quest, and Anne had done so with only seconds to spare.

Jeffery cocked his head to one side. "Hmmm, that's weird. There doesn't seem to be any deadline."

"An open-ended quest?" said Hiro. "I don't think I've ever heard of that."

"And what level is it?" asked Anne.

Jeffery paused again, as though he were listening to a distant voice that only he could hear. "As far as I can tell, Level One. And there are no consequences listed for not completing it, either."

"Unless you count war with the dragons," said Hiro. "Also, I've never heard of a Dragon Slayer quest that's less than Level Eight."

"Jeffery, are you sure?" asked Anne.

"Well, if there's more information than that, this medallion isn't saying," said Jeffery. He hopped onto the gauntlet and gave the medallion a swift kick.

Anne examined the medallion again. "What does it all mean?"

"My best guess is that this quest was designed to allow the dragon queen to live out her life," said Nana. "Basically, it's a quest that kills her by means of natural causes."

"Why would anyone need a quest for that?" said Anne.

"Because as long as the queen is the object of one quest, she can't become the object of another. It effectively prevents any other Dragon Slayer quest from taking effect, thereby protecting her. It's quite ingenious, really."

"But then why does it mention a sword?" asked Penelope. "What's the point of reforging a sword that isn't needed?"

"It's standard," said Jeffery. "Every Dragon Slayer quest requires that a famous weapon be found or remade."

"But that means the queen should be safe then, right?" said Anne. "All we need to do is tell her. She wouldn't go to war over a quest like this, would she?"

"In theory, she shouldn't," Nana said. "Unless, of course, either your thief or the Copper Knights are the designated Official Antagonist. It's the job of the antagonist to work against the hero of the quest, so if your task really is to keep the queen alive, theirs would be to make you fail."

"Jeffery, who's the Official Antagonist?"

Jeffery shook his head. "Sorry, the medallion isn't saying anything anymore. It's blocking me from accessing any of the specific quest information. All I get is an error message saying this quest has been classified. Probably because Dragon Slayer quests are illegal."

A sense of foreboding swept over Anne. Here she was again, thrown into a quest not of her choosing, facing who knew what obstacles.

"What now?" asked Hiro.

Anne looked at the medallion. "Someone has to stop that thief and those Copper Knights."

"So what do we do?" asked Penelope.

Anne fought the panic rising in her chest, knowing what had to be done but wishing more than anything there was someone else around who could do it. Finally, however, she steeled herself and accepted the inevitable.

"The only thing we can do," she said with determination. "We go on the quest."

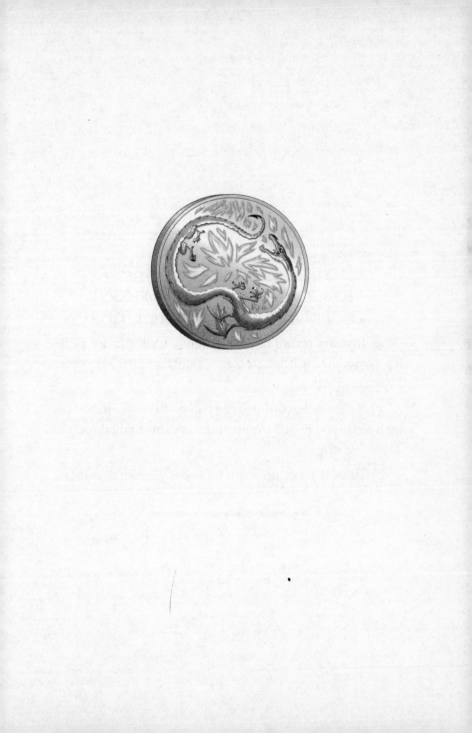

---

*THE ADVENTURER'S GUIDE
TO SUCCESSFUL ESCAPES* OFFERS
THE FOLLOWING ADDITIONAL TIPS:

4) If you're trying to escape from a well-guarded facility, sometimes it helps to create a distraction. (Side note: Fire is distracting.)

5) If the well-guarded facility in question is already on high alert, you might require more unconventional means. Try using magick.

6) Tunnels are death traps. Consider yourself warned.

5

Flight from the Capital

Go on the quest?" exclaimed Hiro. "But we'd be break-ing the lockdown. They might imprison us for life!"

Anne placed a hand on Hiro's shoulder. "I won't deny the risks, but if those knights are determined to kill the queen, then we don't have a choice. Besides, it's not like this is the first time we've done something dangerous."

Hiro groaned. "Don't remind me."

Penelope rubbed her hands together. "I'm loving it already. So what now? Do we distract the guards? Make a run for it?"

"First, we need a plan," said Anne. "Since no one else seems inclined to send a warning, that part is up to us. Nana, what's the best way to gain an audience with the dragon queen?"

"Not be on a Dragon Slayer quest," said Nana.

Anne crossed her arms. "I'm being serious."

"So am I. It's difficult to get in to see the queen at the best of times, even for dragons. This quest isn't going to make it any easier, regardless of its true nature. Probably your best chance is to present her with a gift."

"A gift?"

"Traditionally, when humans want to meet with the dragon queen, they give her a famous weapon. The idea being that before approaching her, they must first weaken themselves in some way. In return, each member of the party can ask her one question, and she'll give you a true answer."

"She can answer any question?" asked Anne.

"Yes. Every dragon monarch possesses an ability called Sight of the Seer. It grants them the power to give an accurate answer to any question, but it only works once for each person."

Anne's first thoughts were to ask the queen about

her origins, about the true meaning of Project A.N.V.I.L. Would she really get the chance?

"Where are we supposed to find a famous weapon?" asked Hiro. "It's not like they're just lying around."

Anne shook herself out of her daydreaming. "The blade of fifteen fingers," she said, recalling the first line of the quest riddle. "Jeffery said every Dragon Slayer quest had a famous weapon, right?"

"Fantastic," said Penelope.

Nana nodded. "I expect that will suffice. Find that weapon, and not only do you have something to present to the queen, you prevent the thief and the Copper Knights from acquiring it and using it against her. You'd kill two birds with one stone."

"I heard that," said Jeffery.

"I intended for you to," said Nana.

"Once we locate the weapon, can you take us to the queen?" asked Anne.

Nana shook her head. "As much as I'd like to help, I'm not permitted to participate in a Dragon Slayer quest, for what should be obvious reasons. In any case, it will be too risky for you to travel around in the open. Once you've figured out where to go, head down to the mines and take the western tunnel to the end of the line. There's a dock. I'll find Copperhelm and tell him to commandeer an airship and meet you there. I can at least do that much."

"Are you sure he'll be able to get one?" asked Anne.

Nana snorted. "At the rate he's taking command of things, he probably has ten airships at his disposal by now."

Anne wrapped her arms around Nana in a big hug. "Thanks for everything."

Nana grunted. "Don't start getting sentimental on me."

Anne stepped back, and the dragon launched herself into the air and soared out through the circular hole in the wall. As Anne watched her fly off, some of the weight lifted from her chest. They were still in a pile of trouble, no question, but at least now they had a plan.

"So how exactly are we supposed to find out anything about this weapon?" said Penelope.

Anne gestured to the rows of bookshelves surrounding them.

Penelope blushed. "Oh, right."

"I can help, too," said Jeffery. "Just let me nibble on a few juicy volumes." Jeffery absorbed the knowledge of any book he ate, and it was a constant battle to keep him from devouring anything with writing on it.

Anne shook a finger at him. "No sampling the royal library."

"But they have so many!" said Jeffery. "They're hardly going to miss one or two. Or ten. Or a thousand." He batted his eyes.

"The first line of the riddle mentions the blade, so we should probably start there," said Hiro. "The section on swords is directly above us."

He led them up the spiral staircase to the third level and located the section in question. Hiro pulled two large books off the shelf, sat on the floor, and began leafing through both of them at the same time.

"How does he do that?" said Penelope, shaking her head.

Anne selected a book for herself and handed another one to Penelope. Anne's happened to be mostly pictures, and she scanned the pages quickly. Halfway through the book, though, she noticed something troubling.

"I'm confused," said Anne. "There's a whole section here on blades that are fifteen fingers long."

Penelope looked over Anne's shoulder. "Blades are measured by fingers. Fifteen is pretty standard."

Hiro looked up from his books. "How do you know that?"

"From my training with Captain Copperhelm," said Penelope. "A blade of twelve to fifteen fingers is a typical length for short swords. A blade of thirty-five to forty-three fingers is standard for a long sword."

Hiro looked back down at the books in front of him. "But if they're that common, there's no way of knowing which one the riddle is referring to."

Anne flipped back to her book's table of contents. "If swords are measured by fingers, then how come my book also has chapters on one-handed and two-handed swords?"

"That's another way they can be classified, although it's much less common," said Penelope. "It's a reference to the length of the hilt instead of the blade, but it basically amounts to the same thing. Five fingers would equal one hand."

"So fifteen fingers would be three hands, correct?" said Anne.

Penelope laughed. "Sure, but there's no such thing as a three-handed sword."

"We won't know unless we look," said Anne.

They settled down to reading again, slowly making their way along the shelf. They read books on swords, books on sword making, and even books on sword swallowing. After several hours of searching, though, they came up empty-handed. They had gone through every book that even remotely had to do with swords, but none of them contained any information whatsoever about a three-handed weapon. It was now late afternoon, and Anne's stomach growled.

Penelope stretched out on the floor. "I told you so," she said. "Three-handed swords just aren't a thing."

Anne kept flipping pages in the book she was holding. "But it has to be. It's our only clue."

"Well, unless one of these books suddenly leaps off the shelf and miraculously opens to a page we missed about a three-handed sword, I'd say we're out of luck."

A big grin spread across Anne's face. "You're right. That's exactly what we need." She reached into the inner pocket of her cloak and brought out a thin red book with a gash in the middle of the cover that had been stitched together.

Penelope sat up. "You brought the guide?"

"I always carry it with me."

Anne had discovered *The Adventurer's Guide* in the Saint Lupin's library. It was a magickal book that provided adventurers with clues to their quests at just the right time. Unfortunately, during their first quest, the guide had been pierced by a sword and damaged. Anne had tried her best to repair it, but she had not been entirely successful.

"Is it working?" asked Hiro.

Anne looked at the cover. It currently read: *The Adventurous Guild for Cooked Broccoli.*

"Um, I'm not quite sure."

She gave the book a shake, and the title changed to *The Adventurer's Guide to Famous Weapons of the Hierarchy.*

"That's more like it."

Anne flipped open to the first page. "Listen to this," she said excitedly, and then read aloud: "The Three-Handed Sword of the Guardian is one of the most powerful artifacts left from the Old World. Forged by a bladesmith known as the Abbot of Swords, it is the only weapon capable of killing a dragon monarch." Anne set the book down and beamed. "That has to be the weapon referred to in the riddle."

"Does it say anything about where to find it?" asked Penelope.

Anne scanned the page. "No."

"That's not entirely true," said Hiro. "It says the

sword was forged by an abbot. That's the title given to someone who's the head of a monastery. If we can figure out which monastery, that would at least give us a place to start looking."

Anne closed the guide and slipped it back into her pocket. "That's enough to get us started. Captain Copperhelm is probably at the dock by now, so we should head to the mines."

They descended the stairs to the main floor and crept to the end of the aisle. They peeked around the corner toward the main entrance. Two guards were on duty.

"How are we supposed to get past them?" asked Hiro in a worried tone.

"Don't worry, I'll handle this," said Penelope, and before either Anne or Hiro could stop her, she stepped out from the end of the aisle and walked over to the guards. Anne and Hiro followed.

"And just where do you think you're going?" asked the first guard.

"We're leaving," said Penelope.

The guards looked at each other and burst into laughter.

"Says who?" said the second guard.

"Says Security Regulation 111 Subsection A. By my calculations, you've been standing here for over three hours. That means you're required to take a three-hour break to match."

Both guards suddenly looked very uncomfortable.

"We already had our break," said the first guard. "A while ago."

Penelope crossed her arms. "And you used your full allocation of time?"

The second guard hung her head. "No. We got bored of doing nothing and decided to come back on duty."

Penelope shook her head. "Disgraceful. I never saw two more useful, non-inattentive guards in my whole life. Maybe someone should talk to your commanding officer about the proper misuse of your time."

"Please," said the first guard. "We promise. This is our first offense. I don't know what came over us. Normally, I love to slack off and get paid for it. I once even won the Sleepy Soldier of the Month certificate."

The other guard nodded vigorously.

Penelope stroked her chin. "Well, we might be willing to overlook your lapse of a lapse, just this once. But we'd need to see some pretty serious loafing about."

The two guards looked relieved. "Oh, we'll get right on it, miss. We can goof off right now. I have some dice in my pocket."

"And we can walk out of here?" said Penelope.

"We never even saw you go," said the second guard.

The guards moved off to the side, and Penelope led Anne and Hiro from the library. They retraced the route back through the palace's many winding hallways and up the central corridor to the palace's main entrance.

As they walked, Anne said, "That was amazing, Pen."

Penelope puffed out her chest. "When you train with Captain Copperhelm, you pick up a few things."

"I'm impressed you knew the proper regulation to cite," said Hiro.

Penelope smirked. "I have no idea what regulation that is. But Copperhelm says most guards don't know them, either. It's all in the delivery."

More guards were milling about the palace entrance, but they either didn't spot the three young adventurers or else didn't care. Anne, Penelope, and Hiro hurried over to the alcove where the mine entrance was located. Anne tried the handle, but it didn't budge. She fished out her new multitool pocketknife (which she'd crafted after losing her old one in the eye of a zombie shark), knelt in front of the keyhole, and began picking the lock.

"Anytime now," whispered Penelope.

"I'm working on it. I'm working on it," Anne said.

One of the guards at the security gate glanced in their direction. "Can I help you kids with something?"

The lock clicked.

"Got it," said Anne, and the door swung open.

"Hey, stop!" yelled the guard. "That area is off-limits!"

The three adventurers quickly slipped through. Anne closed and locked the door again just as the guard grabbed the handle outside.

On the other side, they could hear the guard yell, "Somebody bring the key!"

Inside the mine entrance, a steep staircase illuminated by torches descended farther than they could see. Anne and Penelope started running down the stairs, taking them two at a time, but Hiro remained on the upper landing, staring at the doors.

Anne stopped. "Hiro, come on!"

Hiro licked his lips. "If they come through, it won't take them long to catch up to us. I have an idea." He pulled a thin green book from inside his cloak. Anne recognized it as the latest edition of the Special Order

Spell Catalog that served as his spell book. Hiro said, "This month's catalog includes the Sunspot Spell. I can use it to melt the lock and weld the door shut, just like those knights did with the library gate."

Anne and Penelope ran back up to the landing. "I have a bad feeling about this," said Penelope.

Hearing more shouts from the other side, Anne said, "I don't know if this is the right time to try your magick."

"Trust me, I can do this," said Hiro.

If somewhat reluctantly, Anne nodded. Hiro was the group wizard, after all, and he wasn't wrong: They wouldn't be able to outrun the guards for long. Hiro raised one hand toward the lock and began chanting. A pinpoint of white light appeared, and the lock began to glow.

"Huh, it's actually working," Penelope said in a tone of surprise.

The lock glowed brighter and brighter. Then it began to sag a little. Then a lot.

"Um, great job," said Anne. "But I think that's probably enough."

Hiro ceased his chanting, but the spell didn't stop. There was a hiss as a blob of melted lock dripped onto the floor and began burning the floorboards of the landing. Seconds later, the rest of the lock completely melted and ran down the side of the door. The intense heat from the molten metal caused the thick oak doors to burst into flames.

"Whoops," said Hiro.

"Let's go!" yelled Anne. Penelope grabbed Hiro by the arm and pulled him along. They took the stairs three at a time as the door behind them became a roaring inferno.

"Well, the fire should delay them for a few minutes, right?" said Hiro.

At the bottom of the stairs was a long hallway. They ran to its end and were confronted with two doors. A sign on the first door read:

Welcome
to the
Cave of Marvel

That door was locked.

They tried the second door, which opened and led into a large cavern. Dozens of mining-cart tracks led into tunnels in every direction. Remembering Nana's instructions, they ran to the one labeled WEST TUNNEL.

Footsteps echoed from the stairs and down the hallway. The guards were coming.

"We'll never outrun them on foot," said Anne.

Beside the western track, a mining cart was lying on its side. Penelope ran over to it. "Help me tip this up."

Anne and Hiro joined her at the side of the cart and lifted with all their strength. Slowly, the cart tipped up and over, and with a great clang, it landed perfectly on the rails.

Penelope reached inside. "I'm pretty sure I know how this works," she said. She grabbed hold of the lever on the floor and pushed it forward. As Penelope had guessed, this was the brake, and the cart's wheels unlocked.

However, the cart didn't move on its own, at least it wouldn't until it reached the tunnel entrance, where the tracks sloped down. Anne, Penelope, and Hiro got behind the cart and pushed it along the rails. The stiff wheels squeaked loudly, but not loud enough to cover the shouts of the arriving guards. The three adventurers turned around to see ten guards emerge from the hallway and head straight toward them.

"Faster," grunted Anne. They leaned into the cart, pushing harder, and the cart picked up speed. They were moving at a decent jog by the time they reached the mouth of the tunnel, but the guards had closed in.

"They're here!" shouted Hiro.

Just as the guards reached them, the cart hit the slope. Penelope and Hiro jumped into the cart, but Anne stumbled. Penelope grabbed her arm and helped her into the cart as a hand closed on Anne's shoe. She kicked out with her other foot, and the guard yelped and let go.

The cart instantly picked up speed and hurtled down the tracks.

Penelope wiped her forehead. "Well, that was close."

"I think it's still close," said Hiro.

He pointed behind them. Another cart filled with four burly guards was now pursuing them. Anne studied the path ahead. In the distance, she could make out a switch where the track split. If she hit the switch just after they passed by, it would send the second cart onto another track.

"Quick," said Anne. "We need something we can reach that switch with."

Penelope handed her a metal rod. "How about this?"

Anne took the rod and leaned over the side. The switch was coming up fast, and she would only get one shot. They whipped past the track junction, and Anne swung the rod with all her might, scoring a direct hit. The impact tore the rod from her grasp, stinging her hand, but she had done it. The rails changed position, and seconds later the second cart reached the junction and was sent speeding off in the wrong direction.

Their own cart stayed on the main track, swaying and creaking with every bump and threatening to derail. After a few more precarious minutes of travel, a light appeared at the end of the tunnel.

"There's the dock," said Hiro. "You should probably slow us down so we don't fly off the end."

"I can't slow us down without the brake," said Penelope.

"What happened to the brake?" said Anne.

"Um, remember that rod I handed you? That was it."

Anne gripped the sides of the cart as they hurtled toward the dock. She was about to suggest they jump for it, when a huge, dark shape appeared on the track directly in front of them, blocking out the light.

"Hit the deck!" shouted Anne.

All three of them dove to the floor and braced themselves for the inevitable impact with whatever was out there. Before the cart struck anything, though, there was a deafening roar, and tendrils of red flame licked at the sides of the mining cart.

And then a sudden flash of green.

ACCORDING TO THE DEPARTMENT OF
ROCKSLIDES, MUDSLIDES, SNOWSLIDES, AND
WATERSLIDES, THE TOP THREE CAUSES OF
AVALANCHES ARE AS FOLLOWS:

1) Strong winds

2) Heavy snowfall

3) Crashing your fireball into the side of a mountain

Note: Never start an avalanche without a proper permit.

The Blacksmith and
the Bladesmith

Something was wrong.

The interior of the fireball crackled with energy, which was perfectly normal and not the thing that was wrong. Green flames danced along the inner surface, which was also fine and not the thing that was wrong. What *was* wrong were the dozens of red sparks ricocheting back and forth, scorching Anne's uniform and stinging her hands and face. Before she had time to work up to a really good panic, though, the fireball struck solid ground and began bouncing—once, twice, thrice. Anne tumbled over and over, trying desperately to stay upright. Fortunately, on the fourth bounce the fireball came to a stop. Unfortunately, it did so by exploding. Anne skidded along the rocky terrain and plowed into a snowbank, spraying white fluffy powder in every direction. She leapt to her feet and brushed the icy snow from her clothes.

The fireball had deposited Anne on the side of a mountain. The sky was overcast and the wind howled all around. Behind her the ground was bare and steaming slightly where the fireball had melted the snow. The rest of the slope was covered in deep drifts. Penelope and Hiro were nowhere in sight.

"Hello?" Anne called out.

"Here," came Penelope's muffled voice.

Anne looked down the slope. Penelope's head popped out of a snowbank some distance below. Hiro appeared a little beyond that. Clutching her cloak tightly, Anne climbed over the nearest drift and trudged through the thigh-deep snow to reach Penelope. Hiro walked up from below.

"Were either of your fireballs...different?" Anne asked once they were all together.

"I'll say," said Penelope, holding up a charred sleeve.

"Nana is off her game. This quest must really have her rattled." She looked around. "Speaking of Nana, where is she, anyway? She's usually right behind us."

"She can't take part in a Dragon Slayer quest, remember?" said Hiro.

"Except that she just did," said Penelope.

Hiro shrugged. "Maybe Copperhelm couldn't get a ship after all, and she decided to help us this one time."

Not having Nana with them was a huge blow. Even worse, once word of their quest spread, it was likely that no dragons would be willing to help them at all.

Anne raised her gauntlet-hand. "Activate GPS."

Jeffery appeared in a flash of light. "Wow, you finally brought us to visit the Great Marshmallow. Did you remember a gift? I hear he gets cranky if you don't have something to give him."

"This isn't a marshmallow," said Anne. "Nana dumped us on the side of some snow-covered mountain."

"In that case, if we're having a snowball fight, I want Penelope on my team. She has a wicked throwing arm."

"No snowball fights, either," said Anne. "We need you to tell us where this is."

Jeffery shrugged. "Beats me."

"I thought you were good with directions."

"My access is still blocked." He tapped the medallion for emphasis.

"What?" said Hiro. "You mean you can't help us at all?"

"Well, I can still make inappropriate and sarcastic comments," said Jeffery.

Anne rolled her eyes. "Deactivate GPS."

Jeffery disappeared in another flash.

Anne pulled out the guide. The title read: *The Adventurer's Guide to Places You Didn't Expect to Be*, and there was only one word written inside: *Here*. No amount of shaking changed it.

"I guess we're going to have to figure out where we are and where to go on our own," said Anne, putting the book away.

"I think a more pressing issue is where we're going to find our next meal," said Penelope.

"Actually," said Hiro, "I think the most pressing issue is: Does anyone else feel the ground shaking?"

The moment Hiro mentioned it, Anne and Penelope felt it, too. The ground was trembling with greater and greater intensity, and there was a low rumble coming from above. Looking up, they immediately realized this was due to the fast-moving wall of snow that was about to greet them. Before they could so much as blink, the avalanche swept them down the mountainside. The snow carried them for a long time before it stopped, depositing them in the valley below.

As she pulled herself out, Penelope said, "Well, that was bracing."

Hiro spat out a mouthful of snow. "I think I prefer the desert."

As Anne emerged as well, a shadow fell over the group. The shadow belonged to a man sporting a walrus mustache and dressed in worn leather armor. A sheathed sword hung from his belt. Although he looked shabbier than the royal guards in the capital, the man was unmistakably a Hierarchy soldier.

"Is this your avalanche?" asked the guard.

"P-pardon?" said Anne.

"Do you have a permit to cause this avalanche?" he asked. "I'm guessing not, since any application for such a permit would have had to come through our local office, and I don't recall approving any such requests."

Anne, Penelope, and Hiro could see that the avalanche had brought them to the outskirts of a small village, which was now half-buried in snow and ice. In a few buildings, disgruntled faces peered out through partially covered windows.

"This avalanche isn't ours," said Penelope. "We only just arrived from the capital."

"Joyriding an avalanche without permission, eh? Well, that's normally five years hard labor and a hefty fine, but you're new here, so I'm willing to let you off with a warning this time. Just don't let it happen again."

"Thanks," said Anne, still shaking snow out of her ear.

"Wait a minute, though," said the guard, and he took a piece of paper out of his pocket. "I almost forgot. A notice came into the office this morning. Completely slipped my mind until you mentioned the capital. You said you came from there?"

"Yes," said Anne, feeling suddenly nervous. "Why do you ask?"

The guard unfolded the paper. "Because I believe I have a warrant here for your arrest."

"A warrant?" said Hiro.

"That's right," said the guard. "Standard first-year adventuring group. Two girls, one boy. It's all right here."

"How could there be a warrant out already?" Penelope whispered to Anne and Hiro. "We only just left."

"Except we didn't just leave," Hiro whispered back. "Standard fireballs take eight hours to reach their destination, remember?"

"In that case, shouldn't it be the middle of the night?" said Penelope. "It was only late afternoon when we left, but this guy said it's morning."

If that was true, it meant they might have traveled for as long as sixteen hours—twice the normal amount of time. If that was the case, Nana really was off her game. Unfortunately, figuring out what had gone wrong wasn't going to help them out of their current situation.

Anne pointed to the paper the guard was holding. "Could I see that for a moment?"

"Sure," said the guard, and he handed it to her.

Anne read the warrant with increasing distress. It did indeed have their names, ages, and exact descriptions. Then she spotted something near the bottom of the page that gave her a glimmer of hope. She took a second to compose herself and handed the paper back.

"Everything seems to be in order," she said. "We'd be happy to answer your questions, Constable..."

"Stinkwater," said the guard, and he stared at them intently as though waiting for any hint of a smile or a giggle or even a slightly amused hiccup. Satisfied, he held up the warrant and read from it. "Is your legal name Anvil?"

"Yes," said Anne. Penelope and Hiro seemed tense beside her, but she ignored them and focused on the guard.

"And are you from Saint Lupin's Quest Academy?" he continued.

"Yes."

"And are the names of your companions Hiro Dark-flame and Penelope Shatterblade?" He paused. "Hmmm. Shatterblade. Say, is that any relation to that couple that got everyone killed on that quest all those years ago?"

Penelope turned beet red.

"Yes, those are our names," said Anne, hoping to keep things moving and spare her friend any further pain and embarrassment.

Hiro leaned in close and whispered sharply into Anne's ear. "What are you doing? You're going to get us arrested."

Anne shook her head. "Trust me."

The guard lowered the paper. "Well, you're obviously the group I'm looking for, then."

Hiro was on the verge of hyperventilating, but Anne did her best to keep her face expressionless. "Shouldn't you check our tokens, just to make sure?" she asked.

The guard grunted, as though he didn't appreciate a first-year student telling him how to do his job. "I suppose. Don't want to get caught up on some technicality."

Anne turned to Penelope and Hiro. "Show him your tokens."

Hiro reluctantly dug his token out of his pocket and handed it to the guard. Penelope did likewise, while obviously fighting the urge to shout about how foolish this was.

The guard examined the tokens. "This all seems to be in order. A fighter and a wizard, just like it says here in the warrant."

Anne suppressed a smile as she dug her own token out of her pocket. "And here's mine," she said, handing it over.

The constable read the inscription. "Blacksmith?" He double-checked the warrant again. "But it says here you're a thief."

Anne shrugged. "Hm, well, I guess we can't be the group you're looking for, then. Best of luck finding them. They sound very dangerous."

The guard harrumphed. "Now, see here. Are you asking me to believe there are two adventuring groups from Saint Lupin's Quest Academy with the names Anvil, Penelope, and Hiro who fit your exact descriptions?"

"I'm not asking you to believe anything, Constable Stinkwater," said Anne. "I'm simply pointing out that the information on that warrant isn't a match. I assume that means we're free to go."

The guard sputtered, but he couldn't seem to think

of any counterargument. Anne held out her hand, and reluctantly the guard handed back her token.

"Very well, very well," the guard said. "But if you see anyone who looks like... well, yourselves, and has... your names, and is on some illegal quest to kill the queen of the dragons, make sure you report them right away."

Anne nodded. "Definitely."

As the guard tucked the warrant back into his inner pocket, Penelope and Hiro started walking away before he could reconsider. But Anne paused and asked one last question: "You don't know of a monastery on this tier, do you?"

The guard shook his head. "Nope, sorry."

"Oh," said Anne, feeling disappointed. For some reason, she had been sure his answer was going to be yes.

"There is the abbot, though, of course," he said. "Lives on the other side of town."

Anne perked up. "An abbot lives here?"

"Has for years." He pointed down the street that ran through the center of the village. "Follow the main road into the forest for about thirty minutes until you come to a forge. Big one. Can't miss it. Rumor has it she used to be a swordsmith or something, and a pretty good one, too, if even half the stories are true. But there's not much call for that sort of thing around these parts. Mostly she makes useful bits and pieces for whoever needs them."

"Thanks," said Anne excitedly.

The guard nodded and walked away.

Anne turned back to the others, but before she could say anything, Hiro shook his head. "I know what you're thinking," he said. "But she can't possibly be the same abbot who's mentioned in *The Adventurer's Guide*. She would have to be thousands of years old."

"So?" said Anne. "Sassafras celebrated his thousand and first birthday just two months ago."

"There's a big difference between a thousand years and ten times that. Besides, how would Nana even know we were looking for an abbot?"

Anne remained undeterred. "Listen, the guide said someone called the Abbot of Swords forged the Three-Handed Sword, correct? And that the sword is an Old World artifact? It all adds up. And maybe Nana knew all along but wasn't allowed to tell us. I mean, why else would she send us to this tier if it isn't where we needed to go?"

"But the abbot would have to be as old as the Hierarchy itself," Hiro protested. "How could anyone possibly live that long?"

"He does have a point, loath though I am to admit it," said Penelope.

Anne grinned. "There's only one way to find out."

Anne, Penelope, and Hiro trudged through the knee-deep snow along the forest path until they came to the forge. It was a tall structure with a single large chimney puffing out a steady stream of smoke. There was a stone-walled hut with a thatched roof nearby, as well as several smaller sheds and a three-sided shelter packed with dried and split firewood. As they drew nearer, the air filled with the steady ring of hammer blows.

Someone had recently cleared all the snow from the yard between the forge and the other buildings. Once the trio reached the clearing, they walked easily to the large structure. The double doors in the front of the building were closed, no doubt to keep out the wind, but a side door had been propped open with a stick.

Anne stepped inside. As her eyes adjusted to the darker interior, she studied the room. A large furnace on the far side had a coal bin next to it. Rows of tools hung along the walls, and several chains hung from the ceiling, no doubt for lifting heavy objects.

A large anvil occupied the center of the room, and this proved to be the source of the ringing. A tall woman with pale white skin stood in front of the anvil, her long yellow-gold hair tied back with a leather cord. She wore a dirty leather apron, oversized leather gloves, and a pair of spectacles with dark lenses. In one hand she held a pair of tongs, and in the other a large hammer. She continued hitting the object held between the tongs with a steady rhythm, sending out a cascading shower of sparks with each blow.

As Anne raised her hand to knock on the doorframe, the smith suddenly stopped her hammering, cocked her head to one side, and spoke without turning to face them.

"Valerian, that's no way to welcome guests," she said.

Anne frowned. Had the smith been expecting a visitor and mistaken Anne for this other person? Anne was about to identify herself when out of the corner of her eye she noticed a movement.

It was the tip of a sword, pointing directly at her.

And the person holding the sword was the boy who had stolen her gauntlet.

THE ADVENTURER'S GUIDE TO CLANDESTINE OPERATIONS OFFERS THE FOLLOWING TIPS ON HOW TO PERFORM A SUCCESSFUL SNEAK ATTACK:

Step 1: Sneak up on someone.

Step 2: Attack.

The Abbot of Swords

Anne stood perfectly still.

The boy's arm was shaking, and the tip of the sword waved erratically in front of her. A bead of sweat dripped down his forehead and into his eyes, and he quickly wiped it away with his free arm.

"What are you doing here?" he asked.

Anne frowned. "What do you mean, what are *we* doing here? What are *you* doing here? And what's the big idea, trying to steal my gauntlet? You might be a thief, but that doesn't mean you can just go around stealing everything."

The boy—Valerian, the smith had called him—shook the sword at her. "Go away! You're going to ruin everything."

Anne wavered in the doorway, pulse racing, unsure what to do. She certainly didn't want to get stabbed, but she wasn't about to leave. If that woman was the swordsmith they were looking for, then they needed her to find the sword. But if the boy was here and the smith knew him, which seemed to be the case, exactly whose side was she on?

"Why are you blocking the doorway?" asked Penelope behind Anne. She sidestepped past Anne and into the forge. Hiro followed. Valerian retreated several steps and waved the sword back and forth at all three of them.

"That's why," said Anne.

"Oh," said Penelope. "Good reason."

On the other side of the room, the smith dunked the tongs into a barrel of water, which hissed loudly as a great cloud of steam rose into the air.

"Put the sword away, Valerian," said the smith, who still hadn't turned toward them. She continued with her work, placing the object in the tongs on a nearby bench, seemingly unfazed by the appearance of a questing party or that the boy was threatening its members.

"But they're trying to interfere," said Valerian.

"As well they should," said the smith. "I sent you to Saint Lupin's in hopes that you would make some friends, not activate a pointless quest."

The blade hovered menacingly, and it was starting to make her angry. First this boy, Valerian, stole her gauntlet, and now he was holding her at sword point? Just who did he think he was, anyway? She ignored the fact that she had done the same to him only yesterday.

From behind, she heard the soft rasp of Penelope's sword being loosed from its sheath.

"It's not pointless," said Valerian. "Someone needs to stop the queen."

The smith sighed. "Your intentions are noble, but good intentions alone rarely solve anything. Enough is enough. Put down the sword." This time her tone sounded final and brooked no objection.

Valerian glowered at Anne, but he lowered his weapon as instructed. He slid it carefully into a sheath and hung it on an empty peg on the wall alongside dozens of other swords.

The smith laid the hammer and tongs on a long bench. She walked across the room next to where they were standing, removed her leather apron, and hung it on a wooden peg near the door. Her gloves she tucked into her belt. This close, it was apparent that her skin wasn't merely white, but waxy and smooth like marble. As the smith walked past, she did not so much as glance in their direction, although with her spectacles still on it was difficult to tell.

"Come along" was all she said.

The four children followed the smith across the yard to the small hut. Valerian walked well apart from the rest of them, which Anne found somewhat insulting. If anyone had reason to be wary, they did—and of *him*.

The smith muttered to herself as she walked, almost as though she were counting paces, and when she reached to open the door, she first touched the edge of the frame and then slid her hand over to the handle.

The inside of the hut was simple but immaculate. Six chairs were precisely arranged around a solid oak table. The shelves were lined with even rows of jars along with several stacks of plates and mugs. Herbs and dried plants hung from the rafters in bunches. A fire crackled merrily in the hearth.

"Please, seat yourselves," said the smith, and everyone did—everyone, that is, except Valerian, who remained standing by the wall.

The smith walked over to a shelf and felt her way

along until she reached a section of mugs. Only then did Anne realize that the smith couldn't see. Anne watched as the smith carefully inspected each mug by touch, taking them down one at a time and setting them on the table.

"Valerian," she said, "would you be so kind as to pour some tea for our guests?"

"Yes, Abbot," said Valerian. He moved over to the fireplace, removed the kettle hanging there, and filled each of the mugs with a steaming green liquid. The smell of mint filled the room, and Penelope gratefully cupped her hands around the warm mug and took a drink. Hiro was more cautious, as was Anne, and they did not drink right away.

Anne had noticed the way Valerian had addressed the smith. "Is it true, then?" she asked. "Are you the Abbot of Swords?"

The smith brought out a loaf of bread from a nearby cupboard and began slicing. "I'm afraid there hasn't been an Abbot of Swords in quite some time. The monastery closed years ago."

"But didn't he just call you an abbot?"

"He does that whenever he's unhappy with me. Usually he calls me Mother. My name is Emmanuelle." She offered Anne and her friends a thick slice of bread. Penelope immediately took a huge bite.

"I'm Anne," said Anne. "The other members of our questing party are Penelope and Hiro."

"Nice to meet you all."

"Did you forge the Three-Handed Sword?" Penelope blurted out.

Emmanuelle laughed. "I'm old, young lady, but I'm not that old."

"Do you know the sword's location, though?" asked Anne.

Emmanuelle held up a hand. "Before we get too tangled up in swords, perhaps we should make sure this quest of yours is actually what everyone seems to think it is. Otherwise, we're all making a big fuss over nothing. Set your gauntlet on the table, please." The smith felt her way over to the empty chair next to Anne and sat down.

Anne hesitated. It had already occurred to her that this woman might have sent her son to steal the gauntlet and the medallion in the first place, even if it didn't sound like it.

Sensing Anne's reluctance, Emmanuelle said, "I only wish to confirm the medallion is authentic. But if it would put you more at ease, you may feel free to have one of your friends fetch a sword from the forge and hold it over me, in case I try anything. Might I suggest the one in the black sheath? It's heavier, but better for thrusting."

"Sorry," said Anne. "I wasn't trying to be rude, but we haven't had the best of luck meeting people on quests."

"Understood," said Emmanuelle. "In fact, I applaud your wariness, especially under the circumstances. You did, however, come to me, and you are free to leave whenever you choose. We will proceed or not, according to your wishes."

The woman's forthrightness put Anne somewhat more at ease. Trusting her instincts that Nana wouldn't have knowingly sent them to anyone dangerous, Anne placed her gauntlet-hand on the table. The smith ran her fingers over the surface, pressing and pulling every half inch or so and testing the seams.

"Such craftsmanship," she murmured.

After giving the gauntlet a thorough examination, Emmanuelle traced her fingers slowly across the surface of the medallion. After a few minutes, she stopped and shook her head.

"Oh, Valerian, why couldn't you have left well enough alone?" she said.

Valerian stood rigidly in the corner and stared at the floor.

Finally, Emmanuelle released the gauntlet and rested her hands in her lap. "Well, it's definitely the real thing."

"It's also active," said Anne.

"Yeah," said Penelope. "And your boy Valerian here is working with a group of knights that are trying to mess with the quest."

"They're called the Copper Knights," said Valerian. "And I'm not working *with* them. I *control* them. They do what I say—or at least, they used to."

"What do you mean?" asked Anne.

He glared at her. "They left. They said after what happened at the library, they didn't need me anymore. It was supposed to be my quest, but then you came along and stole it. They were supposed to act as my antagonists, not yours."

"It doesn't matter," said Emmanuelle. "The queen can only be killed by the sword, and it is well hidden. Trust me on that. Not even Valerian knows its whereabouts."

Anne studied Valerian, and as he continued to avoid her gaze, she said, "I'm not entirely sure that's true."

Emmanuelle put down her cup. "Valerian, surely you didn't..."

Valerian raised his chin defiantly. "That's right. I

discovered its location among your notes, and I told the Copper Knights. As far as I'm concerned, the queen deserves everything that's coming to her." He flung open the door and stormed out of the hut.

Emmanuelle bowed her head. Anne, Penelope, and Hiro remained silent, not knowing what to say.

After several minutes, Emmanuelle spoke. "I will take you to the sword," she said. "But only so we can move it to a more secure location."

"We need the sword as a gift for the queen," said Anne. "I have something I need to ask her."

"I'm afraid those are my terms."

Anne looked to her friends. Penelope seemed dissatisfied but said nothing. Hiro nodded readily in agreement. Anne would be saddened not to be able to ask her question, but saving the dragon queen and preventing a war were more important.

"Okay," said Anne. "It's a deal."

"Good. In that case, you'll need this." Emmanuelle took a small card from her shirt pocket and placed it on the table.

Penelope picked up the card and read it out loud. " 'Wise Old Woman.' What's this for?"

"As I'm sure you know, it's illegal for anyone to

interfere with an active quest," said Emmanuelle. "But if you accept me as your mentor, we should be fine."

"*Should* be?" said Hiro, looking alarmed.

"And what about Valerian?" asked Anne.

"I think it best if we keep him with us," said Emmanuelle. "I'll have a talk with him about the knights. He's actually a very sweet boy. He's just having some difficulty accepting that life doesn't always work out the way we want it to."

"So where's the sword?" Penelope asked eagerly.

"Not quite so fast," said Emmanuelle. "First, we need to travel to my old monastery."

"But don't we need to get to the sword as quickly as possible?" asked Anne.

"Yes, but if we want to retrieve it, I'm going to need my eyes."

Anne shifted uncomfortably in her chair. "Er, did you say your 'eyes'?"

Emmanuelle removed her spectacles. Behind them, her eye sockets were two empty black pits. "As strange as it sounds, my eyes are the quickest means of getting to the sword," she said. She replaced the spectacles and took another sip of tea. "You might have noticed my... condition." She rolled back the sleeve of her shirt to display a long white marble arm. "I was once flesh and blood like you, but now I'm turning to stone."

"What happened?" asked Penelope.

Emmanuelle sighed. "It's a long story, and there is little point in dredging up the past."

"The dragon queen was involved, though, right?" said Anne.

"Yes. She and I had a ... difference of opinion on a personal matter. This was the punishment she inflicted upon me for daring to challenge her. I wouldn't mind so much if it were just me, but it's been tough on Valerian. People are uncomfortable spending too much time around me, fearing my curse could somehow pass to them. It's left us relatively isolated out here in the forest." She shook her head. "Children shouldn't have to suffer because of the actions of their parents."

Anne noticed Penelope stiffen in her seat.

"What does any of that have to do with your eyes?" asked Hiro.

Emmanuelle smiled grimly. "The transformation cannot be stopped. Eventually, I will turn into an unmoving statue, leaving me vulnerable. It therefore seemed prudent to ensure the safety of my eyes before I fully succumbed, to make certain no one could take them and use them to obtain the sword. Removing them myself seemed the best option."

Hiro gasped. "You took out your own eyes?"

"Yes, after they turned completely to stone. It's not like they were doing me any good at that point anyway."

"But why—"

Emmanuelle stood. "No more questions. We need to get moving."

She led them back outside and away from the main yard. They tromped through the knee-deep snow beyond the forge to a small ramshackle shed they hadn't seen before. Valerian was nowhere in sight.

"I'll need a hand with these," said Emmanuelle, touching a set of sliding double doors. "It's been a long time since I've bothered with anything in here, and I expect the doors are stuck fast."

Anne and Hiro took one side, and Emmanuelle and Hiro took the other. Anne grabbed the door handle and pulled with all her might. For a long moment, it didn't seem like the doors were going to budge. But then slowly, with great squeals of protest, they began to move. Anne dug her feet into the ground and pulled with every ounce of strength she could muster. Finally, after several minutes of intense labor, the doors opened fully.

The shed's interior was dank and musty. Shelves filled with odds and ends lined the walls. Anne's curiosity, however, settled on the object sitting in the center of the shed. The giant contraption consisted mainly of two wooden rowboats lashed together. Each rowboat had a wide bench across its middle and a large storage trunk at the rear. Attached to the stern of each boat was a large fan, and each had a set of pedals in the bottom, just in front of the bench.

"What is it?" asked Anne.

"It looks like some kind of weird sled," said Penelope.

Hiro glanced around nervously. "I-it's not a wolf sled, is it?"

Emmanuelle laid a hand on the gunwale of the nearest boat. "It's an airship, actually. Of my own design. No antimagick plating, but there are two balloons that attach to give it lift. It also runs on human sweat. Not my preferred form of travel, but it will do in a pinch."

First, Anne, Penelope, and Hiro grabbed shovels and cleared away the snow in front of the shed. Then they looped a rope through iron pins on the front of the rowboats and hauled the airship into the bright sunlight. Following Emmanuelle's instructions, they pulled the two deflated air balloons from the back of the shed and, using a series of ropes and hooks, attached one to each rowboat. Emmanuelle rigged a metal contraption that resembled a weird oil lamp beneath each balloon. She explained that the lamps would heat the air inside the balloons to create the necessary lift.

It took them most of the day to prepare the airship and load provisions. Valerian eventually returned, and while they waited for the balloons to inflate, Emmanuelle took him aside and they had a long talk. Anne, Penelope, and Hiro huddled together on a fallen log in the cool air of early evening and ate a cold dinner consisting of dried meat, cheese, nuts, and berries. The time compression feature of a fireball might trick a person's mind into thinking only a few seconds had passed, but the body still felt the full effects of the passage of time. This meant they hadn't had a solid meal in well over a day, and they gobbled their food hungrily.

"So, do you think it's safe?" Hiro asked between bites.

Anne brushed a few crumbs off her cloak. "What do you mean?"

Hiro pointed to where Emmanuelle and Valerian were sitting. "Do you think we'll be okay traveling with them?"

"Why wouldn't we be?" asked Penelope.

"Are you forgetting it was Valerian who stole Anne's gauntlet and started this whole mess in the first place?"

Penelope shrugged. "He was upset."

Hiro fumbled his cheese. "Upset? He might be responsible for starting a war between humans and dragons."

"The queen hurt his mother. You'd do the same."

"If my mother caught me activating an illegal Dragon Slayer quest, she'd lock me away in a secret prison on the top of some mountain surrounded by assassins, no matter what my reason was."

"So you're not concerned at all, Pen?" asked Anne, who found herself agreeing more with Hiro.

"Look, I'm not saying we should hand him the sword when we find it, but give the guy a break," said Penelope, an edge creeping into her voice. "And even if we can't completely trust *him*, look at Emmanuelle. She tore out her own eyes to protect the sword. We should at least trust *her*."

"You're right," Anne said in a conciliatory tone. "Those are all good points. I think Hiro is just being cautious."

"Caution is fine, but backing out of a quest isn't an option," said Penelope.

"No one said anything about backing out," said Anne.

"Good."

The three friends lapsed into an uneasy silence until Emmanuelle and Valerian joined them.

"Time to go," said Emmanuelle. "It will take us several hours to reach the monastery, so the sooner we get under way, the better."

Valerian and Emmanuelle sat on the bench in one rowboat, while Anne, Penelope, and Hiro squeezed together on the other. Valerian passed them a long pole and showed them how to hook it to the fan in their rowboat.

"For steering," he explained.

"Here we go," said Emmanuelle. She released the ropes holding the airship, which were tied to wooden pegs in the ground. The ship rose rapidly into the air. Soon the tier was far below, visible only by the lights reflecting off the snow in the village where they had first landed.

A swift breeze carried them along for the first hour, which made flying easy, but eventually the wind died down and they had to pedal. They continued in this manner, passing dozens of tiers. Although most were uninhabited and blanketed in snow-covered hills and forests, at least half contained a village or small town or sometimes even a castle or palace with spiral towers. They saw fields of grain, herds of cattle, sheep, and ostriches. As they passed an ocean sphere, flying crabs buzzed around the airship. On one mountainous tier, a large city filled with brightly colored roofs sprawled across the slope.

Eventually, they passed beyond the more populated tiers into a much bleaker region with fewer signs of life. Still, Emmanuelle instructed Valerian to stick to the shadows as much as possible, lest they be seen. She wasn't taking any chances. Well after midnight, drowsiness threatened to overtake Anne. The wind had picked up again, so no one was pedaling. Both Hiro and Emmanuelle had dozed off in their seats. Valerian was staring at the stars, seemingly lost in his own world.

Anne rested her chin on the side of the boat and stared down at the BGFM—the Big Glowing Field of Magick at the center of the Hierarchy. At nighttime, as now, it was much darker, like red embers in a dying fire.

"How does it know?" asked Penelope, leaning over Anne.

"How does what know?" asked Anne.

"The BGFM. It's bright during the day and goes dark at night. But how does it know what time of day it is?"

"I don't know," said Anne. "I guess it's magick."

Anne closed her eyes and began to drift off.

Penelope suddenly sat up straight. "Do you smell something?"

Anne shook off her sleepiness and sniffed the air. "Not really."

"Take a deep breath."

Anne did, and this time she caught the hint of an odor like rotten eggs. She also noticed in the lamplight that the air was filled with small particles, like tiny gray snowflakes.

Anne put her hands over her nose and mouth. "What is that stuff?"

"Beats me. But it's getting worse."

Anne reached across to the other boat and tugged on Emmanuelle's sleeve. She roused quickly. "What is it?"

"Something's wrong," said Anne. "There's a bad smell, and the air is filled with some sort of gray dust."

The smith's eyebrows rose. "Impossible." Emmanuelle turned to Valerian. "Take us out to where you can get a view of things."

Valerian gave the oil lamps a sustained burst, and the airship rose. A group of small tiers were clustered together ahead of them, but Valerian deftly steered the airship through them, almost like he'd been born to fly. The cloud of flakes grew thicker, and there was a strange red glow coming from just beyond the small tiers.

"Do you know what that smell is?" asked Anne.

"Sulfur," said Emmanuelle. "From the volcano."

Penelope coughed. "Did you say 'volcano'?"

Emmanuelle nodded. "That's where the monastery is."

"You built a monastery on a *volcano*?" said Anne.

"A dormant volcano. Or at least it used to be."

As they navigated past the cluster of tiers, the sky lit up in red and orange. A massive tier lay directly ahead. At its center, a huge mountain was erupting. Streams of lava crept down its slopes as jets of gas and rock exploded out of the top.

"We have to turn around," said Emmanuelle. "Now."

"But what about your eyes? And the sword?"

Emmanuelle didn't answer. She reached for the steering pole, but her hand had barely touched the lever when Penelope let out a yelp.

"Incoming!" shouted Penelope.

Anne looked up just as a bright flash of orange streaked by, whistling as it passed.

"Lava rocks," said Emmanuelle.

By now, the airship was traveling above the tier, and another explosion from the volcano below sent more rocks streaking toward them. This time several struck the side of the boats and bounced away, leaving scorch marks. Hiro woke with a shout as one lava rock landed in the rear of their rowboat.

"The trunk is on fire," Anne shouted.

"Dump it," Emmanuelle instructed.

Anne and Penelope tried to lift the trunk, but it was too heavy. Penelope yanked the steering rod out of the fan. "Try this," she yelled.

Using the bench for leverage, Anne, Penelope, and Hiro managed to jam the rod under the trunk and lift it up and over the side, snapping the rod as they did so. The trunk tumbled through the air, spilling out its contents of food and other supplies.

A third explosion was so massive the blast rocked the little airship. Everyone ducked as a spray of lava rocks streaked past. Valerian yelled something no one could hear.

"What?" said Anne.

He pointed upward. The balloon on Anne's side had caught fire, and the airship became lopsided as the balloon deflated and the boat beneath it lost altitude.

"Cut the lines," said Emmanuelle.

"But then there will only be one balloon," said Anne.

"Yes, but at least it won't be on fire."

Emmanuelle held out a knife, but before Anne could take it, a much larger lava rock crashed through the middle of the airship, snapping the ropes and struts holding the two boats together. The instant the boats separated, they set off on different paths. The boat holding Emmanuelle and Valerian rose slightly, bobbing from the commotion, while the boat with Anne, Penelope, and Hiro spiraled downward at an increasingly terrifying speed, trailing flames and smoke. Even if they'd had the lever for the fan, there was no way to control their descent. All they could do was hold on and hope they weren't flung into the night sky.

"Emergency," Hiro gasped.

"That's the understatement of the year!" shouted Penelope.

Hiro pointed to the gauntlet. "Emergency. Signal."

"Oh my goodness, I completely forgot!" said Anne.

For every quest, Jeffery was equipped with one emergency signal. If Anne sent the signal quickly, Nana might be able to rescue them before they hit the ground. Surely, Nana could still help them in an emergency.

Anne held up her gauntlet-hand. "Jeffery!"

Jeffery appeared in a flash of light. "Hey, not to sound like a backseat adventurer, but someone really needs to take flying lessons. Just between you and me, the piloting leaves a lot to be desired."

"Send out your emergency signal!" Anne shouted.

"First of all, there's no need to yell. I'm right here. Second of all, do you really think any dragon is going to respond to a beacon during a Dragon Slayer quest?"

"Just send it!"

Jeffery shrugged. "You're the Keeper." Jeffery's eyes glowed and emitted two small orbs of light that rose into the air. The orbs shot into the sky and transformed into a giant dragon image.

The spinning of the boat was making her dizzy, so Anne squeezed her eyes tight. "Come on, Nana," she whispered.

"Also," said Jeffery, "just FYI, flying with your eyes shut isn't recommended, either."

"Deactivate GPS," Anne said in annoyance.

"Hey, wait just a—" Jeffery said as he disappeared.

"Anne, give me a hand!" shouted Hiro. "Pull on that rope!"

Anne looked to where Hiro was pointing and saw the loose end of a rope dangling from the balloon. She grabbed hold of it and gave it a yank. As she did so, Hiro pulled another rope on the same side. This shifted the mass of the balloon back to the center, and the airship jerked out of its spin, continuing its descent in a more or less straight line. The bottom of the boat clipped the tops of a few trees and narrowly missed smashing into an outcropping of rock. They glided out over a meadow covered in tall grass that had a small toolshed at the end.

"Not the shed, not the shed, not the shed," Anne chanted over and over like a mantra, but it was no use.

They hit the roof of the shed dead center.

And exploded in a ball of orange flames.

THE ADVENTURER'S GUIDE TO REAL ESTATE
OFFERS THE FOLLOWING ADVICE:

There are many excellent locations where one can build a home that will add tremendously to the home's general appeal and overall value. An active volcano is not one of them.

8

Statue vs. Lava Beetle

Smoke hung in the air, and Anne covered her mouth with her sleeve. She was lying on the dirt floor of the shed, but other than a few minor bumps and bruises, she was uninjured. At least, nothing seemed broken. She rose on unsteady feet and wobbled over to the row-boat. The balloon was completely deflated and still on fire, the bench had snapped in two, and the fan attached to the stern was missing, no doubt sheared off when they crashed through the roof—which, as it happened, was also on fire.

Hiro appeared on the other side of the boat, coughing and struggling to rise. Anne moved around to assist him.

"Where's Penelope?" Anne asked.

Another coughing fit overtook Hiro, and all he could do was shake his head.

Anne frantically scanned the room without seeing any sign of her friend. Then she spotted a pair of legs inside the rowboat. It was Penelope, lying in the front under a burning section of balloon canvas. Anne quickly tossed the canvas aside. Penelope's eyes were closed, and her forehead was gashed.

"We need to put out the fire," said Anne.

"No time," Hiro wheezed. "Have to carry her out."

Hiro grabbed the cushion from the bench and threw it down beside the boat to create a softer landing. Then they grabbed Penelope's arms and tried to pull her out, but they couldn't budge her. Anne noticed that one of Penelope's feet was trapped underneath the bench. She reached over and tried to free it, but the bench had jammed itself against the side of the rowboat.

Hiro coughed. "Smoke...getting thicker."

Ignoring the rising heat and creeping flames, Anne climbed into the boat and planted one foot against the side of the bench. She pulled with all her might, but the bench refused to move. Hiro jumped in next to her, holding one of the broken struts. He jammed it under the bench, and together they pushed on it with their combined weight, managing to move the bench a fraction of an inch. With several more heaves, they were able to shift the bench high enough to free Penelope. Once again, they grabbed Penelope's arms and this time levered her over the side. She landed perfectly on the cushion.

"Come on," Anne said through gritted teeth.

Anne and Hiro half-climbed, half-fell out of the boat. Hiro grabbed one corner of the cushion and Anne grabbed the other, and together they dragged Penelope across the floor. The shed door opened easily, and they pulled the cushion into the coolness of the night. They kept going across the grass until they were a safe distance from the burning building. Then they collapsed onto the ground and sucked in deep breaths. The air was still full of ash, but at least it wasn't suffocating them.

Anne and Hiro watched as the rest of the shed roof caved in, sending up a huge pillar of colorful flames that soon engulfed the entire building.

Penelope coughed and her eyes fluttered open. "What happened?" she asked groggily.

"We crashed and you were knocked unconscious," said Anne.

"What? Again?"

On their first quest, Penelope and Anne had jumped from the drawbridge at Saint Lupin's, and Penelope had struck her head and fallen unconscious into the moat. Now, she felt the new lump forming on her forehead. "Well, at least this one is on the other side, so it'll be even now. But I need to be more careful or I'm going to get a reputation."

"What now?" asked Hiro.

The ash from the volcano was growing thicker, and a fresh stream of lava was flowing steadily down the mountainside in their direction.

Anne scanned their surroundings. "Our first priority is to find Emmanuelle and Valerian."

"What about the eyes?"

"They're the only ones who know where the eyes are."

"I can't believe we lost our Wise Old Woman," said Penelope. "She was with us less than a day. That's got to be some kind of record. Jocelyn's going to mark us down for sure."

"Considering we're technically on another illegal quest, I'm not expecting high marks in any category," said Anne.

"Copperhelm will be even worse," Penelope continued. "I can hear him now: 'In my day, we kept better track of our Wise Old Women.' "

Anne rolled her eyes. "This isn't helping."

Hiro pointed toward a set of twin towers. "I think the other half of the airship went in that direction."

Anne nodded. "Then let's get going."

They headed toward the towers. To reach them, they had to cross a second burning field of high grass. The field was surrounded by a wooden fence, and on the far side lay the monastery grounds, which consisted of dozens of buildings connected by various courtyards and gates, all in a state of disrepair and mostly on fire. After a few wrong turns and a few dead ends, they finally reached their destination.

The two towers were separated by a deep trench full of jagged rocks that extended as far as they could see in either direction. Anne, Penelope, and Hiro had arrived at the bottom of one tower, and on the other side of the trench, in the middle of an empty courtyard near the base of the second tower, sat the crashed airship. Though covered by a thick layer of ash, its half-deflated balloon flapping in the wind, the ship appeared surprisingly undamaged. However, they saw no sign of Emmanuelle and Valerian.

To find them, they needed to reach the other side, but the bridge over the trench had been destroyed. High above, though, a walkway connected the towers directly, and so far it remained intact. Even though the doors of the first tower were ominously scorched and hanging loose from their hinges, the adventurers proceeded inside cautiously. The interior was one big open space with a staircase that spiraled around the inner wall. This led to the top—or it used to. Now the staircase was mostly a burning, smoking ruin, with only a few stray steps still jutting out from the walls.

"How are we supposed to climb that?" said Penelope.

"I don't think we can," said Anne. "And I don't see another way up."

They walked back outside. The tower had been built with large, rough, ill-fitted stones. The exterior had been weathered smoother over time, but the seams and gaps between the stones still offered multiple hand- and footholds.

"I think we can do it," said Anne.

"But you just said there was no way up," said Hiro.

"Inside the tower," said Anne. "The outside should work just fine. We can climb this. If we stick to the side facing away from the volcano, we'll also be protected from the heat."

Hiro groaned. "But that's over the trench."

"Look at it this way," said Penelope. "If we fall, we'll only experience a few seconds of sheer terror before getting smashed to pieces."

"The sooner we climb, the sooner we finish," said Anne. She placed one foot on a jutting stone, reached a hand to grab another stone above, and pulled herself up. In no time at all, she was ten feet above the ground.

"Come on," she said. "It's not as bad as it looks."

"Wonderful," said Hiro. Despite his misgivings, Hiro followed behind Anne, using the same handholds and footholds that she had. Penelope came last.

At first, they made quick progress. Then about halfway up, Anne paused. The only available handhold was to the side. She took it, but the next usable handhold was also to the side.

"Why are we going around the tower?" asked Hiro.

"It's the only path I can find," said Anne. "But at least we won't be over the trench anymore."

"This is bad," said Hiro. "Very, very bad."

"Just keep climbing," said Anne.

Anne had to keep going sideways until they were practically to the tower's other side. Though the explosions had abated, it was hotter, the ash fell more thickly, and the air was filled with small burning particles. Finally, Anne found handholds leading upward again, and she climbed swiftly. She had almost reached the upper window when the wall above her became completely smooth.

"What's the holdup?" came Penelope's voice from below. "It's not exactly sunbathing weather out here."

"There aren't any more handholds," said Anne.

Penelope craned her neck to see. "What about the windowsill?"

Anne reached up, but she was at least half an arm-length short.

"It's too far," she called down.

"What if you jumped?"

"What?"

"I said, what if you jumped?" Penelope repeated.

"I could die, that's what!"

"Well, that's pretty much a guarantee if we stay out here much longer."

Anne stared at the windowsill. Her chances of making it were fifty-fifty at best. Then, even if she made the leap, the windowsill might give way under her weight. She shook her head. She could either go back down, hang here all night playing out possible scenarios, or...

Anne leapt.

For one heart-stopping moment she hung in the air. Her hand touched the stone of the windowsill, and she clamped onto it with all her strength. She pulled her body upward and managed to hook her opposite elbow over the sill. Once she did that, it was easy (relatively speaking) to pull herself up and inside.

She didn't stop to rest; she turned around and hung back out of the window.

"I'll catch you," she called down to Hiro.

Hiro reached up. They locked arms, wrist to elbow, and Anne helped him up. Penelope followed quickly behind. Since she was taller, she could just reach the window on her own.

Hiro collapsed against a wall and closed his eyes. "No more climbing."

"Come on," said Anne. "We have to keep moving."

Anne, Penelope, and Hiro ran across the bridge to the second tower, whose interior staircase was undamaged. They flew down the stairs and soon exited out the tower's main door, practically stumbling into the courtyard where the broken airship lay.

Panting, Anne looked around and said, "Where could they possibly have gone?"

Penelope pointed at the ground.

The ash was falling fast and furiously, but they could still see two sets of footprints leading away from the airship and toward a large stone building on the other side of the courtyard. Naturally, the building was engulfed in flames.

"They must have taken shelter in there," said Anne.

Hearing a muffled cry from the building, Anne, Penelope, and Hiro sprinted across the cobblestones and burst through the front door.

Emmanuelle was lying on the floor in the middle of a large room. Valerian was wielding a wooden chair like a lion tamer and trying to fend off a beetle larger than an iron knight. The beetle pulsed with bright yellow, orange, and red light, like a piece of living lava. Every time the chair touched the beetle, the wood burst into flame. Even worse, wherever the beetle stepped, it scorched the floor and left a burning hole. Through these holes they could see that more lava was streaming in beneath the floor and pooling between the foundation walls.

Anne and Hiro ran over to Emmanuelle. She was dazed but still conscious, and they helped her to her feet. Meanwhile, Penelope drew her wooden sword and rushed over to assist Valerian. She swung at the beetle's carapace, but the wooden blade burst into flames on contact. She waved the sword around until the flames went out, and then she and Valerian backed away and joined the others.

"What is that thing?" Penelope shouted over the roar of the flames.

"Lava beetle," said Valerian. "We came in here to get the eyes, but that thing attacked us before we could reach them."

"Where are they?" asked Anne.

"Over there," said Valerian. He pointed to the other side of the room to a giant statue of a woman in flowing robes. The lava beetle stood directly in their path.

"I'll help you remove them," said Emmanuelle.

"You three head for the statue," said Penelope. "We'll deal with this thing."

Penelope and Valerian rushed at the beetle, hollering at the top of their lungs. It lunged at them, but they jumped back in time. Its feet left new sizzling holes in the floor.

Anne and Hiro led Emmanuelle around the perimeter of the room, well away from the holes and the fighting. As they reached the statue, Emmanuelle leaned in close and spoke to them. "I can't reach the head, and there isn't time to find something to stand on, so you two are going to have to do this. You must remove the eyes one at a time, starting with the right one. To extract them, push on the eye and turn it at the same time, first a quarter turn to the left, and then two quarter turns to the right. You only get one chance. Any other movement will lock the eye to the statue permanently."

"Understood," said Anne.

"You'll need this," said Emmanuelle, and she handed Anne a leather bag with a strap. Anne wasn't sure why she would need it, but she slung it over her shoulder anyway.

"We'll help you up," said Hiro.

The statue was easily twice as tall as the average

person, taller even than Rokk. Hiro and Emmanuelle clasped their hands together and boosted Anne up the side of the statue. She held on to the statue's leg and stepped up onto Hiro's shoulders. He grunted but remained steady. From there she was able to swing up into the statue's hand.

The building was burning, and Penelope and Valerian shouted as they fought the lava beetle, which crashed around the room. Anne did her best to ignore the chaos and focus on the task at hand. They needed those eyes. She shinnied up the arm until she reached the head. Then she gasped.

"What's wrong?" asked Hiro.

"The eyes, they're huge," said Anne.

The statue was huge, so in a way it made perfect sense, but it wasn't what Anne had been expecting. The eyes were as big as her fist. She looked down at Emmanuelle. "I thought you said these were your eyes."

"They are," said Emmanuelle. "I had them magickally altered to match the statue. That way, even if someone came here looking for them, they would be unlikely to suspect the statue as the hiding place. But the eyes will still function as needed. Trust me."

Under the circumstances, Anne had little choice. She

studied the statue's face. It looked like a much younger version of Emmanuelle.

"Wait, the right eye is missing," said Anne.

"What do you mean?" asked Emmanuelle.

"I mean it's gone," said Anne. "Someone has already taken it." She didn't want to think about what that might mean.

"We'll worry about that later. Take the other one," said Emmanuelle.

Anne placed her hand on the left eye. It filled her palm. Even though it was made of stone, this still felt like a weird thing to do. She took a deep breath, and in one swift motion pushed inward while simultaneously turning the orb, first a quarter turn to the left, and then two quarter turns to the right. There was a soft click, and the eye dropped out of the socket. It was heavier than Anne had expected, but she caught it and stuffed it into the leather bag.

"Got it," she called down.

"Watch out!" shouted Hiro.

The floor buckled and the statue shifted forward slightly. Anne slid down the arm and dropped to the floor. She and Hiro guided Emmanuelle to the side along the wall, where the floor seemed more stable. The lava beetle was forcing Penelope and Valerian toward the statue.

This gave Anne an idea. "Pen, be ready to move," she shouted.

Penelope raised her sword in acknowledgment.

"Give me a hand again," Anne said to Hiro and Emmanuelle, and they moved behind the statue. Together, they pushed on the base, steadily rocking it back and forth. As the beetle came closer, Anne judged the moment and shouted, "Now!"

Penelope and Valerian dove to the side, and Anne, Hiro, and Emmanuelle gave a final push that toppled the statue over. It struck the lava beetle dead center and drove it through the weakened floor.

Everyone gathered together, huddling in a group. The room was completely engulfed in flames, and the floor was so full of holes there was no longer any safe path back to the door.

"We won't last much longer in here," said Hiro.

"Now would be a great time to answer that emergency signal, Nana," Anne whispered to herself.

No sooner had she spoken than the floor gave way

completely. The boards beneath their feet splintered, and they dropped straight toward the pool of lava below.

Anne opened her mouth to scream—

—only to be cut off by a green flash of light.

Once the fireball had dissipated, Anne found herself standing on a ring-shaped tier with a large hole in the center. There were a few trees and scraggly bushes and not much else. The tier's inner rim was constructed of carefully hewn stones decorated with intricate symbols. Far below, the BGFM was visible. Gauging by the sun, it looked to be late afternoon, meaning they had traveled yet another sixteen hours. One sixteen-hour fireball could probably be attributed to any number of odd occurrences. Two seemed like more than mere coincidence.

A tall gray figure approached.

"Hello, my name is Rokk," said Rokk.

Anne was surprised to see him. "How did you get here?"

The robot surveyed their surroundings. "I do not recall. I am currently experiencing a gap in my memory."

"Don't you see?" said Penelope. "Nana sent him. She

received Jeffery's emergency signal, fireballed us here, and sent Rokk along, too, since she couldn't come with us herself. He just doesn't remember because that blast he took in the library still has him off-kilter."

"I suppose so," said Anne. She turned to Emmanuelle and Valerian. "This is Rokk. He's a...friend of ours."

"Nice to meet you, Rokk," said Emmanuelle.

"So where are we now?" asked Hiro as he dusted flakes of ash from his shoulders.

"Hopefully, exactly where we need to be to retrieve the sword," said Emmanuelle, as Valerian led her by the arm to join the rest of the group.

"This is the right place," said Valerian. "I recognize it from your notes."

"I've never seen a tier shaped like this," said Anne.

"That's because it's technically not a tier. It's an Old World device known as an archway," Emmanuelle said. "They were used as a means of travel." She held out her hand. "The eye, please."

Anne took the large stone orb out of her pocket and handed it to Emmanuelle. In the full light of day, she saw that even though it felt like stone, it was actually semitransparent and the inner structures of the eye were clearly visible.

"Do you think the Copper Knights took the other one?" asked Anne.

"Let's hope not," said Emmanuelle. Anne had originally been expecting Emmanuelle to put the eye back in her eye socket, but given the size of it, this was obviously not possible. "There should be a pillar somewhere on the ring, roughly waist-high and made of black stone."

Everyone except Emmanuelle spread out to look for it. After only a few minutes of searching, Anne nearly walked into just such a pillar as she forced her way through a clump of bushes.

"Over here," she called.

The others joined her. Rokk cleared away the bushes with a single swipe of his hand so that they could fully access the pillar. Emmanuelle stepped forward.

"Activate archway," she said.

A small opening appeared on the top of the pillar, and a black sphere the size of Anne's fist rose out of it and into the air.

"Please stand by for retinal scan," said a voice from the sphere.

Emmanuelle held the stone eyeball up to her face. A red beam of light shot out from the sphere and swept over the eye.

"Identity verified," said the voice. "Now activating archway. For your safety, please remain behind the yellow line until the iris is fully opened."

It was only then that Anne noticed a faded yellow line that edged the stone along the inner rim of the ring-shaped tier. In the center of the hole, a pinpoint of light appeared and grew until it extended to the stone rim. Where moments before there had been only empty space and a long drop, there was now a smooth barrier like the surface of a dark, murky pool.

"So, where's the sword?" asked Anne, with a sneaking suspicion she already knew the answer.

Emmanuelle pointed toward the barrier. "In there."

A BRIEF ORIGIN OF THE
THREE-HANDED SWORD

Once upon a time there was a powerful warrior. She was fierce in battle, and she was fierce out of battle, and she was even fierce when asking someone to pass the salt at the dinner table because that's just how she was. But there was one creature she had been unable to defeat, no matter how fiercely she fought. So she went to the greatest swordsmith in all the land.

"Can you make a weapon to defeat the beast?" asked the warrior.

"I can," said the smith. "It will be the most powerful weapon the world has ever known, the most lethal weapon the world has ever known, and the most beautiful weapon the world has ever known."

The smith set to work. It took an entire year, and when the smith finished, everyone agreed the sword was indeed the most powerful, the most lethal, and the most beautiful weapon ever made. It was also, as it turned out, the most expensive, and the bill for it bankrupted three small kingdoms. The smith gave the weapon to the warrior, and the warrior used it to slay the creature, and the people rejoiced. And then the following week a major earthquake hit and killed everyone because that's the sort of thing that happens when you choose to live on a major fault line.

Meanwhile, far away in another kingdom, a thirteen-year-old girl crafted the Three-Handed Sword one afternoon in a homemade forge in her backyard because she thought it would be "totally awesome."

The Blade of Fifteen Fingers

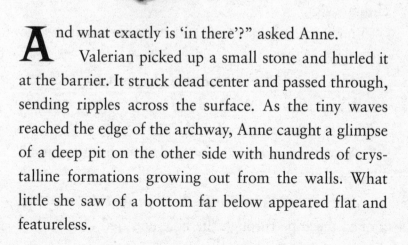

A nd what exactly is 'in there'?" asked Anne.

Valerian picked up a small stone and hurled it at the barrier. It struck dead center and passed through, sending ripples across the surface. As the tiny waves reached the edge of the archway, Anne caught a glimpse of a deep pit on the other side with hundreds of crystalline formations growing out from the walls. What little she saw of a bottom far below appeared flat and featureless.

Penelope whistled. "That's a long way down."

The word *down* echoed strangely off the barrier as the ripples dissipated and the surface became smooth and opaque once again.

"How are we supposed to get to the bottom?" she asked.

The word *bottom* echoed loudly.

"Don't worry," said Emmanuelle. "We managed to rescue at least a few supplies before abandoning ship."

Emmanuelle opened her pack and took out a coil of rope, which she slung over her shoulder. She also produced a long metal peg with a spike on one end and a loop in the other end, like a giant needle.

Hiro turned to Anne. "I thought we agreed no more climbing?"

Emmanuelle held out the peg. "Someone will need to anchor this."

Rokk took the peg from her, stepped back several paces, and rammed it into the ground, causing a minor tremor. "I believe that will hold," he said.

"You're definitely a handy fellow to have around," said Emmanuelle.

Valerian led Emmanuelle over to the peg, and she looped the rope through the hole and tied it off. Then they moved back to the edge and she threw the rope over. Anne watched it pass through the surface of the archway and disappear.

"What if it doesn't reach?" asked Penelope.

"It's all the rope we were able to salvage, I'm afraid," said Emmanuelle. "There should be enough handholds and footholds to get you the rest of the way down if you need them."

Anne's eyes widened. "Us? You mean you aren't coming?"

Emmanuelle shook her head. "Beyond the archway lies a realm separate from this world. If I entered, my condition would accelerate."

"And what about us?" asked Penelope.

"For you it should be safe."

"Why are our quests always so full of *should*s?" said Hiro.

Anne stared at the barrier again. "How do we find it?" she asked. "The Three-Handed Sword, I mean. Once we're down there. Is it just lying around? Is it hidden somewhere?"

"I don't know," said Emmanuelle. "I only know its location. I've never actually seen it for myself." She stepped back from the rim, still holding the eye.

"Are we really going to do this?" Hiro asked in a low voice.

Anne frowned. "What do you mean?"

"Emmanuelle said she's never actually seen the sword, but we're supposed to trust that it's down there? And what about Valerian? How do we know we're not simply helping him finish this quest?"

"Don't mind this one," said Penelope to Anne, while patting Hiro on the back. "He's just nervous."

Hiro glared at her.

"Look, I'm not saying we shouldn't be cautious," said Anne, trying to appease both of them. "But we need to get that sword before the Copper Knights do. Emmanuelle spoke to Valerian, and he fought alongside Penelope against the lava beetle. And if nothing else, we have Rokk with us now."

Hiro's expression remained grim, but he agreed they should go.

Since Rokk weighed the most, he went first, the theory being that if the rope could support him, it could support all of them. Also, Rokk was the least likely to suffer any lasting damage from a fall. Anne followed Rokk, and the others, including Valerian, came after.

Unlike travel by fireball or being transported by a

portal, passing through the archway felt like nothing at all. There was no sense of passing from one place to another. By whatever means the archway connected the two sides, the transition was smooth. The only difference was when Anne had been standing on the tier above the stone ring, she couldn't see into the pit. Once she passed the threshold and she looked back up, however, she discovered she could make out everything clearly on the other side, including Emmanuelle standing at the edge waiting for them.

The crystal formations in the pit were various shades of blue, and many of them reached from one side of the pit all the way across to the other, forming a labyrinth of sorts. As Penelope had feared, though, the rope didn't quite extend to the bottom. Once Rokk reached the end, he stepped down onto one of the larger crystals.

"These structures appear to be sufficiently sturdy," he informed them.

Rokk continued climbing down, and Anne followed him. Though she had to choose a slightly different path among the crystals because she was so much shorter, there were plenty of hand- and footholds. The crystals were smooth and cold, but she managed to reach the bottom without slipping. Moments later, Penelope dropped down beside her, and Hiro and Valerian joined them.

Despite the pit being quite deep, Anne had no trouble seeing. A nondescript blue light emanated from a massive crystal pillar that had appeared in the center of the pit as soon as they touched the bottom. When they approached the pillar, an object appeared in the air above it: a small crystal key.

"Huh," said Penelope. "No offense to whoever made it, but that's one weird-looking sword. Also, very tiny."

"I'm pretty sure it's just a key," said Anne. "It probably unlocks whatever the sword is stored in."

"That's a relief. Because I was going to say, whoever named it the Three-Handed Sword was way off. It would barely fit in one hand."

Rokk hoisted Anne up on his shoulders. She reached out to grab the key, but her hand passed through it.

Valerian gasped. "What's wrong with it?"

"Relax," said Anne. "It's probably just a hologram."

They had encountered a holographic key once before, and Anne knew what to do. She stretched out her gauntlet-hand, and when the gauntlet touched the key, the key disappeared.

Anne brought the gauntlet in front of her face. "Activate key," she said.

The key appeared again, this time above the gauntlet.

Anne reached up with her gauntlet-hand and grabbed it. Even though she knew it was just a projection of light, it felt solid in her grip.

"Look for a keyhole," said Anne.

Rokk put Anne down, and everyone spread out to search.

"Here," called Penelope a moment later from the other side of the pillar.

Anne and the others joined her. About halfway up the side there was a small hole. Anne didn't hesitate; she inserted the key and turned it. The key clicked and the pillar pulsed with blue light.

"Um, is it supposed to do that?" asked Hiro.

The pulsing increased.

"Maybe we should give it a little space," said Anne, and she took a step back. Everyone followed her example.

As the pulsing increased even more, the pillar shook violently.

"Take cover!" yelled Anne, and everyone scattered. Anne tried to run, but she tripped over the uneven ground. Rokk leapt forward and shielded her just as the pillar exploded. Crystal fragments flew in all directions.

Rokk helped Anne to her feet.

"Were you harmed?" Rokk asked. "Did you sustain

any injuries to your head, neck, trunk, arms, hands, legs, feet, and/or attached digits?"

"My digits are just fine, thanks," said Anne. "And thanks for saving me. Are you okay?"

"My body appears to be undamaged."

The top half of the pillar was gone, disintegrated in the explosion. Valerian walked over and examined the remaining stump. "It's hollow," he said.

Anne looked inside. Sitting at the bottom of the hollow pillar was a long, flat, and ornate chest. Rokk reached in, picked up the chest, and set it on the ground. Anne knelt down and opened the lid. The chest contained dozens of pieces of jagged metal.

"It's just a bunch of junk," said Penelope.

"It's not junk," said Valerian. "They're shards from a broken sword blade."

Anne picked up one of the shards. She took another one and held them together. They didn't match.

"Try this one," said Penelope, handing her another piece.

Anne held the fragment against the first one. This time they fit together perfectly, like puzzle pieces.

"I guess we need to match all the pieces to put the sword together," said Anne.

As they began taking pieces out of the chest, it soon became clear there were more than a few dozen. They removed piece after piece until hundreds of shards lay on the ground in front of them.

Hiro scratched his head. "It's impossible that all of those pieces were in there. That chest isn't remotely large enough."

"Except we saw them come out," said Penelope.

"Perhaps the inside of this container is larger than the outside," said Rokk.

"We have an even bigger problem than weird treasure chests," said Anne. "I'm pretty sure there's more than one sword here. I count over a dozen hilts."

"But if there's more than one sword, how will we know which is the right one?" asked Hiro.

"Maybe they're labeled," said Penelope.

"Actually, some of the pieces do have an inscription," said Valerian, and he held out two pieces in his hand. One contained a tiny column of numbers, the other a small square.

They matched the blade shards one at a time— carefully, since many had sharp edges—and slowly reassembled them into swords (albeit still broken ones). It took a lot of time and patience. Rokk scanned the pieces as they held them up, and over an hour later they had thirteen loosely assembled blades laid out on the ground, complete with hilts, all of them over eight feet long and seemingly identical. They stood back to assess their handiwork.

"So, by any chance does one of them say, 'This is the real Three-Handed Sword'?" asked Penelope.

Valerian crouched down and examined the inscriptions on the first two blades. "The numbers on each sword are different," he said. "That must be how we distinguish the real one from the rest."

"But which set of numbers is correct?" said Hiro. "All of the numbers are three digits long, meaning they're already higher than fifteen even before adding them together."

The phrase "three digits" rang in Anne's ear. She looked at Hiro, then at Rokk, and then back at the row of swords.

"That's it," she murmured. "The blade of fifteen fingers."

"We already know that part," said Hiro.

Anne pointed to the remains of the hollow pillar. "When Rokk asked if I was hurt from the explosion, he referred to my fingers and toes as 'digits.' And you just used 'digits' to refer to the numbers."

160

Hiro shrugged. "That's what they're called."

"Exactly. Maybe the riddle really means to look for the blade with fifteen digits—not as in fingers, but as in numbers."

They examined each of the blades and counted how many numbers were on each one. As it turned out, though, none of the blades had exactly fifteen numbers. Most had less.

"So much for that theory," said Anne.

"What about the shapes?" said Hiro. "One of the pieces Valerian found had a square, and I'm sure I saw a triangle and a circle, too, but I don't see them on any of the blades."

Hiro bent down and examined one of the blades. He turned over several shards until he found what he was looking for. "Here's the triangle. And the other side of this blade has ten numbers." He paused. "The number ten plus the three sides of a triangle equals thirteen."

Anne caught on. "If they all have a shape, we must have to add together the total number of digits with the total number of sides on the shape—"

"Until we find the one that adds up to fifteen," finished Penelope.

They reexamined all the blades again, this time

carefully checking the back sides of each one. Hiro scratched the sum for each one in his notebook.

"I think this might be the one," said Anne, holding a shard in her hand. "It has nine numbers on the front, and a six-sided symbol on the back."

"That's the only one that adds up to fifteen," said Hiro, rechecking his notes.

"Woo-hoo!" said Penelope, and she gave Anne a high five.

Even Hiro and Valerian had silly grins on their faces.

Rokk remained as impassive as ever.

Now that they'd located the Three-Handed Sword—or at least the pieces of it—all they had to do was keep it away from the Copper Knights. Anne brought out the leather bag Emmanuelle had given her earlier and carefully placed each piece of the sword inside. Then she closed the flap and tied it securely with a leather cord.

"Scatter the other shards across the ground," said Anne. "We can't fix the pillar, but if anyone else finds their way down here, we might as well make it as difficult as possible to figure out that we've already taken the real sword." They quickly disassembled the other swords and tossed the pieces in all directions.

Even though the leather bag contained the fragments

Possibly a Middlelogue[*]

THE ADVENTURER'S GUIDE TO FANTASTIC STORYTELLING SAYS THE FOLLOWING ABOUT PLOT TWISTS:

A plot twist is an unexpected turn of events.

Example 1: Someone formerly thought dead turns out to be alive.

Example 2: Someone formerly thought dead turns out to be a parsnip.

Example 3: A group of dragons swoop down out of nowhere, pluck up the main characters, and carry them off to who knows where.

---

[*] Some people will tell you that there's no such thing as a middlelogue. Those people, of course, would be wrong, since this is clearly a middlelogue and therefore concrete evidence against all who would claim otherwise. Faced with such overwhelming proof, these same people might, after some thought, point out that even if there is such a thing as a middlelogue, there really isn't any point to it, and in that regard they would be absolutely correct. There is no point to this whatsoever. Please carry on.

THE PALADIN SERIES USER MANUAL
SAYS THE FOLLOWING ABOUT
MEMORY MODULES:

Your PALADIN series robot is equipped with eight high-capacity memory slots. The memory modules are interchangeable and can be used to program your unit for various tasks.

IMPORTANT NOTE: All memory modules should be password-protected. Failure to employ proper security measures could result in someone taking control of your robot.

MORE IMPORTANT NOTE: Please refrain from inserting food or other foreign objects into the memory slots.

10

Prisoners of the Clan

I f travel by fireball was truly the most terrifying form of transportation, traveling in the clutches of a dragon's enormous claws was a close second. Anne had no idea where she was being taken, partly because it was difficult to make out anything through the narrow spaces between the dragon's toes, but mostly because dragon fumes burned her nose and throat and stung her eyes so badly she was forced to cover them with her hands. Apparently, a dragon's body odor included a healthy dose of brimstone dust. The only thing Anne could tell for sure was that wherever they were going, they were getting there fast. The dragon was flying at tremendous speed.

After about an hour, just as Anne was all but gasping for fresh air, she was suddenly and roughly deposited onto the ground. She rolled onto her hands and knees, but her eyes were stinging so badly she couldn't see. When she heard the sound of coughing and gagging nearby, she knew Penelope and Hiro had been dropped as well, and her heart beat a little easier knowing her friends were safe—or at least nearby.

Anne heard the thump of heavy, retreating dragon footsteps, and then a loud metallic clang. Moments later, a terrible screeching filled her ears. Anne wondered if they were being attacked. She tried to rise and run, but she fell as the ground suddenly shifted and swayed wildly back and forth. Two familiar bodies slammed into her.

"What's going on?" yelled Penelope. The three friends clung to one another. "My eyes hurt and I can't open them! Where are we?"

"I don't know," said Anne.

"I'm guessing no place good," said Hiro.

The swaying gradually lessened, although it didn't

stop completely, and the stinging in their eyes abated. Finally, Anne was able to pry open her eyes. Through blurry vision, she discerned their immediate surroundings: They were inside a giant cage. It was dome-shaped, with long strips of metal crisscrossing in all directions and large rusty panels bolted over any significant gaps. The cage seemed to have been built entirely out of scraps.

The cage was suspended twenty feet in the air by a thick chain attached to the end of a towering pillar, which accounted for the swaying motion. The screeching must have come from the pulley. The ground below sloped away, forming a massive bowl shape. It looked to be mostly rock, but some smoother parts looked oddly metallic. Along one part of the bowl, four more enormous pillars rose at regular intervals, curving inward like giant fingers. Anne felt trapped inside a colossal half-clenched hand. She couldn't see much beyond the bowl's edge due to a heavy mist hanging in the air.

Anne stumbled over to the metal strips of the cage's sides and pulled at several, hoping to find a loose one. Despite their haphazard appearance, however, the makeshift bars were firm and refused to budge. Penelope and Hiro tried some of the other strips, but neither had any luck.

"Well, wherever this is, I'm guessing it's a long way from that archway tier," said Anne.

"Not to mention dragons can fly superfast," said Penelope. "We could be anywhere."

Anne brought out the guide. The title read: *The Adventurer's Guide to Cages You Should Absolutely Avoid Getting Locked In*. Inside there was a picture of a cage that resembled the one they were currently standing in. Anne shook the book several times, but neither the title nor the image changed, so she tucked it back in her pocket.

Hiro slapped one of the bars. "I knew we shouldn't have trusted Valerian."

"I don't see how this is his fault," said Penelope.

Hiro whirled on her. "Are you serious? Stealing the gauntlet? The Copper Knights? Not to mention trying to activate the quest in the first place? He isn't responsible for any of that?"

Anne was taken aback by the intensity of Hiro's reaction.

"Calm down," said Penelope. "I only meant I doubt he summoned the dragons."

"Oh, well, I guess that makes everything okay, then."

Hiro crossed his arms. "I can't believe you're still defending him."

"I don't think Pen is defending anyone," said Anne, hoping to ease the tension.

"I can speak for myself, thanks," snapped Penelope.

Anne felt an edge of anger creep in. "In that case, why *are* you defending him?"

Penelope put her hands on her hips. "Oh, so you're taking Hiro's side, are you?"

"I'm not taking sides," Anne said. "I'm just trying to understand."

"That's just it, though. You can't possibly understand." Penelope clenched and unclenched her fists several times. "Valerian is suffering because of something that happened between his mother and the dragon queen. I'm not saying what he's done is right, but neither of you know what it's like to have other people constantly look down on you because of something your parents did."

"So you think it's okay for Valerian to kill the dragon queen?" asked Anne.

"Maybe he's right," Penelope said. "Maybe she deserves it."

Before Anne could say anything else, Penelope

stomped off to another part of the cage, and Hiro marched to the opposite side.

Anne's heart sank. She didn't know what to say to either of her friends. She wasn't even sure who she agreed with. Hiro wasn't wrong: Valerian had betrayed them. But Penelope also had a point: They didn't know his full reasons for doing what he'd done, and she highly doubted he had intended for his mother to be harmed. Anne shuddered to think what had happened to her in the pit.

After several hours of restless sitting and waiting, the thump of approaching footsteps reverberated through the mist. Anne stood. As the footsteps drew nearer, she imagined any number of horrible fates. She gripped the bars and prepared herself for the worst. At first, she could only make out a large dark form, but as it neared the cage, Anne's fear turned to joy. There was no mistaking those black scales and those deep-green eyes. A flood of relief washed over Anne.

"Nana!" she cried.

Penelope and Hiro leapt to their feet and came rushing over.

"I hate to say I told you so," said Nana. "Actually, that's not true. I rather enjoy saying it."

Anne was so happy to see Nana that she was grateful even for the dragon's cantankerous demeanor.

"How did you know we were here?" asked Anne.

Nana shrugged. "News travels fast. Dragon news even more so."

"And you came to rescue us?" Hiro asked hopefully.

"Because of your deep affection for us?" Penelope added.

Nana smiled. "While I hate to admit it, you three have grown on me. Mostly like pieces of fungi, but then, some fungi are very hard to remove. You're like irremovable pieces of fungi."

"Nana, what's going on?" asked Anne.

"Yeah," said Penelope. "Those dragons threw us in here, but they haven't done anything else—including feeding us, by the way. We've missed breakfast and lunch already today, and we're on the verge of missing dinner as well. Isn't there some sort of regulation against that?"

Nana yawned and made a show of stretching out on the ground. "You've been declared guilty under dragon law of conspiracy to murder the queen of dragons."

"What?" said Anne. "How can we be found guilty when there hasn't even been a trial?"

"It's standard practice," said Nana. "All prisoners are declared guilty before going to trial. But don't worry. I've been appointed to defend you."

"And you can convince them that we're innocent?" asked Hiro.

"Not a chance."

"But—but then why did you tell us not to worry?"

Nana shrugged. "It seemed like the sort of comforting thing someone appointed to defend you would say."

Anne felt her anxiety return. "So what happens now?"

"You appear before the queen, who basically tells you what I just told you, and then they execute you," said Nana. "But after that there's a barbecue, and those are typically a lot of fun."

Penelope crossed her arms. "And how exactly are we supposed to enjoy a barbecue if we're dead?"

"I meant fun for me," said Nana, smacking her lips.

"Nana!" cried Anne.

Nana grinned. "You three are a little high-strung, you know. You should try to relax. Trust me. I have it all figured out. After the queen declares you guilty, she'll ask if you have any last requests. That's when you ask to take the dragon trials."

Anne perked up. "What are the dragon trials?"

"They're basically a big test involving riddles and sword fighting and maybe even a bit of magick and whatnot. Nothing you haven't done before. And if you pass the trials, they let you go free."

"Why can't you just bust us out?" asked Penelope.

"I told you, I can't interfere. But I'm sure you'll do fine."

"Has anyone ever successfully finished the trials?" asked Hiro.

"Technically, no," said Nana. "But there's always a first time."

Anne's heart sank into her stomach.

Two more dragons appeared out of the mist. One was large and yellow and had a long snout. The other was short, blue, and squat and had large ears.

"The queen will see you now," said the yellow dragon.

Instead of releasing Anne and the others, the dragons simply detached the cage from its chain, grasped the bars between their claws, and flew off. As they rose into the sky, Anne got a clearer view of their prison. It was indeed a hand—a colossal hand attached to an equally colossal arm. The arm protruded from the side of an immense tier, and Anne wondered if there was even more of the body buried inside the floating island. If so, its size would be staggering.

They crested the top of the tier and continued onward. The landscape was dry and bleak, with sharp peaks and deep trenches. Without warning, the dragons dropped suddenly into one of the shadow-filled valleys. They descended rapidly until the light overhead shrank to a thin crack. Finally, they came to a stop and landed.

They were on a ledge, and in front of them the trench cut even deeper into the rock. Spanning it was a bridge made entirely of bones. None of them asked where the bones had come from.

The dragons opened the cage, and Nana motioned for them to come out. Neither of the dragon guards seemed overly concerned about keeping Anne, Penelope, and Hiro close, maybe because there was nowhere to run. They proceeded across the bridge and into a domed cavern. It was moderately spacious, although Anne couldn't imagine more than a few dozen dragons Nana's size fitting in there comfortably all at once. A massive crystal formation rose from the center of the room, and the guards guided them over to a spot in front of it. Nana stopped behind them.

Through an entrance on the other side of the cavern came yet another dragon, a silver one. It was big, although no bigger than Nana. Anne had certainly seen larger. It moved regally, though, and with definite purpose. The silver dragon walked to the center of the room and climbed atop the crystal structure.

"Behold," said the yellow dragon guard. "Her Majesty, Kassandra Dawnbringer, Queen of the Dragons, Rightful Heir to the Heartstone, Seventh Marvel of the Modern World."

The queen nodded to the two dragon guards. "You may go," she said. Her voice was not loud or threatening. In fact, it was almost quiet, and yet it conveyed a strength that was not to be underestimated or trifled with. The guards left.

The queen's eyes swept across those present until finally coming to rest on Anne.

"So," she said at last, breaking the silence. "This is the Keeper of the Sparrow who dared to break the treaty between the dragon clan and the Hierarchy by brazenly activating a Dragon Slayer quest."

"I didn't dare anything," Anne said defensively. "I didn't seek the medallion or know what kind of quest it contained."

The queen shook her head. "Ignorance of the law is no excuse. Do you deny activating the quest?"

"I didn't do it on purpose," said Anne.

"I find that answer to be evasive."

"Nana, aren't you going to say something?" asked Hiro.

"Like what?" said Nana. "I thought it was evasive, too. Seriously, you really need to up your game if you're hoping not to die."

"Your Majesty," said Anne, "if you would hear me out, I have troubling information you must know."

The queen leaned back. "Proceed."

They didn't have a gift to present, so Anne couldn't ask her question, but she could at least warn the queen.

Anne took a steadying breath. "As I said, I never intended to activate that quest, but someone else did. There's a group of knights, known as the Copper Knights—"

"I am aware of them," said the queen.

"You are?" said Anne. "I mean...that's great. It's

great that you already know. Anyway, they are, or they were, working with a boy named Valerian. I'm not quite sure anymore because it turns out that they seem to be more in control of him than he is of them. Anyway, long story short, we think they're trying to kill you. They even have the Three-Handed Sword. Or, I mean, all the broken pieces of the sword. They haven't reforged it or anything, at least as far as we know, but who knows what they're capable of if they've already made it this far, right?"

"Is that everything?"

Anne thought for a moment. "Actually, we also wanted to speak with you about a swordsmith we met named Emmanuelle—"

"Enough!" bellowed the queen. Her eyes were wide and red with rage. "You will not speak of that person in this chamber."

"But she told us about your disagreement, and I really think if you—"

"I said, Enough!"

The queen was livid. She paced back and forth across the top of the giant gemstone. Anne opened her mouth to apologize but then thought better of it. There was no telling whether that would make things better or worse.

"From your own mouth you condemn yourself. You admit to activating the Dragon Slayer quest. You admit to associating with the Copper Knights. You admit to conspiring and colluding with a sworn enemy of the dragon clan. And you do so freely in this chamber, this most hallowed place of the dragons. Have you no humility? Is there no end to your brazenness? Even worse, you express false concern for my well-being, when it is widely known that there is no weapon in existence that can kill me."

The queen raised herself to her full height. "You have been found guilty. The penalty for your crime is death, to be carried out immediately. Do you have anything to say for yourselves?"

Penelope nudged Anne, and it was enough to bring her out of her state of shock.

"We...we request the dragon trials," said Anne, her stomach flip-flopping.

"What?"

"Th-the dragon trials," Anne repeated. "It is our right as prisoners to choose the trials for the chance to prove our innocence."

The queen's eyes flickered over to Nana and back

again. She didn't say anything, but she was obviously displeased with this turn of events.

"Very well," said the queen, her jaw clenched tight. "At dawn tomorrow, you will be taken to the arena. There you will face the dragon trials. And there you will die."

The night passed slowly.

Nana had brought them some food after their meeting with the queen, but despite her full stomach and overall exhaustion, Anne had trouble falling asleep. Hiro tossed and turned in his corner of the cage. Penelope didn't make any sound whatsoever. No one seemed quite as angry anymore, but Anne could tell their fight was still a sore spot.

Anne's thoughts drifted to Emmanuelle. Even if she hadn't been injured in the fall, she was now stuck in that...place. She said going there would speed up her transformation. Anne couldn't imagine being trapped there, all alone, life slowly ebbing away. And what must Valerian be feeling? Anne was furious with him for his betrayal. Even if what had happened to his mother hadn't been his fault, hadn't he chosen to work with the

Copper Knights in the first place? And hadn't he lied about continuing to have contact with them? Anne had little sympathy for him.

It was all too much for her to untangle. Tomorrow, they first had to face the dragon trials, and then she could worry about the rest.

She closed her eyes and fell into a fitful sleep.

A NOTE ON DRAGON LAW:

Little has been written about the dragon legal system (since most defendants are arbitrarily declared guilty and become dinner). Less still has been written by dragons themselves (since dragons are typically too busy enjoying dinner). In fact, the only known book by a dragon on the subject of their own laws, *So You've Broken a Dragon Law and Are About to Become Dinner*, of which there was only ever one copy made, was mistaken for a fancy dessert at a posttrial dragon barbecue and swallowed whole by the judge, who declared it "delicious."

The Dragon Trials

The next morning was unusually bright and sunny. Anne wasn't sure what she was more anxious about: the upcoming dragon trials, or the fact that every minute wasted was yet another minute not spent finding a way to stop the Copper Knights. The dragon queen seemed confident that any attempt on her life was doomed to fail, but if she was wrong, the consequences could be disastrous.

The yellow and blue guard dragons arrived to escort the three adventurers. They returned to the same ledge, but they didn't cross the bridge again. Instead, the guards led them down a steep, curving stairway that descended into the depths of the tier. Eventually, they arrived at an enormous rocky cavern. A large hole occupied the center of the floor, and the roiling waves of the BGFM were visible far below.

Multiple ledges ran around the perimeter and were filled with dragons of every size, color, and class, from tiny yellow hummingbird dragons to colossal bright-pink elephant dragons, from fiery red dragons with a row of spikes down their backs to blubbery blue dragons whose continuously jiggling bodies were mesmerizing. There was even a tiny green dragon the size of a flying ant that Anne didn't notice until it buzzed past her nose, and there was a scaly brown dragon that looked like it had been carved out of rock, which Anne mistook for a statue until it moved while she was looking at it. She stared at all the dragons in amazement.

The guards led them around the hole in the floor, which Anne realized resembled the archway through which they had traveled to fetch the Three-Handed Sword. In fact, it looked identical in every respect, save two: a low wall ran around the perimeter, and a large disc hung from the ceiling directly above it. Anne couldn't guess what was on top of the disc, but she felt certain it must relate to the dragon trials.

On the far side of the archway an enormous green dragon stood atop a pillar. The dragon nearly reached the ceiling of the cavern, and it took Anne a moment to realize it was only a statue. Seven much smaller pedestals formed a semicircle in front of it, but these were empty. Each of the smaller pedestals had a letter and a number carved into it: A1, A2, and so on to A7.

The queen stood directly beneath the pillar with the dragon statue, and the guards brought Anne, Penelope, and Hiro to stand before her. She appeared to have regained her composure from their previous encounter, and her manner was once again quiet and resolute.

"So, do you still desire to face the trials?" asked the queen, a definite edge to her voice.

"Do we have a choice?" asked Anne.

The queen smiled at this. "I suppose not." She turned to the black pillar next to her. "Activate archway."

The pillar opened and a small black sphere rose into the air. "Please stand by for retinal scan," said the sphere.

A red beam of light scanned the face of the dragon queen and stopped on her eye. While the sphere performed its scan, Anne wondered again about the connection between the dragon queen and Emmanuelle. Why did their eyes, and only their eyes, open the archways?

"Identity verified," said the sphere. "Now activating archway."

Anne heard the archway activate, but the wall around it blocked their view.

"What's down there?" asked Penelope.

"A place of death and decay," said the queen. "It is the only place we dragons fear to go, and with good reason. No one, dragon or otherwise, has ever entered and returned. We call it the Never-Ending Maze."

"Well, at least it has a fancy name," Penelope quipped. Despite the brave front she was putting on, Anne could tell her friend was nervous.

"Lower the platform," called the queen.

There was a dull thud somewhere off to the side, and the large disc hanging from the ceiling descended. It stopped level with the top of the wall, covering the archway completely. A set of steps materialized out of thin air.

"Up you go," said the guard.

Anne walked slowly up the steps, and Penelope and Hiro followed. The top of the disc was sectioned off into a five-by-five grid of square tiles, and in the center of each square was a different symbol. Anne didn't recognize any of the symbols, but she suspected they were part of some dragon system of writing.

"What do we do now?" asked Anne.

"It's really quite simple," said the queen. "You walk to the other side, proceeding as a group. The only rule is that the same person may not choose two tiles in a row."

Off to the side, Nana seemed about to say something, but remained silent.

Anne studied the grid suspiciously. "That's it?"

The queen smiled. "It's possible you might encounter a few obstacles along the way."

Anne turned to Penelope and Hiro. "What do you think?"

Penelope shrugged. "I say straight across."

Hiro nodded in agreement.

Anne stepped onto the first tile in the center column, and all the dragons in the arena roared with delight. Despite the vastness of the space, it was like encountering a physical wall of sound. The symbol in the center of the tile began to glow, and a wispy blue form rose up in front of them in the shape of a fire lizard. A ghostly form of the symbol from the tile hovered over its head.

The dragons ceased their roaring. They seemed keen not to miss whatever was about to happen.

"What has an eye but cannot see?" asked the fire lizard.

Anne furrowed her brow. "What?"

She scanned the arena for some hint of what they were supposed to do, but the silent dragon faces betrayed nothing. When she looked back to the fire lizard, she noticed that the symbol above its head had changed and was continuing to change, switching forms every second.

"What has an eye but cannot see?" the fire lizard repeated.

"It's a riddle," said Hiro. "It wants us to answer the question."

"And does anyone happen to *know* the answer?" asked Penelope.

Hiro nodded. "I've heard this one before. The answer is a needle."

"That is correct," said the fire lizard, and it dissipated back into nothing.

"Wow," said Penelope. "That was almost too easy."

Penelope and Hiro joined Anne on the first tile, and then Penelope stepped forward to the next one.

"Wait!" said Hiro, but it was too late. Penelope's foot had touched the second tile, and the symbol in the center began to glow. Another fire lizard rose up, and again the symbol from the tile appeared over its head.

"I cannot live without light, yet wherever I touch light, I die," it said.

The symbol above it began to change form just like the previous one had. Oddly, Anne thought she recognized a few of the forms.

"What? What did I do?" asked Penelope.

"I studied some dragon script at my old school," said Hiro. "And I think these are numbers." He pointed back to the first tile. "I'm pretty sure that one is sixty. I'm guessing it meant we had sixty seconds to answer the first question." He pointed to the symbol on the second tile. "I think that one means fifty."

"Then stop wasting time and answer the question," said Penelope. "How can something both need light to live and die when light touches it?"

Hiro pressed his hands against his temple. "Think. Think."

The "numbers" continued changing in a steady rhythm. Anne stepped onto the second tile beside Penelope to study the changing symbol, wondering if it could possibly hold a clue. A tiny black shape moved across the tile. When she looked up, she saw that it was only the tiny green dragon passing by again. But that meant the black shape on the tile had been its—

"Shadow," she said. "The answer is shadow. You need a light source in order to cast a shadow, but a shadow can't actually exist in the light itself."

"That is correct," said the fire lizard, and it faded away.

The three of them sighed with relief.

"Hiro, you're next," said Anne.

Hiro studied the tiles around them. He pointed to the one straight ahead. "I think that one stands for forty. And I'm pretty sure the one after it is the number for thirty. And I bet the last one is twenty. That means this row decreases by ten seconds for every tile we go forward." He pointed to the tiles in the next rows over. "But the tiles in these rows only decrease by five seconds each time, leaving more time for each question."

"Yeah, but going to the side also means doing at least one extra question," said Penelope.

"Sure, but more time means—"

The first tile disappeared and Hiro dropped. Penelope dove and caught his arm with a grunt. The dragons in the arena cheered.

"Help," said Penelope.

With the tile missing, Hiro dangled directly above the barrier. As with the other archway, the surface was dark. Anne grabbed Hiro's other hand, and together she and Penelope pulled him up onto the second tile with them.

"Thanks," said Hiro, his eyes wide with fear. "That was a little too close."

"What happened?" said Penelope. "Why did it do that?"

Anne surveyed the grid. "I'm guessing that either the tiles get removed as you progress across the board, or else we only have so much time between tiles. Meaning we'd better keep moving. Hiro, choose one and let's get going."

Hiro nodded and stepped on the tile to their right. Anne and Penelope followed immediately. As soon as they left the second tile in the center column, it disappeared.

"The more I eat, the longer I live, but one drink of water would kill me," said the third fire lizard.

"Everything needs to eat in order to live longer, doesn't it?" said Anne.

Hiro scratched his head. "Good point. And are there creatures that are allergic to water?"

"It's fire," said Penelope with confidence.

"How did you get that one so quickly?" asked Hiro.

Penelope stuck out her tongue. "You're not the only one who reads books."

Anne started forward, but Penelope grabbed her arm.

"What's the matter?" said Anne. "We need to get moving before the tile disappears."

"That fire lizard hasn't yet disappeared, though."

Penelope was right. Instead of fading away to nothing, the fire lizard turned red and burst into flame.

"That can't be good," said Hiro, and he took a step back.

The fire lizard swooped at them and they ducked. Anne could feel its heat on her neck as it passed.

"Now what are we supposed to do?" yelled Hiro.

"It must be related to the riddle," said Penelope as she ducked another attack. "It turned to fire, so we need to hit it with water. Quick, Hiro, use a water spell."

"The current issue of the spell catalog doesn't have one!"

The fire lizard turned for another attack. Acting out of impulse, Anne leapt forward and spit at it. The fire lizard ceased its attack and immediately faded away.

"Seriously?" said Penelope. "You spit?"

Anne grinned. "I'm surprised you didn't think of it first."

"Good point."

Hiro tugged on their sleeves. "We'd better get moving."

Anne was about to step on the next tile forward, but Hiro stopped her. "I'm guessing each tile in this column includes an attack after we solve the riddle," he said. "I recommend we move back to the center column."

"How? The tile we left is gone."

"True, but now that I think about it, there was no rule against moving diagonally, correct?"

Anne thought it was risky, but then, the whole thing was risky. She took a deep breath and stepped diagonally to the third tile of the center column. Hiro and Penelope quickly followed, and the tile they left disappeared like the others.

"I am forever approaching, but never arriving," the next fire lizard said.

"Remember, only forty seconds for this one," said Hiro.

"But no pressure, right?" said Penelope. "Anyway, no worries, because the answer is the horizon."

"No!" said Anne. "That's not it!"

Hiro pushed them forward to the next tile, their fifth, just as the one beneath them exploded. They landed hard and were pelted by flying bits of ceramic. The dragons roared with delight, and the fire lizard bore down on them.

"Tomorrow!" shouted Anne. "The correct answer is tomorrow!"

The fire lizard melted away.

"What happened?" said Penelope. "Horizon was a great answer."

"The horizon doesn't approach you, you approach it," said Anne. "As time moves forward, tomorrow is always approaching, but it never comes because when it gets here, it becomes today."

Penelope nodded. "Oh, right. Good one. Thanks for the save, by the way," she said to Hiro.

Hiro nodded back. "I owed you one."

Anne was glad everyone had decided to put aside their differences, at least for the time being. They stood as the next fire lizard appeared, along with its symbol.

Anne put a hand on each of their shoulders. "No quick answers this time, okay?"

"What gets wetter and wetter the more it dries?" said the fire lizard.

"Thirty seconds." This time it was Penelope who reminded them.

Anne ran the riddle through her head. The sun dried things but never got wet. A fire that got wetter went out. What had the ability to dry things yet got wet while doing so?

"A towel," said Hiro firmly.

The fire lizard disappeared.

"My father leaves his wet towels all over the house," Hiro explained. "Drives my mother crazy."

Hiro led them onto their sixth tile, the final one in the column. A hush settled over the arena once again as the fire lizard rose.

"Wait, that's not the symbol for twenty," said Hiro, sounding panicked. "That's the symbol for ten."

"You mean we've only got ten seconds?" said Penelope.

This time, the fire lizard sang out an entire verse:

I am owned from birth until death,
Neither borrowed nor stolen can I be.
Yet I am used most often by others
And only rarely by the one who possesses me.

"What did it say? I didn't even catch all of that!" said Penelope.

"There was something about being borrowed and stolen," said Hiro. "And also something about a thing you own from birth until death."

Penelope clutched her head in her hands. "I can't think. None of it makes any sense."

The numbers had almost counted down to one, but instead of panicking, Anne smiled. "The answer is your name," she said confidently. She had spent too much of her life wondering about her own real name not to put those clues together.

At first nothing happened, and for a brief moment Anne worried that she had in fact answered incorrectly. Then the fire lizard faded, and the arena erupted into cries and jeers. Anne ignored them. She stepped off the last tile and down a second set of wooden stairs that had materialized. Penelope and Hiro followed her, and they walked back over to the spot in front of the dragon queen.

The arena quieted again, although Anne could still hear mutterings.

"Congratulations," said the queen. "You're the first prisoners to ever make it all the way across the disc."

"So are we free to go?" asked Anne.

"No," said the dragon queen. "I'm afraid you did not follow the rules. The instructions were that you had to take turns, but your male pushed you and the other female onto the fifth tile when it was the other female's turn."

It was true: Hiro had gone out of turn. Anne wracked her brain for a loophole. "You only said we had to take turns," she said triumphantly, "not that we had to follow a set order."

"True," said the queen. "But then he also chose the final tile after having chosen the fifth."

The queen was right. Technically, Hiro had chosen twice in a row.

"Guards," called the queen. "Prepare the prisoners for execution."

As the guards moved forward, a large black shape dropped in front of them, blocking the way. It was Nana.

"I really hate to interrupt the proceedings," she said, "especially since I just won big in the betting pool, but I'm afraid I can't let you go through with any executions."

The queen looked shocked. "You would dare to defy your queen?"

Nana bowed her head ever so slightly, which was the most Anne had ever seen her defer to anyone. "You and I both know that the rule about taking turns is not part of the original laws governing the trials. That is your own creation. They completed the trials fairly and according to our most ancient customs, and they should therefore be free to go."

"See, this is what happens when you spend too long among humans," the blue dragon guard muttered to the yellow dragon guard.

"What are you waiting for?" the queen roared at the guards. "I said, prepare the prisoners!"

The guards took a hesitant step forward.

"Perhaps I didn't make myself clear," said Nana, stretching her wings and rearing back. "I wasn't asking. I was telling. Leave them alone, or suffer the consequences."

The queen shook with rage. "I will not be spoken to in this manner! Guards, seize that—"

—was all she got out, for in that instant Nana released a huge red fireball. The fireball struck the crystal formation the queen was sitting on and then split into dozens of smaller fireballs, each flying off in a different direction. The arena erupted into a chaos of roars and the frantic flapping of wings as the other dragons fled for cover. Even the queen was forced to retreat.

"Run!" bellowed Nana.

Anne scanned the arena, which was wall-to-wall with dragons.

"Where to?" yelled Anne. "Can't you fireball us out of here?"

"Not from inside."

Nana let loose another round of fireballs, and then she swung her tail at a brave guard who rushed forward, knocking him into two others who had sensibly decided to stand back and do nothing.

Nana used her tail to bat two incoming fireballs from other dragons, returning them to their senders. "Look, I don't know what to tell you," Nana said to the trio. "But you'd better figure something out because it's about to get ugly in here."

"You mean this isn't already ugly?" said Penelope. "Wow, dragons are intense."

"What about you?" asked Anne.

"I'll find my own way out," said Nana.

A mad, desperate idea formed in Anne's head. It

defied all common sense, but if they stayed there a minute longer, they were going to get burned to a crisp or torn limb-from-limb.

"Head for the disc," shouted Anne.

Anne ran over to the wooden stairs and up to the outer rim of the disc. Penelope and Hiro followed closely behind. The entire middle column of tiles was now gone, but the archway was still active.

"Great idea, but how do we raise it back up to the ceiling?" said Penelope, obviously thinking Anne intended to use the disc itself to escape.

"We don't," said Anne.

She grabbed each of their hands tightly and pulled them forward with her as she stepped off the edge, forcing them to fall into the archway below.

‒‒‒◦◦◦◦◄·►◦◦◦◦‒‒‒

THE ADVENTURER'S GUIDE
TO EXECUTIONS OFFERS
THE FOLLOWING TIP:

Generally speaking, it is best to skip executions whenever
possible, especially if the execution in question is your own.

‒‒‒◦◦◦◦◄·►◦◦◦◦‒‒‒

The Never-Ending Maze

They appeared in a cave.

Or more accurately, they fell into one.

Lucky for them, the archway was only ten feet above the floor and the ground was soft and mossy, being covered in lichens and some sort of fungus. Anne rolled onto her back and stared up through the archway. Fireballs were still flying about the arena on the other side, and several dragons circled high overhead. Moments later the archway closed and Anne found herself staring at a ceiling instead.

This was not the arena cavern they had left only moments before. For one thing, the ceiling was considerably lower, and the air was a lot cooler. Anne wrapped her cloak tightly around herself. The real giveaway was the walls and ceiling. They were not made of the arena's brown and gray rocks. They were smooth and black.

"This must be the Never-Ending Maze," said Hiro.

Penelope looked around. "It doesn't look like a maze."

"You can't tell what a maze looks like when you're inside it," said Hiro.

"Then how do you know it's a maze?"

"Because that's what the dragon queen called it."

Penelope put her hands on her hips. "And do you believe everything the dragon queen tells you?"

"Wherever this is, we need to find a way out," said Anne.

"Just a minute there, missy," said Penelope. "I'm not done with you yet, either. What's the big idea of jumping in here with us without so much as a word of warning?"

Anne shuffled her feet. She knew they'd be upset, and she didn't have a good explanation. It was a huge risk, and who knew if they would find a way out. She had acted on pure instinct.

"Look, I'm really sorry," said Anne, "but I didn't see any other options. I didn't think we would last much longer in that arena full of dragons, and I knew they wouldn't follow us in here." Anne braced for a barrage of harsh words. Instead, Penelope wrapped her arms around Anne in a big hug and lifted her off the ground.

Penelope set her back down. "I'm sorry, too, about the whole thing with Valerian. You were both right. I shouldn't have trusted him so easily. As far as bringing us here, with the way those fireballs were flying around, the truth is you saved our skins."

"I agree," said Hiro. "That was quick thinking."

"And you're also sorry for the things you said to me, yes?" Penelope said to Hiro.

Hiro frowned. "Well, technically, I was correct, so..."

Penelope punched him in the shoulder.

"Okay, yes, I'm sorry, too," said Hiro, rubbing his arm.

"And don't you forget it."

No matter what they faced now, Anne was happy to know they'd be facing it as a team again.

"Which way should we go?" Anne asked them both.

"Why don't you ask Jeffery?" said Hiro. "Maybe he knows something."

"Good idea." Anne raised the gauntlet. "Jeffery?"

There was no response.

"Why isn't he coming out?" said Penelope.

Anne studied the cave again. She'd seen black walls like this before: They were the same as the interior of the Infinite Tower and the secret laboratory beneath Saint Lupin's, which they had visited during their first quest. They were obviously related to the Old World, but Anne couldn't begin to guess their significance.

"I think it's these walls," said Anne. "I don't know what they're made of, but somehow they prevent Jeffery from coming out of the gauntlet."

"Great," said Penelope. "We can't even consult our GPS. Does the guide have anything to say?"

Anne took the guide from her pocket. The cover read: *Fishmongers of the World Beware!* She gave the book a shake, but the title didn't change. The inside pages were completely blank.

"Looks like we're on our own," said Anne.

"Well, we might as well do some exploring, then," said Hiro. "Maybe we'll find a clue somewhere that will tell us how to get out."

They picked the closest tunnel. It led down a short

hallway that opened onto a much longer corridor, and the mossy floor of the cavern gave way to smooth stone tiles. Neither direction looked better than the other, so Anne turned right and kept walking. As they went along, she wondered what was so bad about this place that the dragons refused to enter.

Several minutes later, they came to a side corridor. Anne walked around the corner to have a look and stumbled back.

"What's the matter?" said Penelope, who took a look herself, with Hiro and Anne behind her.

Down the side corridor was a dragon. Or rather, a statue of a dragon. It looked impressively realistic, and it must have taken the artist a very long time to complete in such fine detail. For some reason, its face had an incredibly sad expression.

"That's amazing," said Penelope as they drew closer.

Hiro frowned. "Why put a statue in the middle of nowhere?"

Penelope shrugged. "Why not? It gives people something to look at."

"In a never-ending maze?"

Anne agreed with Hiro. As interesting as it was, it

seemed an odd place to stick a piece of art. But there was no point dwelling on it.

"So back the way we were headed, or down this way?" said Anne.

Penelope shrugged. "Does it matter?"

They kept walking down the side corridor for another ten minutes until they hit a cross tunnel, where they discovered even more dragon statues.

"That's really strange," said Hiro.

"Even worse, though, is that now we have to choose from four directions," said Penelope. "Left, right, straight ahead, or back the way we came? We've been in this maze less than thirty minutes, and already I'm sick to death of it."

They continued forward and walked for well over an hour before encountering any more side tunnels. They passed three more statues, and at the first new intersection they elected to stop and rest. The only provisions they had were some biscuits Penelope had stuffed in her pocket from the previous night's meal.

"Shucks," she said as she split off pieces for everyone. "I totally could have eaten these for breakfast."

As Anne sat eating, she felt a momentary wave of

despair. Here they were, yet again, stuck on a quest none of them had chosen and weren't prepared to deal with. And no matter the outcome, they would undoubtedly be facing serious consequences.

A faint echo interrupted her thoughts. She stopped chewing and listened. It sounded like approaching footsteps.

"Do you hear that?" Anne whispered.

Penelope leapt silently to her feet and snuck along the wall. She paused at the intersection, and then signaled with her hand, pointing down the corridor to their right. Something was approaching from that direction. Anne motioned her back. Was this the thing in the maze the dragons so greatly feared? Should they try to make a run for it? Could they even outrun whatever it was?

The footsteps grew louder. Anne tried to keep herself from shaking, but she wasn't having much success. Considering the two trembling bodies next to her, neither were Penelope and Hiro, and that somehow made Anne feel a little better. The footsteps reached the corner, and a boy stepped out of the side corridor and stopped. It was Valerian.

Before Anne could even open her mouth, a large blur sped past her and tackled Valerian to the ground.

"Help!" shouted Valerian, struggling against Penelope. "Get her off me!"

"Not likely," said Penelope, as she pinned his arms. "At least not until I've given you a good thumping."

Valerian struggled to get free, but it was no use. No one escaped Penelope's clutches unless she wanted them to.

Valerian looked imploringly at Anne. "Please."

Anne glared at him. "What makes you think I'm on your side?"

Valerian tried to wriggle out from under Penelope's elbow, but she smooshed his face into the ground.

"I didn't mean for any of this to happen," he said. "You have to believe me. As soon as I got the chance, I escaped from the Copper Knights and came back here to find my mother."

Anne looked around. "What do you mean you came 'back here'? Where is 'here' exactly?"

"We're in the same realm where the Three-Handed Sword was hidden. Or the same plane of existence. Or whatever you want to call it. It's all connected in one long, extended series of rooms and tunnels and has multiple exits. It's an Old World system of travel known as an archway network."

"I didn't see another exit when we were down in the pit," said Anne.

"That's because the archway was active," said Valerian. "Once it shut off, a passageway opened beyond it. I found my mother at the bottom of the pit. She isn't injured, but her condition has grown much worse."

"So why didn't you take her out of here?"

"The knights smashed the controls to that archway and it wouldn't open. I tried to get her to another one, but she collapsed on the way." Valerian stared pleadingly into Anne's eyes. "Please. I only left her and came here because I heard voices. She needs help."

"You betrayed us," said Penelope. "Why should we trust anything you have to say?"

Valerian stopped struggling. "You're right. You shouldn't. It's all my fault you're in this mess in the first place. I have no right to ask anything of you. But I'm not asking you to help me. I'm asking you to help my mother."

"How did you even get here?" asked Anne. "The Copper Knights took the eye."

"Check my pack."

While Penelope kept Valerian pinned, Hiro reached into his pack and pulled out a large round stone.

"The other eye!" exclaimed Penelope.

Valerian nodded. "After I discovered where my mother had hidden them, I went to the monastery and took one. Ever since, I've been using it to open the archways and travel." He bowed his head. "I'm sorry I didn't tell you about it earlier. I thought if I took possession of both eyes, I could regain control of the Copper Knights since they were the only way to the sword. But I see now that they were only using me."

"Let him go," said Hiro.

"What?" said Penelope. "You of all people should want to see him get a good thrashing."

Hiro shrugged. "I believe him. I mean, I'm not saying he doesn't deserve some form of punishment for everything he's done, but Emmanuelle shouldn't have to suffer because of his poor decisions. Besides, the Copper Knights have everything they need. Why else would he come into the maze voluntarily?"

"Are you sure?" asked Anne.

"As sure as I can be."

Anne didn't like it. They'd been fooled by Valerian once, and she wasn't about to let it happen again. Still, they outnumbered him three to one, and Penelope could always sit on him again if he caused further trouble.

Anne nodded.

Penelope rolled off Valerian and rose to her feet, but she stood over him a moment longer. "Did you hear the story about the boy who cried?"

"You mean the boy who cried wolf?" asked Valerian.

"No, I mean the boy who cried because I beat him with my sword for being a big, fat liar."

"I—I understand," said Valerian, and the fear in his eyes looked believable enough.

Penelope stepped back, and Hiro helped Valerian to his feet, handing him back the eye as he did so.

"Where's your mother?" asked Anne.

"Not far from here."

Valerian headed down the passageway, followed by Hiro. Anne grabbed Penelope's arm, holding her back.

"Keep your sword loose, okay?" said Anne.

Penelope nodded.

Valerian walked with the determination of a person with something to lose, and Anne and Penelope ran to catch up. They passed another dragon statue.

"Why are the dragons so afraid to come here?" asked Anne.

"Isn't it obvious?" said Valerian, pointing to the statue. "Just look what it does to them."

Anne was stunned. "You don't mean those are real dragons?"

"They were. Banished here by the queen for various reasons. In the maze, they slowly turn to stone."

Anne's mind was spinning as the puzzle pieces came together. Coming here caused the dragons to turn to stone. Emmanuelle was also turning to stone. Did that mean—

"In here," said Valerian, and he ducked through a doorway.

This room was smaller than the one they had landed in, and much of the space was taken up by yet another statue. Or at least, Anne thought it was a statue. This one was beautifully carved out of pure white marble. She was about to reach out and touch it when the dragon drew a deep, ragged breath. It was alive.

"It's a trap," yelled Penelope, and she tore her sword out of its sheath.

Valerian stepped between Penelope and the white marble dragon and held up his hands.

"I didn't lie," he said. "And it's not a trap."

He placed his hand on the dragon's white scales.

"Everyone, this is my mother."

The dragon's eyes were closed and her breathing was uneven, as though she were sleeping fitfully.

Penelope squinted. "Um, no offense, but I'm pretty sure that's a dragon."

"My mother *is* a dragon," said Valerian.

"That's a bit harsh," said Penelope. "I thought your mom was actually really nice."

Anne placed her hand on Penelope's shoulder. "Pen, he's saying this is Emmanuelle. She is literally a dragon."

Penelope studied the white dragon more closely. "I don't see the resemblance."

"Some dragons have the ability to take human form," Valerian explained. "But only in our world. Not here."

Hiro raised his eyebrows. "Does that mean you're a dragon, too?"

Valerian shook his head. "I'm only a half-dragon. I can hold my dragon form for a few seconds at the most, but sometimes that's all I need. I'm...actually the one who fireballed you from the capital tier, after you escaped from the library. The Copper Knights abandoned me at the docks where their airship was waiting. Since I couldn't exactly continue on to Saint Lupin's, I was sending myself back to my mother. You three got caught in the wake of my fireball."

"I didn't think dragons could travel by fireball," said Hiro.

"Full dragons can't," said Valerian. "But if I time it right, I can shoot out a fireball in my dragon form, and then switch back to my human form and ride it. I'm not very good at them yet, though. They tend to be somewhat unstable and I can never seem to get the timing right."

"That would explain the sixteen-hour fireballs," said Penelope.

"When we almost died on the volcano tier, that was you, too?" said Anne.

Valerian nodded.

More pieces of the puzzle fell into place.

"The queen banished your mother here," said Anne.

"Yes," said Valerian.

"Why?"

Valerian met her eyes without wavering. "Because of me and what I represent. Because my mother dared to love a human. Because of the shame this brought on her sister and the family legacy."

Anne's eyes went wide. "Your mother and the queen are sisters?"

Valerian nodded. "My mother is the older of the two and was actually supposed to become queen. She created that medallion herself, thinking it would save her and me from harm, but her sister acted before she ascended the throne."

"If you're a dragon, how come you're not turning to stone here in the maze like all the others?" asked Hiro.

Valerian gave a harsh laugh. "The advantages of being only half dragon."

"Did you really believe activating the Dragon Slayer quest would change any of this?" asked Anne.

Valerian sighed. "It can't change what's happened to my mother, but that wasn't my only reason for activating it. It's no secret that dragons believe themselves to be superior to humans, but some believe it more strongly than others. My aunt, the queen, has been working on a plan to take control of the Hierarchy."

"If you were banished, how do you know all of this?" asked Penelope suspiciously.

"There's a hidden archway in the dragons' throne room, high up near the ceiling. You can hear everything that goes on."

"So why not tell someone?" said Hiro.

"I tried, but no one would believe me. Among the dragons I'm an outcast, and among humans I'm merely a child. Activating the quest seemed like the only option, but I figured if I was the one who did it, then it wouldn't cause any trouble for the Hierarchy. The dragons could hardly blame humans for a crime committed by a fellow dragon, even a half-dragon like me."

"Where do the Copper Knights come into all of this?" asked Penelope.

"They belong to the dragons. They were gifts from the Hierarchy long ago. I knew I wouldn't be able to complete the quest on my own, but I also knew no dragons would help me, so I took control of the knights. Or I thought I had, anyway."

"And what about Rokk?" asked Anne. "What did the knights do to him?"

Valerian hung his head. "I honestly don't know anything about that."

Anne placed a hand on his shoulder. She was still mad about Rokk and about getting dragged into yet another quest against her will, but she felt bad for Valerian and what had happened to him and Emmanuelle.

The white dragon moaned. "Valerian."

Valerian rushed over to her side. "I'm here, Mother," he said.

"Valerian…the time is…nearing."

He threw his arms around her neck. "No. Please, not yet. Just hang on a little longer. We'll find a way to get you out of here."

The dragon shook her massive head. "It's too late… for me…but there is still time…for you to do the right thing.…Help them stop the knights."

"I will," said Valerian. "I promise."

The dragon sighed one last time and ceased moving. She had turned completely to stone. Valerian fell to his knees beside her and wept, his tears dripping onto her cold marble scales.

Anne, Penelope, and Hiro watched silently. Anne wished there was something she could do to ease Valerian's pain. She didn't pretend to understand everything that had happened, but Emmanuelle had died trying to help them, and for that Anne was grateful. She could only imagine the overwhelming pain of losing Penelope or Hiro.

As they stood there, a soft orange glow emanated from the dragon's chest. It grew brighter and brighter, emerging from beneath Emmanuelle's scales like a ghost. A small crystal pulsing with light fell to the ground with a soft clatter.

Without thinking, Anne reached down to pick it up. When the fingers of her gauntlet-hand closed around the crystal, a great jolt of energy surged through her body. The force of it threw her backward, and she slammed into the wall.

Someone called her name, but it sounded as if it were coming from very far away.

Anne's vision grew blurry, and then everything went dark.

13

A True Heir's Final Breath

Warmth.

      Light.

Color.

Anne felt shapes she could not see.

Saw shapes she could not feel.

Then flames.

Red eyes.

And the roar, the roar, the roar, the roar...

"Why is she still unconscious?" asked a voice that sounded like Penelope.

"I told you, I don't know," said another voice. That was Valerian. "Humans touch the stones all the time. There's no reason that should have happened."

"So what do we do now?" asked a third voice that was definitely Hiro.

"Keep her warm and comfortable," said Valerian. "And hope she wakes up soon."

Someone knelt beside her and took her hand.

Anne struggled to say something, anything, to reassure them. She was there, right there with them. She tried to move even a finger, anything at all, to let them know she could hear them. But her body would not obey. She couldn't even open her eyes.

"Anne, I don't know if you can hear me or not," said Penelope. "I just want you to know you're not alone."

She gave Anne's hand a squeeze.

Anne drifted once more into oblivion.

Anne was walking down a hallway, but she still wasn't in control of her body. It was like she was looking through someone else's eyes. She opened the door to the laboratory. She didn't know how she knew it was a laboratory. She just did. The door bore an image of a dragon. The image seemed familiar, but she couldn't quite place it. A plaque next to the door read: DR. ZARALA COLE.

Inside, a young man with pale white skin stood at the end of a long counter studying something under a microscope. He was tall and thin and had unruly dark hair. His lab coat was crisp and his loafers freshly shined. When the door clicked shut, he looked up.

"Ah, good morning, Dr. Cole," he said.

"Good morning, Dr. Grey," she heard herself say. "What were last night's test results?"

The young man scowled and gestured at the instrument in front of him. "The same as all the others. We're getting nowhere fast."

"Did you run the results through the spectrometer?"

"I've run them through every piece of equipment in this lab. Twice. They always come out negative."

He seemed about to say more, but held back.

"Was there something else?" she asked.

"I just...I think we need to reconsider adding a catalyst into the matrix. I'm certain if we just—"

"We've talked about this," she said. "It would introduce an unstable variable into the equation, and the results would therefore be unpredictable."

He became visibly annoyed. "I don't deny there are risks, but the council is becoming impatient. We need to show some progress, or they're going to start questioning the value of their ongoing support."

"I understand your concerns, but the answer is still no. I'm sorry, Oswald, but that's my final word on the matter."

The young man nodded curtly and didn't pursue the matter further, but she could tell he wasn't satisfied. She would have to keep an eye on him, just in case he decided to take matters into his own hands.

As Anne drifted off again, she thought she heard a crow cawing.

Her last image was of a single black feather.

Anne opened her eyes. It felt like she'd been asleep for an eternity. She tried moving her hand, and to her surprise it responded. She fanned her fingers and then balled them into a fist. Next, she wiggled her toes. When she tried to sit up, however, she became instantly dizzy and collapsed back. Fortunately, someone had placed a cloak under her head for a pillow.

A face appeared above her.

"Careful," said Valerian. "You've been out for nearly two days."

"Two days?" exclaimed Anne. "But—but how is that even possible?"

"Be thankful it was only two. At first, we were worried you might not wake up at all. You've been breathing a lot easier today, though, and I figured it was only a matter of time before you came around."

It all seemed like a dream now, fading away quickly.

Valerian helped her into a sitting position and offered her some bread and water. She was ravenous and immediately bit a large hunk off the bread. While she chewed, she examined her surroundings. The room they were in was smaller than the one where they had visited Emmanuelle.

"Where are we?" she asked.

"Not far from where you collapsed. I...couldn't stay there."

"I'm sorry," said Anne. "About your mother, I mean."

"Thanks," said Valerian.

"Where are Pen and Hiro?"

Valerian knelt and placed his hand on top of hers. "The Copper Knights have them."

The bread fell from Anne's hand. "What happened?"

"The maze isn't as lifeless as it looks," said Valerian. "Some of the rooms contain food. We were scavenging in an orchard not too far from here when the knights showed up and took Penelope and Hiro hostage."

Anne's eyes narrowed. "Why didn't they take you, too?"

"I don't know. I told you I escaped from them after they took Rokk and the sword, but the truth is once the airship landed, I simply walked away and they didn't try to stop me. I can't explain why."

Anne frowned. With all that had happened, she couldn't help but be suspicious of Valerian's account. On the other hand, if he had wanted to, he could have simply led the Copper Knights back here and let them capture her as well.

"Where are they now?" she asked.

"Still in the orchard. It's not far from here," he said. "The knights have offered a trade."

"For what? They already have the sword."

"True," said Valerian, "but they still need that." He pointed to Anne's gauntlet-hand, and she realized she'd had it clenched the whole time. She relaxed the fingers. In her palm lay the pulsing crystal that had emerged from Emmanuelle after she had died.

"What is it?" asked Anne.

"It's a bit complicated. In the dragon meeting hall, there's a large crystal formation—"

"I've seen it," said Anne. "The queen sat on top of it."

Valerian nodded. "It's called the Heartstone. Whenever a monarch gives birth, they lay the child on the stone, and one of these smaller crystals forms inside the baby dragon. That's why humans refer to the crystals as dragon stones."

"What does that have to do with the quest?" asked Anne.

Valerian swallowed. "The crystals emerge from the dragon upon death, as you saw with my mother. Because of that, dragons refer to them as a dragon's last breath."

Anne gasped and whispered the second line of the quest riddle. *"Anoint it with a true heir's final breath."*

"Exactly."

Anne looked at him. "Do you have one inside, too? One of the dragon stones?"

Valerian nodded. "That's the real reason the queen banished my mother. Because she dared to lay me, a half-dragon, on the Heartstone. I was going to use mine to anoint the sword."

"But to get your stone, wouldn't that mean you would have to…"

Anne left the rest unspoken.

"Now you understand why I needed the Copper Knights," Valerian said. "To complete my mission, once I was…no longer able to."

Anne shook her head. "We can't give them your mother's stone."

"But your friends—"

"We'll think of a way to help them, but if the knights reforge the Three-Handed Sword, I think there's a good chance they could kill the queen, no matter what she believes."

Valerian thought about this. "Once we give them the crystal, there would still be time to stop the knights. They can't repair the sword just anywhere. My mother's notes mentioned the location of the one forge capable of remaking such a weapon. We need only beat them there and destroy it."

"But they'll have a head start," said Anne.

Valerian grinned. "There's another archway near the orchard that the knights don't know about. And it so happens that it leads to the tier where the forge is located."

Anne felt torn. It was a huge risk giving the Copper Knights a dragon stone. On the other hand, she couldn't abandon her friends.

"Do you believe them?" she asked. "The Copper Knights, I mean. Do you believe they'll honor the trade?"

Valerian hesitated. "I honestly don't know. But what choice is there?"

"Well, I don't trust them. It's sure to be a trap of some sort."

"So what do we do?"

An idea formed in Anne's mind, and a smile slowly spread across her face.

"Easy," she said. "We spring the trap."

Valerian took the lead as they made their way along the black tunnels of the maze. After a dozen or so turns, Anne couldn't tell which way they were going. But

Valerian continued forward without hesitation. After about ten minutes, he finally slowed and pointed down a side tunnel.

"That's our exit," he said. "At the end of that corridor, there's a small chamber. The archway is in there." He took off his bag with the eye in it and handed it to Anne.

"You're trusting me with this?" asked Anne.

"Completely," said Valerian.

He took them down several more corridors, and Anne did her best to keep track of the sequence of turns, just in case she needed to find her way to the exit on her own. Finally, they entered a large cavern that contained a grove of apple trees. The Copper Knights were waiting at the entrance to a tunnel on the opposite side. Penelope and Hiro were there as well, with their arms tied securely. Anne couldn't contain a smile upon seeing her friends.

Also standing with them was Rokk.

"Rokk, you don't have to do this," said Anne. "Remember your encounter with the Matron? How you resisted her? You can do that again. You can resist the Copper Knights."

Rokk remained unmoving. He didn't so much as look in her direction.

"You're wasting your breath," said one of the Copper Knights. "He's with us. Now give us the stone."

"First release our friends," said Anne.

The knight nodded, and another knight undid their ropes.

The first knight pointed to Valerian. "Now the stone."

Valerian hesitated but brought out the glowing crystal. He and Anne walked to the center of the grove and waited. Rokk escorted Penelope and Hiro to meet him. Valerian placed the dragon stone in Rokk's massive hand. A green beam shot out of Rokk's eyes and scanned it.

"Well?" said the first knight.

"Analysis complete," said Rokk. "This is a true piece of the Heartstone."

"Excellent."

The knights raised their staffs and advanced on Anne, Penelope, and Hiro. Rokk didn't move or join them, but he didn't stop them, either.

"Wait," said Valerian. "We had a deal."

"And we kept it," said the first knight. "The deal was the safe return of your comrades in exchange for the dragon stone. We made no promise about what would happen after the trade was complete."

"Fair enough. But of course, neither did we," said Anne, and she turned to Valerian. "Now!"

It happened in the blink of an eye. One moment Valerian was standing there, and the next moment a large red dragon stood in his place. The dragon opened its mouth and spewed out a jet of red flame, forcing the knights to retreat.

"Run!" boomed the dragon. "Get to the archway!"

When Anne hesitated, Penelope grabbed her and Hiro and hauled them toward the tunnel that Anne and Valerian had come from. Once out of the cavern, Anne took the lead, and the three of them sprinted down corridors and around corners, zigging and zagging, with Anne doing her best to remember the correct route. Valerian's roaring became more distant. Anne could only hope he was okay.

Soon they reached the side corridor that Valerian had shown Anne, and they ran down it at full speed. At the end was a much smaller cave with an upright stone archway. Anne hurried over to the black stone pillar next to the archway and took Emmanuelle's eye out of the bag.

"Activate archway," she said.

The stone opened, and the glass sphere appeared.

"Please stand by for retinal scan," said the voice from the sphere. Anne held up the eye, and the red beam swept over it. "Identity verified."

The archway opened. The other side of the barrier showed a grassy field.

Penelope stepped in front of the archway and motioned for Anne and Hiro. "Come on," she urged. "Before they catch up."

Anne shook her head. "We can't leave without Valerian." She pointed at Hiro. "Be ready with your Minor Exploding Spell."

"That one isn't in this month's issue, either. The catalog does have a Tremor Spell, though."

"Use it. If they're chasing him, that might be our only means of stopping them."

As the seconds ticked by, she became increasingly worried that they had miscalculated, and feared they would have to leave Valerian behind. She didn't want to, but Valerian had made her swear to it. Getting to the forge and finding a way to prevent its use was their top priority.

Just when she was about to give up, there was a commotion from the other end of the corridor.

"Incoming!" yelled Penelope.

Valerian, back in his human form, stumbled around the bend. Anne and Penelope rushed over to assist him.

"They're right behind me," he mumbled. Anne heard clanking footsteps approaching from the corridor.

They helped Valerian to the archway.

"Now, Hiro!" shouted Anne.

Hiro quickly read the spell from his catalog.

The ground shook.

The walls crumbled.

And the cave collapsed.

THE POPULAR DO-IT-YOURSELF
GUIDE *HOW TO COLLAPSE A TUNNEL
WITHOUT KILLING OR MAIMING YOURSELF*
PROVIDES THE FOLLOWING DETAILED,
STEP-BY-STEP INSTRUCTIONS:

1) Don't do it.

14

The Sign of Zarala

Anne, Penelope, Hiro, and Valerian made it through the barrier just in time, followed by a clatter of falling rocks.

"Deactivate archway!" said Anne.

The archway behind them closed.

They were standing in the middle of a field of gray grass. The sky was overcast and gray. The rocks were gray, including the stones used to construct the archway (but excluding the ones that had fallen through the archway with them). Ahead of them, far in the distance, was a range of cold, gray mountains. In the other direction, much closer, was a collection of tall gray structures. It all looked familiar. Too familiar, in fact.

Jeffery appeared in a burst of light. "It's about time. I was starting to feel a little claustrophobic in there. Those gauntlets aren't exactly designed for comfort, you know." He looked around. "Hey, haven't we been here before?"

That was precisely what Anne was thinking. During their first quest, they had visited a cold gray tier just like this one. It was known as a dead tier. Dead tiers were the result of a failed Level Twelve quest, and no life grew on one ever again. This did not, however, mean there were no dangers, and Anne recalled only too well being chased by a swarm of mechanical dragonflies. The memory made her shudder.

"Do you really think this is the same dead tier we visited during the last quest?" asked Hiro.

Jeffery shrugged. "I don't know, but how many of them can there be?"

"Anne, over here," said Penelope.

Penelope was kneeling on the ground next to Valerian, who was lying flat on his back. Anne rushed over. His face was pale, and when Anne placed her hand on his, it felt cold and clammy.

"What happened?" she asked.

"I don't know. He just collapsed."

Anne gently shook his shoulder. "Valerian, can you hear me?"

After a moment, Valerian began to stir.

"I'm okay," he rasped. He sat up slowly. "I could go for a drink of water, though."

Hiro handed Valerian the water skin from his pack, and he took a long drink. After a few minutes his color seemed to return, and he stood up again.

"Sorry about that," he said. "I've never tried to hold my dragon form for that long." He looked around. "Did everyone get out?"

"Yes," said Anne. "Thanks to you."

He smiled. "Thanks for waiting for me."

"So where's this forge, anyway?" asked Penelope.

Valerian scanned the horizon and pointed to the structures in the distance. "The city. The forge is there."

They headed out, with Anne and Valerian taking the lead and Hiro and Penelope following behind. Jeffery scouted ahead and reported back every few minutes on the upcoming terrain. Unsurprisingly, it was all gray. The only nongray point of interest came from the city itself, where there were intermittent flashes of light.

Around midday, after nearly two hours of walking, they stopped in the cool shade of a gray oak tree. Valerian shared some edible fungi he'd gathered while in the maze. It was tough chewing, but it had a nutty flavor that was not unpleasant.

"By my calculations, the knights are probably out of the maze by now," said Valerian. "They need to travel here by airship, though, so we should still have lots of time."

After everyone had eaten their fill, they set out again. It was another hour of walking before they reached the outskirts of the city. The buildings were impossibly tall. Anne had no idea how someone could construct something so large. The flashing lights turned out to be reflected light. Each building was covered entirely in mirrored glass, which reflected sunlight in all directions. The farther into the city's interior they went, however, the darker it became. And colder.

"Look there," said Valerian.

A small brown bird perched on the doorframe of one of the buildings. The bird didn't make any sound, but it peered at them curiously.

"Where did that come from?" said Penelope.

"Jeffery, I thought nothing could live on a dead tier," said Anne.

"I didn't think anything could, either," said Jeffery. "Of course, if you'd let me eat more books, I could provide you with more thorough and up-to-date information."

"Nice try," said Anne.

"I have a bad feeling about this," said Hiro.

Anne agreed. They walked across the wide avenue to the next street. When Anne looked back, the bird was still watching their every step.

"Don't look now," said Penelope, "but we have more company."

Perched over the door of the building directly ahead was another small brown bird, identical to the first. In fact, Anne looked back to make sure it wasn't the same bird, but the first one was still watching them on the other side of the street.

"They look like sparrows," said Valerian.

Anne studied the bird in front of them. "I think you're right," she said. "Jeffery, I don't suppose you want to try talking with them?"

"You are correct," said Jeffery, "in supposing that I don't want to."

"But you're a sparrow, too," said Anne.

"I was told never to talk to strange birds."

"Who told you that?"

"I told myself, and I trust me implicitly."

They continued forward while keeping constant track of the birds. Then they rounded a corner and were greeted by another dozen or so perched on various doorframes and ledges.

"This is a bit unnerving," said Hiro.

"Well, they haven't tried to swarm and kill us yet," said Penelope, "which means that so far this dead tier rates above the first one we visited. Unless this *is* the first one, in which case never mind."

"Over here," said Valerian. He led them off the main avenue and into a small park surrounded by a low stone wall. The branches of the trees were filled with sparrows.

In the middle of the park was an obelisk. It was slightly taller than Penelope and appeared to be made of the same black stone as the pillars that operated the archways—which, now that they had been in the Never-Ending Maze, reminded Anne of the black walls there as well.

"This is it," said Valerian.

Anne looked around. "What is?"

Valerian pointed to the obelisk. "This monument. This is where the forge is."

"You mean this pillar is the forge?" asked Penelope.

"No, it's the doorway to the forge," said Valerian. "I don't know how it works, though."

They walked around the obelisk. Three sides were bare, but the fourth side had a message inscribed in some strange script. None of them could read what it said, not even Hiro, who had studied a few ancient languages. Below the inscription, near the bottom of the obelisk, was a tiny plaque with a carved image. Anne knelt to get a better look. It was a dragon—and not just any dragon.

"Look at this," she said excitedly.

Hiro crouched beside her. "The Sign of Zarala."

"What does that mean?" asked Valerian.

"It means we're close," said Anne. "It's the same as the image on the medallion. On our first quest, that symbol on a map helped us locate one of the major destinations, a place called the Infinite Tower."

Anne inspected the dragon image more closely. A series of very faint, curved scratches were visible on the main pillar around the plaque. "There are some marks here," she said.

Hiro inspected them. "It looks like they were caused by something rotating. And technically the dragon image is on its side. Maybe it turns?"

Anne grabbed the plaque and tried turning it in both directions, but it didn't budge. "I guess not."

"Maybe it's locked," suggested Penelope.

They examined the rest of the obelisk for any sign of a locking mechanism but found none. After checking the obelisk a third time, they decided to fan out and see if there might be any hints in the rest of the park. Other than dead gray grass and bushes, however, there wasn't much to see.

The birds in the trees continued to watch them curiously, but otherwise they did nothing to interfere.

"Check this out," called Penelope. She was standing near a corner of the park's stone wall. Everyone joined her, and Penelope pulled back some gray vines to reveal another small plaque containing yet another dragon image. It, too, was sideways and had scratches around it.

"Try turning this one," said Hiro.

Penelope grabbed the plaque and gave it a twist. At first it resisted, but with effort she was able to turn it until the image was straight. There was a distinct click as it locked into place.

The sky suddenly filled with sparrows screeching and diving at them.

"Duck!" yelled Anne.

Everyone hurried across the park to the obelisk. Anne tried to turn the plaque again, and this time it moved a fraction of a turn.

"There must be more," she shouted over the din. "Check the other corners."

Penelope, Hiro, and Valerian ran to the remaining three corners of the stone wall as the sparrows chased after them.

"I've got one," yelled Valerian.

"Me too," said Hiro.

"Me three," called Penelope.

Some of the sparrows dove at Valerian as he crouched down, but a sudden flare of light sent them scattering. Jeffery swooped through the air, zigzagging back and forth, chasing the sparrows away. Valerian turned the plaque and ran back over to Anne.

"Done," he said.

Anne tried the plaque on the obelisk again, and it turned a bit more.

Then Hiro arrived, breathing heavily. "All finished," he said.

Anne turned the plaque again. It was almost in place.

Penelope was having trouble, in part because she kept having to stand up and swat away the sparrows. Now that three of the plaques had been turned, all the sparrows were concentrating on her.

Anne, Hiro, and Valerian ran over.

"It's stuck," said Penelope.

Valerian knelt down to help her with the plaque. Meanwhile, Anne removed her cloak and used it to shoo away the sparrows. Hiro did the same. Penelope and Valerian both strained until Anne thought their heads would explode, but finally the plaque turned.

They returned to the obelisk. Anne closed her eyes and made a silent wish for it to work. She grabbed the plaque and gave it a final twist. It turned smoothly and clicked into place. Then the entire obelisk slid backward to reveal a hidden stairway leading underground.

The sparrows flocked together and swarmed, digging at them with claws and beaks.

"Everyone inside!" yelled Anne.

Penelope went first, followed by Valerian and Hiro. Anne went last, but before she dropped belowground, she reached up and turned the plaque sideways again. The obelisk immediately slid back into place, nearly taking her head off.

The stairs led down to a long corridor that would have been completely dark were it not for Jeffery's glowing feathers. Anne could hear the sparrows chattering outside, but with the obelisk closed, the noise was considerably muffled. She was about to ask how everyone was doing when the hallway suddenly filled with a cloud of sparrows, screeching and diving.

"How did they get through?" yelled Hiro.

The group ducked and ran down the corridor, which led to a door that opened into a room filled with strange equipment. Once everyone was inside, Anne slammed the door shut, but that didn't stop the sparrows. The birds passed directly through the solid barrier.

"What's going on?" shouted Valerian.

"I think they're holograms," said Jeffery.

"If they're holograms, then how come they hurt so much?" said Penelope, as she fought off half a dozen at once. "I thought holograms were made of light."

"We can figure that out later," said Anne. "Right now we need to get rid of them."

"Turn off their emitter," said Jeffery.

"Their what?"

"The thing that makes them appear," said Jeffery. "Remember on our first quest when the Matron smashed that gray box and the Construct disappeared?"

"What's 'the Construct'?" asked Valerian.

"Never mind," yelled Penelope. "Just look for a gray metal box!"

Everyone fanned out and searched the room. In one corner, buried beneath some crates, Anne found it: a tall, gray metal box with a completely smooth surface.

"It's here, but I don't know how to turn it off," she said, running her hands over it.

"Stand back," said Penelope. "I'll turn it off." She lifted a metal chair over her head.

"I'd really prefer if you didn't do that," said a voice behind them.

Penelope froze, and Anne spun around.

In the center of the room, in the middle of the chaos, stood a young woman. She wore a simple tunic and pants and a thin, knee-length white coat, and she appeared to be Anne's exact twin, except that her eyes were brown, not yellow.

Anne, Penelope, and Hiro had met her once before.

It was the Construct.

THE HANDMAIDEN'S TWIN

Once upon a time, there was a handmaiden whose job it was to spin yarn for her mistress. Day after day, all she did was spin, spin, spin. She got a break only once every other Saturday to play a rousing game of rugby.

Deciding there had to be more to life than spinning yarn, the handmaiden invented a duplicating machine and created a twin of herself. She set her twin to work and then spent a leisurely day walking through the forest, swimming in a stream of clear water, and arm wrestling the occasional bear.

When the handmaiden returned home, however, she discovered that her twin had not done as instructed. Instead, the twin had used the machine to create even more twins, who were all now arguing over whose job it was to spin yarn. Rather than becoming angry, the handmaiden saw an opportunity. The twins formed a theater troupe, made a small fortune, and used the money to buy the world's largest radish.

There is no moral to this story.

15

The Forge

Anne stared at the young woman, who had a faint aura around her that flashed briefly whenever it caught the light. It was a little like looking at a ghost. Anne's twin ghost.

"I thought you were dead," said Anne. "You disappeared when the Matron destroyed that gray box."

The Construct smiled. "Dying would be very difficult considering I have never actually been alive. That box was merely a remote terminal, and while its destruction prevented me from appearing, my actual program is located elsewhere."

Penelope cleared her throat. "Um, not to interrupt this happy little reunion," she said while crouched on the floor next to Hiro and Valerian, "but could you maybe do something about these birds?" The holographic sparrows hadn't stopped attacking.

"My apologies," said the Construct. She tilted her head slightly and her expression went momentarily blank.

The sparrows disappeared.

The Construct smiled. "There, all taken care of."

Anne's ears were ringing in the sudden silence, which was wonderful. Penelope, Hiro, and Valerian rose to their feet, still slightly wary, half-expecting the sparrows to reappear at any moment and continue their attack.

"What are they?" asked Anne.

"A security program," said the Construct. "They act as my eyes and ears and let me know when potential intruders are approaching. Unfortunately, they can get a little carried away."

"Tell me about it," muttered Penelope. "How come they can touch us?"

The Construct walked over and poked Penelope in the shoulder. "You mean like that?"

"Hey, how did you do that?"

"The other terminal you encountered was less sophisticated. The terminals here are more powerful. They emit what you might call solid holograms."

"They're solid, all right," said Hiro, rubbing the scratches on his arm.

"Sorry if I'm being rude, but who are you?" Valerian asked.

"I am known as the Construct. I serve as the interface for the computer."

"Er, the what?"

"We'll fill you in later," said Penelope.

Valerian looked back and forth between the Construct and Anne. "But why do the two of you look alike?"

"I was designed to look this way," said the Construct. She studied Anne with curiosity. "So, Anvil of Saint Lupin's, Keeper of the Sparrow, another quest so soon?"

Anne frowned. "I wasn't planning on it, but yes, another one got activated. This one is a Dragon Slayer quest."

The Construct smiled and shook her head. "That is how the quest has been presented to you, of course. In reality, the name is an anagram."

"A what-a-what?" said Penelope.

"Anagram," said Hiro. "It's when the letters from one word or phrase are rearranged to spell something else."

"What does *Dragon Slayer* stand for, then?" asked Anne.

"It's really a Send Array Log quest," said the Construct. "After the Write Error Check from the first quest was performed, this second quest was designed to assess the integrity of the World Engine Array—the part of the computer that created the Hierarchy. The log verifies if the Array is operating correctly."

"And where does killing the dragon queen fit into all of this?"

"The dragon monarch carries the array log within her."

Valerian's eyes widened with realization at the exact moment Anne also figured it out. "The dragon stones," they said in unison.

"Correct," said the Construct. "Dragons were the original protectors of the computer, even though they long ago forgot their true purpose. Each dragon stone carries the necessary information. You need only take one of the stones to an upload terminal."

"We can worry about that part later," said Anne.

"Right now we need to shut down the forge that's located here. Can you do that for us?"

"I am unable to access it from here," said the Construct. "For security reasons, the forge operates on a stand-alone network. But you should be able to lock out the knights by changing the security code. I will take you there."

The Construct turned and walked through the wall. A moment later she reappeared.

"My apologies," she said. "After ten thousand years on my own, I tend to forget not everyone can do that."

The Construct took them through a different door to a room whose only feature was a white pillar, which reminded Anne of a device called an elevator. She'd only ridden in one once, when she, Penelope, Hiro, and Rokk had descended from the top of the Infinite Tower during their first quest.

A seam appeared, and a set of doors slid apart.

The Construct gestured inside. "Down we go."

The Construct entered, followed by Anne, Penelope, and Hiro, but Valerian hesitated.

"It's fine," said Anne. "We've done this before."

He nodded and stepped inside, still looking a little uncertain despite her reassurances.

The doors closed again and the elevator descended. Unlike the previous elevator, this one had a window, and Anne peered through it. They were in an enormous cavern that dwarfed even the arena on the dragon tier.

"During your first quest, I take it you found Zarala's lab at Saint Lupin's," said the Construct.

"Yes," said Anne. "Unfortunately, it got destroyed in my final battle with the Matron. But I did learn about Project A.N.V.I.L. Can you tell me anything about that?"

"It is unimportant."

"Unimportant? But I was going to ask the dragon queen about it."

"I cannot make your choices for you, but my advice would be not to waste your question on such a trivial matter."

Anne couldn't believe her ears. She had obsessed about Project A.N.V.I.L. for the past two months. How could the Construct expect her not to be curious about it?

"Can you tell me about it, then?" asked Anne.

"That information has been locked inside a coded file. Do you have the password?"

"No."

"Then I cannot help you."

It irked Anne to be this close to the information she so badly wanted, yet be unable to get it. After several minutes, the elevator reached the bottom. Upon exiting the elevator, the Construct pointed to a large, square building of gray stone in the distance.

"The forge is inside that structure," she said.

The group crossed the cavern, but as they neared the building, the Construct slowed.

"What's wrong?" said Anne.

"Something isn't right," said the Construct. "I'm not receiving a signal from the security grid."

"Um, isn't that a good thing?" said Penelope.

"Even when it is dormant, it sends out a signal to indicate that the program is working properly. But I'm not picking up any signal at all."

They continued forward cautiously. When they reached the building's front door, they found it ajar.

"Does anyone else hear that sound?" asked Hiro.

Anne listened, and indeed there was a low humming noise. As they stepped inside, the humming became even louder. Beyond the entrance was a long, black corridor. Jeffery began to shimmer.

"I think you'd better go back inside the gauntlet for now," said Anne.

"I agree," said Jeffery, his voice modulating, and he disappeared.

They proceeded down the corridor, and the humming grew louder still. The corridor wasn't long, and at the end, another open door led into a dark room. The only visible light was a red strobe on top of a structure directly in front of them. The structure was a massive cube, twenty feet to a side. The side of the cube facing them held a vault-like metal door, easily twelve feet high, with a single word inscribed across its surface:

F.O.R.G.E.

"Behold, the Finite Optimized Replication Generator," said the Construct.

"Um, that only uses four of the letters," said Anne.

"It takes both the *g* and the *e* from *generator*," said the Construct. "Apparently, someone struggled in coming up with a good acronym."

"That's the forge?" said Valerian, sounding surprised. "I thought it would be, you know, an actual forge."

"It looks like an Old World device," said Hiro.

"Yes," said the Construct. "And it's been activated."

Anne scanned the surrounding space. The flashing red light made it hard to see, and the corners of the room remained in deep shadow. However, she could make out catwalks crisscrossing the space above them.

"Does the forge operate on its own, too, like the security grid?" asked Anne.

"No," said the Construct. "It most definitely does not."

The humming grew to a crescendo and then abruptly ceased. The flashing light changed from red to green, and somewhere a bell chimed. Everyone stepped back as the giant door swung slowly open. Inside, rotating in the air in the center of the cube, hung an eight-foot gleaming blade.

The Three-Handed Sword of the Guardian had been reforged.

"Wow," said Penelope. "That's the most awesomest sword I've ever seen in even my whole life."

"Too awesome for proper grammar, apparently," said Hiro, and Penelope elbowed him in the ribs.

"But—but how did it get in there?" asked Anne.

"I do not know," said the Construct. "This is very troubling."

Suddenly, a large figure emerged from the shadows behind them.

It was Rokk.

"Please stand aside," he said.

As before, Rokk didn't show any sign that he knew who Anne, Penelope, and Hiro were.

"Why should we?" said Penelope.

While Anne appreciated Penelope's courage, she wasn't sure it was such a great idea to provoke a ten-foot-tall robot that hadn't exactly been functioning properly as of late. That was the sort of thing that got you squashed.

"I am the Guardian," said Rokk. "The Three-Handed Sword belongs to me."

"And what are you going to do with it?" asked Anne.

Rokk's eyes glowed red. "Kill the queen."

*Psychopathic killer robots
don't make good friends.*

—Lyrics from "Psychopathic Killer Robots Don't Make
Good Friends," by the bard formerly known as That Guy
Who Played in the Local Tavern One Time

The Knights of Saint Lupin's

"We can't let you do that," said Anne.

"You cannot stop me," said Rokk.

"He's got a point there," said Hiro.

Something clanked above them, and Anne looked up. The six Copper Knights were standing on a catwalk directly overhead. They leapt off and landed next to Rokk. Each held its staff at the ready, prepared to send out a lightning bolt at the least provocation.

"Do as he commands," said one of the knights. "Step aside and give us the sword."

"Or else what?" said Penelope.

In reply, the knight fired a bolt of lightning from its staff, hitting the floor and leaving a black scorch mark.

Penelope nodded. "Fair enough. I was just confirming."

Valerian leaned over and whispered into Anne's ear. "Like before. You three grab the sword. I'll deal with them."

Before Anne could reply, Valerian transformed into a red dragon and charged at Rokk and the knights. Even though Valerian had done the exact same thing to the knights only a few hours before, the surprise attack still caught them off guard. Valerian bowled over three of the knights and sent Rokk stumbling backward before they could react. Rokk quickly recovered, however, and tackled the red dragon around the neck, twisting him and forcing him against the wall. The three knights who had managed to remain on their feet each grabbed a leg and tried to pull the red dragon to the ground.

"We need to help him," shouted Penelope.

"No," said Anne. "Come with me."

Anne charged into the forge and grabbed for the sword. As soon as she touched it, the sword dropped out of the air, but it was too heavy to hold. The hilt struck the floor, and the sword toppled over and clanged onto the ground. Penelope ran over, and they tried to lift it. Hiro joined them, but even with the three of them lifting, they were barely able to raise it an inch. Finally, they dropped it.

"How are we supposed to get out of here with that thing?" asked Hiro.

The Construct approached Anne. "I might be able to gain control of the Copper Knights. There is a terminal in here that will allow me to link directly with the forge's network. It has a small button at the back. You need only press it."

"Why can't you do it?"

"My programming does not allow me to take a course of action that could potentially damage this structure."

Anne scanned the room. "Where is it?"

The Construct pointed to a gray box next to the back wall, past where Rokk and the knights were fighting with the red dragon.

"It figures," said Anne. She turned to Penelope and Hiro. "Get the sword out of here."

Anne peeked out the door. The red dragon had one knight clutched in each of his front paws, and he expelled a burst of fire at Rokk, who rolled away to avoid the flames.

It was now or never. Anne dashed for the back wall, leaping over a fallen knight and ducking under a twirling staff that bounced off the wall. She reached the gray box and ran her hand down the back until she located a small indentation. She pressed in with her finger and felt it lock into place.

"And just what do you think you're doing?" said a voice.

One of the knights reached for her, but she spun out of its grasp and ran back to help Penelope and Hiro with the sword. The knight gave chase, but it was forced to stop its pursuit when the red dragon landed across its path. The dragon righted himself and swung his tail at the knight, knocking it off its feet.

Anne reached the Construct.

"It's done," said Anne.

The Construct nodded.

"Okay," said Anne. "Anytime now."

"Yes," said the Construct.

Anne could tell Valerian was tiring from his battle with the knights and Rokk. He had already held on to his dragon form far longer than before, and Anne doubted he had much more fight left in him.

"Are you going to take control of the knights or not?" she asked.

"I am trying," said the Construct.

Anne frowned. "I thought you said you could stop them."

"I am unable to establish a connection."

Anne looked on helplessly as the battled raged. The red dragon pounced on two of the knights, but they rolled aside and targeted him with their staffs. The dragon howled in pain as the lightning bolts struck his flanks. Two knights grabbed Penelope and Hiro and held them captive.

"There is another possibility," said the Construct. "An electromagnetic pulse might temporarily sever the connection and incapacitate them. You did it once before, when you destroyed the dragonflies on your previous quest. Be aware, however, that it will also adversely affect any unshielded electronics in the vicinity."

"Does that include Rokk?" asked Anne, suddenly fearful for the robot's life.

"I cannot be certain. You must decide which is more important right now: your friend, or preventing the knights from completing their mission."

How could Anne possibly choose? In their short time

together, Rokk had become a good friend. More than that: He had become like family. How could she knowingly hurt him? And yet, if he could speak for himself in this moment, his true self, she knew he would tell her to do whatever she had to in order to stop the knights, even if it meant hurting him.

Anne looked at Rokk and whispered, "I'm sorry."

Anne tried to remember how she had sent out the pulse before. She recalled feeling utterly overwhelmed and just wishing the attacks would stop. She willed the pulse to activate, but nothing happened.

"Activate electromagnetic pulse," she said, but still nothing happened.

Rokk delivered a devastating blow, and the red dragon fell to the floor, where he transformed back into human form. One of the knights picked up its staff and walked over to the prone form of Valerian. It aimed the staff directly at him.

"Stop!" screamed Anne.

A wall of blue energy burst forth from the gauntlet and swept through the room. The knights froze in place, and Penelope and Hiro escaped from their grasp. Anne had done it. Or had she? One of the figures still moved:

Rokk.

Anne was equal parts relieved and terrified—Rokk had survived the electromagnetic pulse, but what would he do next? As if in answer, Rokk stepped past Anne to where the Three-Handed Sword lay on the floor. He picked it up with ease, his three hands wrapping around the hilt perfectly. Then one of his hands opened a panel in his side, reached in, and brought out the dragon stone. Emmanuelle's last breath. Before Anne could speak, Rokk inserted the stone into the pommel of the sword. There was a brief flash, and the entire blade glowed blue. Without a word, Rokk turned and sprinted from the room.

Anne started after him.

"Wait!" said the Construct.

"But he's getting away," said Anne.

"You will not be able to catch him. Even if you could, you would not have the strength to overpower him."

Anne slumped against the door of the forge. "Then they're still going to win."

"Not necessarily," said the Construct. She motioned for Anne to follow her.

The Construct approached a Copper Knight and pointed to a small circle on the back of the knight's collar.

In it was an engraving of a bird with its wings outstretched, and beneath the circle were inscribed four words:

MAGICKAL ALL-TERRAIN RECONNAISSANCE VEHICLE

Next to the words were a letter and a number: A1.

"Do you see this image?" asked the Construct.

Anne shrugged. "It's a sparrow, I think."

"Watch this."

The Construct pushed on the circle, which turned out to be a button. With a hissing noise, a seam appeared down the center of the knight's back, as if by magick. The armor plates on either side of the seam retracted, creating an opening. Without warning, a man fell backward out of the knight. Anne jumped aside to avoid being squashed as the man collapsed onto the floor. He was pale and disheveled, but Anne recognized him.

It was Niles Twinkletoes, the Lord Chamberlain of the Sapphire Palace.

--·—◇❈◇—·--

Anne knelt next to the Lord Chamberlain. His chest was rising and falling. Oddly, he was still in the same clothes he had worn to the awards ceremony several days ago.

Penelope peered over Anne's shoulder. "Hey, it's that old guy from the royal palace. How did he get in there?"

How, indeed? Anne's mind reeled.

"I suggest checking the other knights as well," said the Construct.

Anne, Penelope, and Hiro quickly hurried over to the other knights. Each knight was labeled as the first one, except each one had its own unique number, A2 through A6. As they pressed the buttons, five more people tumbled out of the other metal suits. They all turned out to be committee members from the awards ceremony.

"How did they end up inside the knights?" said Penelope. "Is this who we've been fighting all along?"

Anne, Penelope, and Hiro looked at Valerian, who was now conscious and sitting up.

"I had no idea there were people inside," he said. "I thought they were empty."

Anne recalled the events in the library. "You arrived while the ceremony was going on. The committee members definitely weren't inside them then. They were still on stage."

"And they were still there after the knights left, too," added Penelope.

"Maybe the knights returned to the capital and kidnapped them later," suggested Hiro, "while Valerian was traveling with us."

"Maybe," said Valerian, but his tone was doubtful. Nor did Anne believe that was the case. She felt certain something else was going on, but she couldn't put her finger on what. She turned to the Construct.

"How did you know they would be in there?" said Anne.

"I didn't," said the Construct.

"But you at least knew there *could* be people inside."

"Of course. What you refer to as iron knights, or in this particular case as Copper Knights, are in reality Old World power suits. They can be operated manually by someone called a pilot. If necessary, each power suit can place its pilot in temporary stasis, which is like freezing them in time. Given the current condition of the committee members, I would suggest this is what happened."

"But if the committee members were frozen this whole time, how were the knights moving and talking?"

The Construct smiled grimly. "I believe the answer to that question will prove very interesting."

The Lord Chamberlain roused. Anne and Penelope helped him into a sitting position.

"Where am I?" he asked groggily.

"On a tier very far from the capital," said Anne. "What's the last thing you remember?"

He reached up a wobbly hand to scratch the side of his head. "I remember getting dressed for the awards ceremony. Walking onto the stage. After that? Not too much, I'm afraid."

"Do you recall being attacked by the Copper Knights?"

A look of concern crossed his face. "There's been an attack?"

"I don't think he's going to be much help," said Penelope.

Anne agreed, and she realized they didn't have much time. Rokk was on his way to kill the queen. If they couldn't stop him, they at least needed to find a way to warn her.

Anne turned to Valerian. "Can you send us to the dragon tier by fireball?"

Valerian shook his head. "Sorry, but I can barely stand, let alone transform again. I need time to recover."

They couldn't wait. Then another way sprang to Anne's mind.

"Valerian, you said there was an archway above the throne room that none of the other dragons know about," said Anne.

"Yes," said Valerian. "What of it?"

"How long would it take to reach it?"

Valerian thought about this. "Well, we collapsed the cave behind us, so we can't go back through the archway that brought us here. The next-closest archway is at least a six-hour hike from the city. Then it's another three hours through the Never-Ending Maze from that point to get to the archway that leads to the throne room. By that time, we'll be too late."

"Not necessarily," said Anne with a smile.

Six Copper Knights exited the city at a dead run. Anne took the lead, followed by Penelope, Hiro, and Valerian. Because they would be going out of the range of the remote terminal, the Construct uploaded herself into the fifth knight in order to accompany them. The Lord Chamberlain was operating the sixth. He had recovered sufficiently to travel and decided that operating one of the Copper Knights "looked like a hoot." Although the remaining committee members had also regained consciousness, there were no more suits available, so they had to remain behind.

Much to Anne's amazement, the knight she was piloting fit her perfectly. As soon as she climbed inside, the knight seemed to shrink to fit her body, even though Penelope assured her that from the outside it looked the same size it had been all along. Everyone else reported a similar phenomenon. The interior of each knight transformed to fit its pilot. Perhaps they were like the treasure chest that had contained the pieces of the Three-Handed Sword: The inside didn't necessarily match the outside.

After the back of the knight closed behind Anne, a series of panels on the interior of the helmet lit up all around her, showing her images of the outside. Then a band of light appeared around her head, and she found herself instantly in control. When she walked, the knight walked, and when she spoke, everyone could hear her.

They covered ground quickly and reached the archway in a little over thirty minutes. This one was built into the side of a hill. Once in the maze, it took them only another fifteen minutes of travel to reach the archway Valerian had said led to the throne room.

"Are you sure you want to do this?" asked Valerian. "You'll be returning to a tier full of angry dragons who tried to execute you."

"We're the Knights of Saint Lupin's!" cried Penelope. "We laugh in the face of danger!"

Anne smiled. It was hard to argue with that.

She exited her knight just long enough to activate the archway's black pillar and allow the glass sphere to scan the eye. The archway opened, and they proceeded through in single file. The space on the other side of the archway was dark and cramped, especially for six Copper Knights.

"Hey, quit shoving," said Penelope.

"Sorry," Hiro replied.

The "wall" in front of the group consisted of large scraps of metal and giant coils of wire and tubes. Light filtered through various cracks, and Anne found one large enough to provide a mostly unobscured view of the throne room.

"Is it clear?" asked Valerian.

Their plan was to enter the throne room when it was empty, seek out the queen, and present her with everything they knew (or at least everything they thought they knew). Unfortunately, the throne room was packed with dragons.

"No," Anne responded. "It looks like something's happening."

A dragon guard entered and took up a position near the door.

"Your Majesty," said the guard. "The committee from the Hierarchy has arrived."

"Show them in," said the queen.

The guard spoke to someone outside the door, and a moment later a group of people entered. Anne recognized them as the members of the awards committee, but that didn't make sense. How could the committee members possibly have beaten them here, especially without any form of transportation? Even more baffling, the Lord Chamberlain was with them. How could he be in two places at once?

"Imposter!" said the Lord Chamberlain next to Anne with indignation.

The Lord Chamberlain in the throne room stepped forward and unrolled a scroll. As he did, Anne caught a glint of light. When she looked at the other committee members, brief flashes of light came from them as well. Was it just the way the torchlight was striking them?

Then it struck her. "I—I think they might be holograms," she said.

"Who?" asked Penelope.

"The committee members in the throne room. When they move a certain way, I can see brief flashes of light, like when the Construct moves around."

"I am not aware of any other active holograms," said the Construct. "Although it is not impossible."

"If they're solid holograms, no one would know the difference," said Hiro.

The Lord Chamberlain down in the throne room cleared his throat and began reading. "We, the duly elected representatives of the Hierarchy, do hereby utterly and without reserve acknowledge the breaking of the treaty between our two peoples with the activation of a Dragon Slayer quest. Therefore, as of this moment, we enact Section 5, Article 12, of the treaty, as is our duty, and submit ourselves for your judgment."

The dragons in the throne room let out a deafening roar.

"What just happened?" Anne yelled over the din.

"Nothing good," said Hiro. "The committee just surrendered the Hierarchy to the dragons."

ACCORDING TO *THE ULTIMATE GUIDE TO DRAGON SLAYERS*, THE THREE MOST FAMOUS DRAGON SLAYERS IN THE HISTORY OF THE HIERARCHY ARE:

1) Kork the Orc, famous for fighting dragons by ramming them with his airships. Credited with nine kills and fifty-seven destroyed ships.

2) Wistonia Carpediem, known for slaying dragons using only the finest tweed.

3) Sir Squeaksalot, famous folk leader during the Great Squirrel Uprising, who defeated the colossal dragon known as Q the One-Eyed by impaling him upon a slightly moistened toothpick.

17

The Queen of Dragons
on Her Throne

"We have to get down there," said Anne.

"But if we go back and try to locate another archway, we'll be too late," said Hiro.

"I'm not suggesting we find another archway. I'm suggesting we go down there now."

"How?" said Penelope. "We're stuck behind tons of junk here."

"Yes, but we also have six Copper Knights that have ten times our strength." Anne maneuvered her knight in front of the largest metal panel. "Everyone form a line," she said. "If we push together, we should be able to create an opening."

Everyone moved into place and began pushing on the panel. At first, nothing happened, but then slowly, inch by inch, the panel began to move.

"Keep pushing," Anne called out.

Finally, they managed to shove the panel over the lip, at which point gravity took over. A large pile of scrap metal fell with the panel, which slammed into the floor of the throne room with a thunderous clang.

Anne didn't waste any time or give any instructions. She simply stepped to the edge and jumped, landing in the midst of the rubble. Moments later, five other knights landed beside her. Aiming for the Heartstone, Anne managed two steps before her knight suddenly stopped and everything went dark.

"What happened?" said Anne. "Hello? Anyone?"

No one answered.

"Activate GPS," said Anne.

Jeffery appeared in front of her face in a burst of light. "What's up, buttercup?"

"My power suit stopped working."

"Um, power suit?"

"Long story. The Copper Knights are really something from the Old World called power suits. We're inside one now, but it stopped working."

Jeffery inspected the interior of the helmet. "Well, I've only known about power suits for all of seven seconds, but in my expert opinion, I'd say it's been deactivated."

"Can you fix it?" asked Anne.

"I can try," he said, and he dove into the panel directly in front of her in a splash of light, leaving her once again in darkness.

Anne strained to hear what was going on outside the suit. Without the display panel, she couldn't see anything. She heard footsteps approach—large ones, if she wasn't mistaken—and then the queen's voice called out:

"Open!"

To Anne's surprise, the panel in front of her retracted so that her face was exposed. She quickly glanced to either side. She couldn't see all the other knights, but the few she could see were also frozen in place, and the fronts of their helmets were also opened. They were completely surrounded by dragon guards. The dragon queen herself, however, was still seated on the Heartstone.

Anne could see anger burning in the queen's eyes, and Anne's heart beat faster.

"Well, well," said the queen in a quiet voice. "Our wayward prisoners have returned."

"Your Majesty, hear me," said Anne. "Those representatives from the Hierarchy are imposters. We think they're something called holograms. The real members of the committee were captured by the Copper Knights."

"Lies!" said the fake Lord Chamberlain. "Your majesty, this is preposterous! Outrageous!"

"Please, Your Majesty," Anne continued. "The real Lord Chamberlain is here with us, right there inside one of the Copper Knights."

"You mean *my* Copper Knights?" said the queen. "You would dare use my own weapons against me? How foolish of you, for I wield ultimate control over them. As you can see, no one may use them without my permission, especially not some ragtag band of humans."

"We're not attacking you," said Anne. "We came here to warn you."

"Silence!" bellowed the queen. She stared at Anne with loathing. "Once I have concluded my business with the Hierarchy, I shall enjoy watching your execution. And this time there will be no trials."

Anne gulped.

Looking around desperately, Anne happened to glance back up to the ledge, high above the throne room, from where she and the others had dropped. There stood Rokk. He must have followed them through the archway, which she realized now they had forgotten to deactivate. His hands grasped the Three-Handed Sword, which pulsed with blue light. Even from a distance, it looked powerful. Anne harbored no doubts that it could slay a dragon.

Rokk raised the sword and pointed it at the queen. "I bring you a message," he said. "A message of death." With that, he leapt from the ledge.

The third line of the riddle ran through Anne's head: *Kill not the queen of dragons on her throne.*

Time seemed to slow. Anne willed her legs to move, so that she might reach the queen and push her out of the way, but her knight remained frozen. Several dragon guards moved toward the queen, but it seemed as though they were running underwater. Only Rokk appeared immune to the slowing of time. He fell from the ledge like a spear, and Anne sucked in a breath as she anticipated the blow.

But it never landed.

Just before the blade dispatched the queen, a blur intercepted Rokk and carried him away. The timing was impossible. Mere seconds had passed. Rokk and the blur crashed onto the ground and immediately struggled for control of the sword. It was the Construct. She had found a way to reactivate her knight.

For a moment, Anne thought the Construct might prevail, but Rokk kicked out with his mighty legs and sent her stumbling back. He surged to his feet, raised the sword above his head, and drove it straight down into the heart of the Copper Knight.

The knight exploded.

The blast rattled Anne's knight and sent Rokk flying backward into the wall. He fell to the ground and didn't move. The Three-Handed Sword also went flying, but in a completely different direction. For several heartbeats, everything was still. Pieces of the knight lay strewn about in a wide circle. There was no sign of the Construct, and Anne feared she was gone yet again.

"Your Majesty!" shouted a guard.

The guard pointed to where the Hierarchy committee had gathered in front of the Heartstone. The Three-Handed Sword had found a target. Not the queen; the sword hadn't even come close to her. Instead, the

292

sword had impaled the fake Lord Chamberlain through the chest and pinned him to the ground. The same Lord Chamberlain whom Anne had thought was a hologram. Except he wasn't. Though wounded, he didn't bleed, but he was also not made of light. Something else poured from him: a thick, black, oily smoke.

Just like during the first quest, with an archaeologist named Mr. Shard at the top of the Infinite Tower.

And just like the Matron when she had cut off her own arm.

Anne again noticed a glint of light coming from the Lord Chamberlain, but now she could see that it wasn't an aura like the Construct. The light was smaller, more focused, and coming from a crystal hanging around the Lord Chamberlain's neck.

The pierced Lord Chamberlain looked up at the throne. "We throw ourselves at your mercy, My Queen."

The queen said nothing.

The Lord Chamberlain reached out a shaky hand. "Your Majesty, I beg you, let us complete our business here. There is still time to—"

He never finished. The queen sucked in a lungful of air and spewed out a column of red fire. It engulfed the Lord Chamberlain and the other members of the committee.

Anne went rigid inside her knight, hardly believing what she was seeing. The committee members didn't cry out in pain. In fact, the fake Lord Chamberlain smiled as he burst into flame. The fire quickly turned to black smoke as all six of the committee members dissolved into nothing. When the queen ceased her assault, all that was left were a few smoldering scraps of clothing on the ground, the sword, and six sparkling crystals. It struck Anne how very much the crystals resembled dragon stones.

"Hand me the sword," said the queen.

One of the dragon guards picked up the Three-Handed Sword in its mouth and laid it before the queen. As Anne watched this happen, the kaleidoscope of events of the past several days—everything from the attack in the royal library, to the bodies of the committee members being rearranged, to the Copper Knights not obeying Valerian, to this very moment—suddenly formed into a picture in her mind.

"This whole thing has been your idea from the beginning, hasn't it?" Anne said boldly. She hadn't quite fit everything together yet, but she knew that she was on the right track. "You said earlier that no one could use the Copper Knights without your permission. That means Valerian couldn't possibly have taken the Copper

Knights unless you allowed it. You only let him *think* he had control. You wanted the Dragon Slayer quest activated so that the dragons could have a reason to be outraged—because it would break the treaty with the Hierarchy and weaken their position. But you yourself, *not* Valerian, controlled the knights. You used them to kidnap the real committee and replace them with those imposters, so they could surrender quickly to you without a need for war. That was your plan all along."

Anne expected another angry outburst, but the queen sat quietly, staring down at her. In fact, Anne thought she looked impressed.

"Bravo," said the queen. "I will grant that you have a sharper mind than most—for a human, anyway. You are correct. I have been involved from the beginning. But you left out the most important piece of the puzzle."

"Which is what?"

"I'm the Official Antagonist," said the queen. "The prospect of gaining control of the Hierarchy was merely a bonus, something I reached for because the opportunity presented itself, but what I most desired was this sword."

Having spoken thus, the queen clasped the Three-Handed Sword between her front paws and thrust herself upon it. The glowing blue blade sliced easily into the heavy scales of her chest, just as it had been designed to do. It cleaved through flesh and bone and pierced her dragon heart. Her eyes rolled back in her head, and she collapsed on top of the Heartstone, where she let out one final, rasping breath.

The dragons in the hall stared in disbelief.

Suddenly, Anne's knight opened again and she leapt out. Penelope, Hiro, Valerian, and the Lord Chamberlain did the same, and together they rushed over to the crystal formation. Valerian climbed up and placed his hand on the queen's side, feeling for a heartbeat. Anne already knew he wouldn't find one.

Finally, Valerian stood and faced the entire throne room.

"The dragon queen is dead," he said.

No one moved.

Anne became acutely aware that their group was standing unarmed in a room full of dragons whose queen had just died. That she had died by her own hand might not matter to the dragons. Anne walked over to where Rokk lay unconscious, hoping she might revive him, but unsure, even then, if he'd help should the dragons attack.

She knelt beside him and noticed that a panel on the side of his head had popped open. An object lay on the ground next to him. Another dragon stone. Anne remembered when Rokk had been knocked down in the royal library, and one of the Copper Knights had knelt beside him. Had the knight inserted this stone into Rokk? Was that the source of his erratic behavior? She picked up the stone and stuffed it into one of the pockets of her cloak.

Someone shouted from the throne room's entrance, interrupting Anne's thoughts. Jocelyn and Lord Greystone entered the throne room, accompanied by two long columns of council soldiers. The soldiers immediately formed a tight ring surrounding the Heartstone. Valerian descended from the Heartstone and joined Penelope and Hiro, while Lord Greystone climbed up to examine the queen's body.

Jocelyn walked directly over to Anne.

"How did you get here?" asked Anne.

"We came with the council ships," said Jocelyn. "There's an entire armada outside."

Anne stared at the queen's lifeless form. "We tried to protect her. I didn't know she would do that."

Jocelyn said nothing as she dug several papers out of her satchel and handed them to Anne.

Anne took them but couldn't focus on the words. "What's this?" she asked.

"As you well know," said Jocelyn, "so long as you three are students at Saint Lupin's Quest Academy, I am required to evaluate your performances."

Anne couldn't believe what she was hearing. The dragon queen had just taken her own life, and Jocelyn was worried about evaluations?

"We were trying to prevent a war," said Anne.

Jocelyn nodded. "A very noble purpose. However, the specific details of any given quest do not change the rules. The quest required that the dragon queen die of natural causes. She did not. I'm afraid this cannot be overlooked."

Anne frowned. "Meaning what?"

"Why, isn't it obvious, my dear? You failed."

ALL QUEST ACADEMIES EMPLOY THE FOLLOWING GRADING SYSTEM:

P   Pass (congratulations, you passed!)

B   Burnt to a Crisp (a dragon set your homework on fire)

Q   Quack (your homework was graded by a duck)

V   Vacation (your teacher has taken a leave of absence because of how badly you performed)

F   Fail (or, if there were crumbs on your paper, possibly Fruitcake)

18

Failing Grade

I t took a moment for Jocelyn's words to sink in.

"But I tried to save her," said Anne.

Lord Greystone leapt down from the Heartstone. "Trying is irrelevant. You activated a quest and didn't complete it, and now you must deal with the consequences." He removed a slim notebook from the inner pocket of his cape. "First, as I'm sure you know, failing a medallion quest while still attending a quest academy means failing the academy."

Anne turned to Jocelyn. "You're not really going to let him expel me, are you?"

"I'm afraid there's very little I can do about it, my dear," said Jocelyn. "He's the Minister of Questing, and well within his rights."

"But I *own* Saint Lupin's," Anne said. "You can't kick me out of my own home."

"Don't count on it," said Greystone. "Even if we're lucky enough to prevent a war with the dragons, the Wizards' Council will be looking for a scapegoat. At best, I'd say you're looking at a life sentence in a council dungeon cell. If they decide to hand you over to the dragons, then it will be the same verdict but with a much shorter life span, I expect."

"Anne, look," Penelope interrupted.

"Not now, Miss Shatterblade," said Jocelyn. "We will deal with you and Mr. Darkflame in a moment."

"Um, I think you're really going to want to see this," said Hiro.

Anne, Jocelyn, and Greystone looked to where Penelope was pointing. At the top of the Heartstone, the body of the dragon queen was glowing.

"What's happening?" asked Jocelyn.

Anne knew. They'd witnessed it before when Valerian's mother, Emmanuelle, had died. Now that the queen was dead, the dragon stone inside her would emerge. The light became more and more focused as the crystal neared the surface, until finally the crystal passed out of her chest and fell onto the Heartstone—

—and disappeared.

For a heartbeat nothing happened. A wave of uneasiness swept over Anne. Valerian had explained how newborn dragons were laid on the Heartstone so that a fragment of the stone would grow inside them. But he never said anything about what happened if a crystal was returned to the Heartstone once a dragon had died. Then Anne recalled the Construct's words, something about taking one of the dragon stones, which was really an "array log," to an upload terminal.

"Where did it go?" asked Penelope.

Hiro scanned the ground. "Maybe it rolled off or someth—"

A blinding pulse of light shot out from the Heartstone. Anne turned away and shielded her face. When she turned back, the Heartstone was gone.

"Where did it go?" said Valerian in a panic.

A vast rumbling arose among the dragons in the throne room. Apparently, they didn't know what had happened to the Heartstone, either. The queen's body now rested on the cold, hard ground. The Three-Handed Sword still protruded from it, but the dragon stone in the pommel had fallen out. Emmanuelle's dragon stone. When Anne looked around for it, she saw that it had rolled close to her, and while everyone was focused on the missing Heartstone, she bent over and picked it up. She couldn't help reflecting on how the spirit of one sister had been used against the other.

The floor shook.

"What was that?" asked Hiro nervously.

Anne thought about the dragon stones. When a dragon died, the stones came out. But it wasn't all gory and messy. They simply passed through the dragon, like a spirit passing through walls. If the Heartstone possessed that same property, and if that property were to be suddenly activated by, say, coming into contact with a dragon stone, where would it go?

"It would pass through the floor," Anne murmured, looking down.

Penelope frowned. "What are you talking about?"

"I'll explain on the way," said Anne. "Follow me."

Jocelyn reached out for her. "Now, just a minute, young lady—"

Anne ignored her and ran over to her Copper Knight. The council could punish her later; she didn't care. Without hesitation, Penelope, Hiro, and Valerian followed her lead and ran to their knights as well.

Anne climbed in—her knight was still open—but nothing happened.

"Why isn't it working?" she cried.

Jeffery alighted on the knight's shoulder. "The stones in the helmets are dragon stones," he said. "I figured it out when I inspected yours earlier. That's what the dragon queen used to control the knights. They were tuned to her stone."

Anne leaned out of the knight. "But those stones are white, not crystal."

"I'm just telling you what I know," said Jeffery.

Just like Rokk, then, Anne thought.

And just like the fake doubles of the committee members, too.

Somehow everything was connected to the dragon stones.

"If we remove the stones from the helmets, will the knights start working again?" asked Anne.

Jeffery shook his head. "The dragon stones are also what power the knights."

Anne dug the two dragon stones out of her pocket, Emmanuelle's and the one that had fallen out of Rokk. "You said the knights were tuned to the queen's stone. Can you tune them to one of these instead?"

"No, they require a living, thinking being in order to receive commands," said Jeffery. "Curiously enough, though, I am picking up another signal in this chamber that they could be tuned to."

"What signal?" Anne asked suspiciously.

"Your gauntlet."

Anne stared at the gauntlet and only hesitated for a moment. "Do it," she said. "Connect all of them."

Jeffery saluted. "Yes, ma'am," he said, and he took off, hopping from knight to knight, stopping only briefly on the top of each helmet. Anne reentered her knight and concentrated on making it work. It didn't take long. Seconds later the back of the knight closed, the circle of light appeared around her head, and the panels lit up around her.

"What about the empty one?" called Penelope.

Only five power knights remained, now that Rokk had destroyed the one the Construct had used. However, the Lord Chamberlain was busy talking with Lord Greystone and hadn't reentered his.

"Jeffery, can you operate that thing?" asked Anne.

"You don't have to ask me twice," he said. Jeffery flew over to the empty knight.

"Where are we going?" asked Hiro.

"The arena," said Anne.

Their activities were finally noticed. Greystone shouted for them to stop, but before the council soldiers could react—and the dragons, meanwhile, seemed so confused and upset that they weren't paying attention—Anne, Penelope, Hiro, Valerian, and Jeffery ran at full speed out of the throne room, across the bridge, and down the long stairway, and entered the vast space of the arena. The disc used for the dragon trials had been returned to its place near the ceiling, and the archway had been deactivated. Through the large hole in the floor, they could see the BGFM far below. Sparkling waves crashed together, sending up sprays of magick that swirled together in a mesmerizing dance.

"This power suit thingy is awesome!" said Jeffery. "I'm never, ever doing anything else ever again except driving this thing around. For always. I would even give up eating books to make that happen."

"What now?" asked Valerian. "There's nothing down here."

"Oh, I wouldn't necessarily say that," said Anne.

She pointed to the far side of the arena at the dragon statue. At the colossal, ten-story-high, thickly armored dragon statue. Except it wasn't a statue anymore. It was moving.

"So, you figured it out, did you?" thundered what was now a living, giant metal dragon.

Yet the dragon's voice sounded very familiar.

"Why is that thing alive?" yelled Hiro.

"It's the queen," said Anne. "The Heartstone absorbed her last breath, and then it dropped through the floor and into that thing."

"That's right," roared the giant metal dragon queen. "And now I will take my rightful place as ruler of this world. For too long dragons have lived in the shadow of insignificant humans, following their insufferable rules. No more. I will destroy the Hierarchy and build a new world in my own image. Humans will serve dragonkind as they should, and I will become the greatest marvel this world has ever seen!"

The word *marvel* echoed in Anne's head.

"*But let wonder bring the harbinger of death*," said Anne.

"What about it?" said Hiro.

"One of the queen's titles is Seventh Marvel of the Modern World," said Anne. "*Marvel* is another word for *wonder*. We've had it wrong. The line in the prophecy means the queen will bring the messenger of death—death for the entire Hierarchy. At the hands of a giant metal dragon. And our quest just helped her do it."

"Are you saying this is what was supposed to happen all along?" said Penelope.

"Actually, I think the quest was trying to suggest this would be a bad idea."

"That much I agree with."

The dragon queen stepped off her pedestal, and when her foot came down, the force shook the entire arena. She headed directly toward Anne and the others.

"Run!" yelled Anne.

All the knights scattered—all except one.

"Leave my friends alone, you big bully," said Jeffery.

He raised his staff and shot out a bolt of lightning. The bolt merely glanced off the heavy armor plating of the dragon queen's foot and struck the wall. In response, however, the queen lifted her foot and brought it down directly on top of Jeffery's knight, crushing it. There was a muffled explosion.

Anne was about to charge at the queen to help Jeffery when a bright rainbow streak shot through the top of the queen's foot. In an instant, Jeffery appeared inside the helmet of Anne's knight. "I take back the part about not eating books anymore," he said.

Anne reversed course, away from the dragon queen, but she had hardly taken ten steps when the dragon's giant tail whooshed through the air. Anne ducked, but someone behind her wasn't so quick. The tail sent the knight flying across the arena and into the wall. Anne didn't even know who was in it. Another knight leapt onto the dragon's pedestal, and from there it leapt onto the dragon queen's back and used the staff to hit her with bolt after bolt of lightning, but to no avail.

"You dare challenge me?" roared the dragon queen.

"Oh, I dare, all right," Penelope replied from within the knight.

Penelope ran up the dragon's back to her neck and continued attacking her. The dragon queen thrashed about, and Anne watched in horror as Penelope struggled to hold on. Penelope managed to grab the edge of a panel high on the dragon queen's back.

"Hang on!" said Hiro.

Hiro stepped forward and grabbed the dragon queen's tail from behind. This proved unwise, as the dragon dislodged him with a quick flick.

"Anne, we need to remove the Heartstone," said Valerian.

Anne knew he was right. They could never defeat the dragon queen in a direct confrontation. But if they could get to the Heartstone, she would become just an empty statue again—or so Anne hoped.

"You go for it," she said. "I'll distract her."

"Watch out, Anne!" screamed Hiro.

Penelope was falling. The large metal panel she'd been holding had torn loose. Anne tried to catch her, but the panel slammed into Anne first and sent her crashing to the ground. She was dazed but unhurt. Inside her helmet, an error message appeared, and the panels flickered. Anne had no desire to be trapped inside a dead knight, so she yelled, "Exit!" and the back opened. Anne crawled out and surveyed the damage.

Jeffery's Copper Knight was crushed. Penelope's

wasn't moving, and Hiro's knight still lay slumped awkwardly against the back wall. The only active knight seemed to be Valerian's, and just at that moment, the dragon queen scooped it off the ground, ripped the head clean off, and threw the knight's body into the hole in the floor. Valerian's Copper Knight sailed into the void beyond and tumbled end over end toward the BGFM.

"No!" screamed Anne.

The dragon queen didn't stop to gloat. She simply dropped through the hole herself, but instead of falling, she spread her massive wings and soared out of sight.

For a moment, Anne stood in a stupor. Valerian couldn't be gone. Somehow, he had to have survived. She shook herself and ran toward the rim of the opening.

"Anne!"

She stopped short.

Valerian was walking up behind her.

Anne clutched her hands to her chest. "But—weren't you inside that knight?"

Valerian shook his head. "The knight was dying, so I jumped out and hid behind one of the pedestals."

"What about Hiro and Penelope?"

"Hiro's okay. I don't know about Penelope. But they're both trapped in their knights until we can break them out."

Just then, dozens of dragons and council soldiers poured into the arena. Everyone swarmed around Anne, Valerian, and the fallen Copper Knights, though at first no one did anything. The soldiers and dragons were too busy arguing (and nearly coming to blows) over who had jurisdiction.

Without wondering whether they would listen to her, Anne ordered several soldiers to help remove the helmets from Penelope's and Hiro's knights. Perhaps some of Captain Copperhelm's personality had rubbed off on her, because the soldiers instantly obeyed. After a few minutes, the soldiers managed to pry open the helmets of both knights. Hiro was groggy, but Penelope seemed to be in good spirits, all things considered. However, it was going to take a while to completely free them.

Anne walked back to Valerian just as Jocelyn arrived. She didn't look very happy.

"Well, I guess you can't fail me after all," said Anne. "Technically, the queen is still alive." Anne couldn't help the snarky tone that had crept into her voice; she felt Jocelyn deserved every bit of it.

"I'm afraid things are more serious than that," said Jocelyn.

Lord Greystone walked over and joined them. He said, "You and the rest of your group may consider yourselves under arrest, effective immediately."

"You already arrested us once this quest," said Anne.

"Consider yourself under double arrest, then," said Greystone. "Also, given recent events, I've ordered a full investigation into this quest. The Wizards' Council is going to be taking a very close look at how Saint Lupin's is being run, and I suspect there is a good chance it will either be shut down or taken over by the council."

Anne grabbed Jocelyn's arm. "You can't let that happen."

Jocelyn hung her head and sighed deeply. "As much as it pains me to say so, I think this might be for the best. Just consider what's happened over the past few months," she said. "Level Thirteen quests, near destruction of the world, setting loose a rampaging giant metal dragon queen. At some point, I have to face the facts: I'm simply not cut out to run an academy."

"That's ridiculous!" said Anne. "You're fantastic! I mean, I'm not super happy with you right now, but you're a great professor. Any student would be lucky to study with you. And the same goes for Captain Copper-helm and Sassafras, too."

Jocelyn patted Anne's hand. "That's very kind of you, my dear, but I think our record together speaks for itself."

What was going on? Anne had only known Jocelyn for a couple of months, but in that time she knew her to be fiercely protective of both her academy and the students under her care. This wasn't at all like Jocelyn.

Then she saw it. A glint of crystal hanging around Jocelyn's neck.

"Where did you get that?" asked Anne.

"What? This?" said Jocelyn, and she seemed suddenly nervous.

"I've never seen you wear it before," said Anne. "But your sister, the Matron, had one just like it."

"I—I borrowed hers. I thought I would wear it in her memory to the awards ceremony."

"You're lying," said Anne. "The Matron's crystal was lost with her when she fell from the Saint Lupin's tier."

"I think that's quite enough out of you," said Greystone. "Considering the trouble you're already in, another outburst will only make it worse."

Anne couldn't stand it anymore. She was furious at

the whole mess and sick of these dragon stones. Without thinking, she leapt at Jocelyn and grabbed the crystal. Jocelyn stumbled back, but Anne didn't loosen her grip. The chain around Jocelyn's neck snapped, and the crystal came away. Jocelyn immediately collapsed to the ground. She gripped her face and began convulsing.

"What's happening to her?" asked Valerian.

Anne dropped to her knees and pried Jocelyn's hands away from her face, only to shrink back in horror. Black, oily smoke poured from Jocelyn's eyes and nose, and when she opened her mouth, all that came out was more black smoke. It even started to seep through the pores of her smooth brown skin. Jocelyn reached for Anne, but Anne scrambled back out of reach.

Jocelyn continued to shake. The smoke became so thick it soon enveloped her entire body. In mere minutes, she melted away completely. All that remained were her clothes lying flat on the ground and a few wisps of black smoke.

Anne was speechless.

One of the council soldiers ran over. "Lord Greystone, the dragon queen has escaped. She destroyed most of the armada and is now on a direct course for the capital."

"To arms!" cried Greystone, and he turned his attention to gathering and organizing the soldiers in the arena.

"I can't believe Jocelyn was an imposter," Anne said, looking at the spot where she had melted. "Just like the committee members."

"Too bad all the Copper Knights were destroyed," said Valerian.

Anne looked up with a sudden realization. "They weren't," she said. "There's still one left."

"What do you mean?" asked Valerian.

Anne leaned closer so as not to be overheard. "We need to return to the archway."

"What? It's high up, nearly to the ceiling of the throne room."

"The walls are rough. I'm sure we can climb it."

"More climbing? But what for?"

"Is there an archway anywhere on the capital tier?"

Valerian stared at her. "Several. But why do you want to go there?"

"Because there's another Copper Knight back in the royal library at the Sapphire Palace, remember?" said Anne.

"Nana incapacitated it, but maybe we can get it working again."

Valerian looked alarmed. "The capital is where the queen is headed. And in case you hadn't noticed, she just destroyed five of the knights without breaking a sweat, not to mention an entire armada of council airships."

"Penelope ripped a panel off the back of the metal dragon queen. That might provide access to the Heartstone. I have to at least try."

Valerian nodded. Greystone and the soldiers were still busy organizing themselves, and they didn't notice as Anne and Valerian quietly edged over to the wall and made their way closer to the entrance. Once they got close, they sprinted for the staircase.

"Hey!" called a guard. "Someone stop those kids!"

Anne and Valerian bolted past the entrance guards before the soldiers realized what was happening. They took the stairs two at a time and then ran down the corridor and out onto the bone bridge. Unfortunately, the guards on the far side of the bridge had heard the shouting and were coming to investigate.

Anne and Valerian stopped. "We're not going to make it through," Valerian said.

Anne looked up at the thin crack of light high above. "Can you fireball me to the capital from here?"

Valerian gazed at the crack. "I don't know if I can transform yet."

Soldiers were now blocking both ends of the bridge.

"I need you to do this," said Anne. "It's our only hope."

"I'll try. But no guarantees."

Valerian closed his eyes in concentration. The guards moved closer.

"Come on," whispered Anne. "You can do it."

Valerian took several slow, steadying breaths and squeezed his fists into balls.

The guards were almost upon them.

This time Anne saw the transformation as it happened. Valerian's neck became long and slender, and his skin turned red and scaly. His arms and legs grew into powerful limbs, and wings sprouted from his back. He became a red dragon and rose up, wings outstretched, scales glistening in the thin stream of light coming from the surface. Out of the corner of her eye, Anne saw the guards stumble back into one another.

Then Valerian's wings shrank, and his front feet gave way beneath him, sending him crashing to the bridge.

The guards became emboldened, drew their swords, and started forward once again.

"Valerian!" Anne called.

The dragon turned toward the sound of her voice. The strain on his face was obvious, but he straightened and rose to his feet, slowly, deliberately. Anne thought for sure Valerian would collapse or lose his dragon form, but with a mighty effort, he sucked in a huge lungful of air and blew out a bright green fireball.

Anne was on her way.

THE ADVENTURER'S GUIDE TO DRAGONS
(AND WHY THEY KEEP BITING ME)
SAYS THE FOLLOWING:

If you don't wish to get bitten by a dragon, don't stick
your head in its mouth.

19

The Harbinger of Death

W here exactly Anne was on her way *to*, of course, was another question entirely.

Once the fireball deposited her and the smoke cleared, she took stock of her surroundings. Tall buildings were all around, so it certainly seemed like Valerian had managed to get her to the capital. She was standing in an exterior courtyard, but nothing looked familiar. Maybe this wasn't surprising given how little of the capital she'd actually seen. Anne ran up a nearby set of steps to an upper terrace to get a better view.

Her heart sang. The Sapphire Palace was only a few blocks away.

Moreover, it was still late afternoon, meaning not only had Valerian fireballed her to the right place, he had apparently managed to create a premium fireball and send her there almost instantly.

With no time to waste, she hurried back down to the courtyard, charged through the nearest exit—

—and ran headlong into someone. They both fell to the ground. Once Anne caught her breath, she found herself staring into a familiar face.

"Captain Copperhelm!" she cried.

He had several guards with him, and they had all drawn their swords and were pointing them at her.

"Where in the blue blazes did you come from?" said Copperhelm, climbing to his feet and mumbling to himself. "I come to investigate a rogue fireball and nearly get run over by a wanted fugitive."

Anne grabbed him by the shoulders. This seemed to excite the guards even more, but she ignored them.

"Captain Copperhelm, I need you to take me to the Copper Knight that was left in the royal library."

He brushed off his vest. "Well, hello to you, too."

"We might not have a lot of time. There's a giant metal dragon coming to attack the capital."

He pointed behind her. "You mean like that one arriving right now?"

Anne turned. High in the sky, and closing fast, was the giant metal dragon queen. The few council airships that had remained behind at the capital attempted to form a barrier, but the dragon queen punched through them like a stone through wet paper.

Anne turned back to Copperhelm. "Where's that knight?"

Copperhelm motioned to the guards. "Begin evacuating the capital. Cut the moorings of the outer tiers so they can float away. If there are any warships left, get them to harass that thing and try to distract her, but tell them not to engage directly."

The guards saluted and ran off.

Copperhelm pointed to Anne. "You, come with me."

He led Anne into the building. They took a winding path, up and down stairs, until they came to a tower with a barred door. Copperhelm motioned to a guard, who let them through.

"Down here," he said.

They descended several flights until they arrived at a small office.

"Where's the prisoner?" Copperhelm asked the guard seated inside.

"Last cell," came the reply. The guard escorted them to the end of the hallway to a giant barred door. Anne peeked through the slit in the door. Inside the cell stood the seventh Copper Knight. She could even make out the A7 engraved on its collar.

"Let me in there," she said.

"Now, just a minute there, young miss," said the guard. "Those things are dangerous. Six of those knights injured dozens of guards when they escaped from the palace several days ago."

"Has this one moved at all?" asked Anne.

"Well, no, but if it suddenly springs to life again, how is a little girl like you going to stop it?"

"Open the door and I'll show you."

"You heard her," said Copperhelm, waving one of his emergency command cards at the guard. "Now open it."

The guard unlocked the door and hurried quickly away down the hallway. Without hesitation, Anne stepped over to the Copper Knight, with Copperhelm close behind. She jumped onto the top bunk and examined the knight's helmet. As she had expected, there was no dragon stone. It must have been knocked out when Nana attacked, but they missed spotting it due to all the glass beads from the broken display case. She took out the dragon stone that had fallen out of Rokk and inserted it into the helmet.

"Jeffery, can you tune this stone to the gauntlet?" she asked.

Jeffery appeared in a flash of light. "Already done."

Anne reached over and pressed the button on the collar. As with the other knights, a seam appeared down the back and it opened.

And out fell Jocelyn.

The real Jocelyn, Anne hoped.

"Help!" said Anne.

Copperhelm reached out just in time, and they caught Jocelyn together and lowered her onto the bed.

"That was quite the magick trick," said Copperhelm. "Are you sure you aren't the wizard of the group?"

Anne grinned. "You haven't seen anything yet."

Copperhelm grunted.

Jocelyn began to rouse. "Dear heavens, whatever is going on here?" she said. She looked around the cell. "Have I been arrested?"

"Do you want to close the quest academy?" Anne asked her. "Do you want me to sell Saint Lupin's?"

Copperhelm stared at her with uncharacteristic shock. "Close the academy? Sell it? What are you talking about?"

"I need to be sure this is the real Jocelyn."

"Who else would she be?" he said.

"Believe me, there are several possibilities."

Jocelyn raised herself into a sitting position. "My dear, as always, Saint Lupin's is yours to do with as you please. But if you think selling it will somehow get me to close the academy or get you out of doing your chores, allow me to disabuse you of that notion right now. You are my student no matter where the academy is located."

Anne hugged her. "You're definitely the real Jocelyn."

"What's this all about?" asked Copperhelm.

"I can't explain it all because I don't understand it all yet myself," said Anne. "But right now I need to take this knight and stop the dragon queen."

Copperhelm nodded. "Fair enough. Don't worry about us. I'll see that everyone gets safely out of here."

"I know you will."

Anne climbed into the knight and the back closed behind her. She experienced a momentary panic in the dark interior, but then the circle of light appeared around her head and the panels lit up.

Jeffery appeared in the helmet. "Hey, wait for me."

Anne maneuvered the knight out of the cell. It must have suffered some damage in its encounter with Nana because it didn't move nearly as well as the other knight she had piloted. Anne pushed it into a jog. Surprised guards leapt out of the way. A few were too slow and got knocked over, but Anne didn't slow down.

When she arrived outside, everything was in chaos. True to her word, the dragon queen had landed at the far end of the city and was busy tearing through buildings and ripping apart any airships that drifted too close. The knight lurched down the avenue and rounded the corner. The Sapphire Palace lay straight ahead, but several towers had collapsed and the streets were filled with rubble. Anne tried to jump over it, but the knight stumbled and didn't seem able to comply. It must have been more damaged than she thought. It would take her forever to get across the city like this—at least, it would if she traveled on the surface. The mines, on the other hand, would allow her to pass unhindered.

She ran up the palace steps and into the entrance hall. In the alcove, a guard was turning a key in the lock of a brand-new set of mine doors. When he saw Anne—or rather, a Copper Knight—bearing down on him, the guard whipped out his sword and prepared to fight.

"Open," said Anne, and the front panel of the helmet opened.

At the sight of her, the guard relaxed and lowered his sword. "What's a young girl like you doing in that contraption?" he asked.

"Open the door!" yelled Anne.

The guard shook his head. "I'm under strict orders not to let anyone down there. Some kids were messing with the mine carts and burned down the old door. Can you believe it?"

No one could say Anne hadn't asked nicely. Anne closed the panel and charged the knight straight at the doors without stopping. The guard dove out of the way. She hit the doors dead center, tearing them off their hinges.

"Hey! You're going to pay for those!" the guard yelled after her.

Anne took the stairs ten at a time. The steps crunched under the weight of the knight every time she landed, but they held. Anne was having trouble keeping the suit running straight, and several times it veered sideways into the walls. Upon reaching the bottom, she headed down the long corridor, which ended in two doors.

Anne charged through the same door they had entered last time, the one that led into the main cavern. If she could get another mine cart on the tracks, she could get there even faster.

"What's the 'Cave of Marv dash E one'?" asked Jeffery.

"What did you say?" Anne brought the knight to a halt.

Jeffery pointed back at the hallway. "I was just reading that sign back there on the other door."

"But why did you pronounce it like that?"

"Uh, because that's what it says."

Anne jogged back to the hallway to look at the two entrances.

"No, see, it says 'Cave of Marvel,'" said Anne.

"Look closer. That's not a lowercase *L*. It's the number *one*. And there's a faint dash between the *V* and the *E*. So, 'Marv dash E one.'"

Anne studied it again. Jeffery was right.

Marv dash E one.

MARV-E1.

Anne remembered the inscription on the back of the Copper Knights:

Magickal All-Terrain Reconnaissance Vehicle, or MARV, for short.

"Jeffery, you're brilliant!" said Anne.

"Well, that much is obvious."

Using her knight, Anne kicked the door open, splintering the frame.

"Our door budget for this quest is going to be very high," said Jeffery.

Anne almost couldn't believe her eyes. In the center of yet another massive chamber, and standing on a pedestal just as large as the one that once displayed the giant metal dragon statue, stood a hundred-foot-tall knight. It had a giant E1 inscribed on its chest plate. In its hand was a massive sword.

"Wow," said Jeffery. "We definitely have to try that thing."

Anne ran over to the pedestal, but her knight couldn't make the jump. She called for the exit and stepped out.

"So much for that one," she said. "Luckily, we seem to have a spare." She gazed up at the giant knight. "I'm sure Hiro is glad he isn't here for this."

There was a staircase behind the pedestal, and she ran up. Like the metal dragon, the knight was constructed of hundreds of interlocking panels. Anne set her foot on the first panel of the leg and began climbing. She made swift progress up the side of the leg and then jumped across to the wrist. Anne pulled herself hand-over-hand up the arm until she reached the shoulder. From there she clambered around to the back of the knight's neck, where she spotted what she'd hoped to find: a large circle with the sparrow image on it. She pushed on it with all her strength. A hatch on the back of the knight opened and Anne jumped inside.

As with the Copper Knights, she felt the sensation of the interior space adjusting itself to fit her. After that, nothing happened.

"Jeffery, why isn't it working?" she asked.

"Just a second," said Jeffery, and he dove into the panel, leaving her in total darkness.

The seconds ticked by.

"Jeffery?" she called out. "Are you still there?"

Suddenly the interior of the knight disappeared around her and she found herself standing inside a black cube, roughly ten feet to a side, lit by a single white light in the ceiling.

"What is this place?" she asked.

"I've temporarily shut off the pilot interface. Do you see a hatch in the floor?" asked Jeffery.

She located a circular panel with a recessed handle. "Yes."

"Open it."

Anne pulled on the handle and swung the hatch upward, and Jeffery came shooting out.

"I think you'll find what you need down there," he said.

Anne peered through the hatch opening. There was another chamber below, and in it lay a giant crystal formation identical to the Heartstone.

Anne dropped into the chamber. She pulled out Emmanuelle's dragon stone and placed it on top of the crystal. At first nothing happened. Then the dragon stone merged with the larger crystal. Anne climbed back up. A moment later the chamber disappeared and the knight re-formed around her. A ring of light appeared around her head, the panels around her lit up, and suddenly she was a hundred feet tall.

"This is awesome," said Anne.

Operating the giant metal knight was the same as operating the Copper Knights, albeit on a much larger scale. It responded to her impulses. She just had to think about what she wanted to do, and the knight obeyed.

She made the knight step down from its pedestal and walked it over to the wall.

"How are we supposed to get out of here?" said Anne.

"Well, the dragon is up, so I vote for up," said Jeffery.

There was a certain, simple logic to that, so Anne sent the knight's left fist upward into the ceiling, bringing down a shower of dirt and rocks. After several more strikes, the knight's fist broke through to the main floor of the palace above. Anne used the giant sword to widen the hole and then climbed up. As the knight raised itself, it smashed through all six floors of the palace. Once it was standing on solid ground, as gingerly as possible (for a hundred-foot knight, that is) Anne climbed out of the palace. This brought down the front wall of the building, and behind her the remainder of the roof collapsed. Anne winced, but she couldn't worry about it now.

The dragon queen was two tiers over. Anne walked the knight forward, still getting a feel for how it moved. Worried that the bridges would not support the weight of the giant metal knight, she simply leapt the gap when she reached the edge of the tier. The knight landed with a crash, taking out several single-story buildings.

She only hoped the guards had been successful in evacuating everyone from the capital.

Anne pushed the knight into a run, down a wide avenue that ran the length of the tier, and then jumped, sailing over the next gap with ease.

The dragon queen noticed her now.

Lifting the sword high over the knight's head, Anne thundered forward. The dragon queen held up her front leg to block, but when the sword came down, it cut deeply into her armored scales. The dragon queen roared, almost as if in pain, and lashed out with its tail. Anne had been expecting this, however, and she dodged to the side—unfortunately crashing into yet another building.

The dragon queen head-butted the knight and sent it reeling backward into a stone tower, which crumbled beneath the weight. Before Anne could get the knight back on its feet, the dragon queen sideswiped it with her tail. This time Anne couldn't dodge the blow. The tail hit the knight in the shoulder and drove it across the ground, taking out an entire city block.

As Anne tried to rise, the dragon queen leapt onto the knight's back, slamming it to the ground yet again.

"That isn't very nice," Anne said.

She struck out wildly with the sword and caught the

dragon queen with a glancing blow. The dragon stepped back unsteadily, which gave Anne enough time to get the giant knight back on its feet. The two titans exchanged a quick succession of blows, each one landing like a thunderclap.

Anne swung the sword again, but this time the dragon queen bit down hard on the knight's wrist, crunching deep into its armor plating. The sword tumbled from Anne's grasp. The dragon queen spun the knight around, swept up the sword, and drove it into the knight's back as far as it would go. The blade passed fully through the body and burst out of the knight's stomach. Alarms started blaring all around.

Anne ducked under the dragon queen's outstretched limbs and twisted around behind her. She wrapped the knight's arms around the dragon's torso and pulled it tight against the knight's chest, where the end of the sword was protruding. Anne stabbed into the dragon queen's back, pinning them together, and then she leapt forward, so that the knight landed atop the dragon, driving the sword in even deeper.

More alarms blared, and the words CRITICAL FAILURE scrolled across the panel in front of Anne.

It hadn't worked.

For the moment, the dragon queen was pinned.

But the giant metal knight was dead.

Anne exited through the knight's back hatch.

The dragon queen struggled to rise, but due to the damage she had suffered and the weight of the giant knight, she couldn't. Anne knew that wasn't likely to last long.

"Any thoughts?" Anne asked Jeffery.

"Attack?" he suggested.

"Jeffery, there's no way I could put even a scratch on that thing."

"Who said anything about attacking it from the outside?" said Jeffery.

"You want me to go *inside*?"

"It's not as preposterous as it sounds. Penelope ripped off that panel, so get in there and do enough damage to shut it down. That's pretty much your only chance."

"But I don't even have a weapon."

"Improvise."

Anne looked up at the massive dragon. "After this, definitely no more quests."

She clambered swiftly around the knight's collar. From

there she was able to drop straight down onto the dragon queen's back. She spotted the opening where the missing panel had been attached, but before she reached it, the dragon began to toss and jerk. Anne moved forward cautiously, one slow step at a time, until she reached the opening. The dragon continued to pitch back and forth, and it was all Anne could do to stay on her feet. She took a deep breath and dropped inside.

Although the dragon queen continued to thrash, Anne found plenty of handholds. This part of the interior was filled with gears and support beams and dangling wires. She moved forward, with no particular idea where she should be headed other than inward.

"Help...me."

Anne stopped. Who could be calling out?

"Help...me," said the voice again.

"Hello?" she called out. "Is someone there?"

The voice sounded as though it was straight ahead. She climbed over more cables and gears and had to squeeze through a narrow passage.

"Help me," said the voice, sounding closer.

Anne crawled ahead toward a light source coming from a small opening, and she eased herself down into a large chamber identical to the one in the knight. The Heartstone lay in the center of the space.

"Help...me," said the voice, which came from the Heartstone itself.

"Your Majesty?" said Anne.

"You must...kill...this abomination."

Anne looked around. "You mean this metal dragon?"

"Yes."

"But...isn't that asking me to kill *you*?"

"Not me...someone else...took...control."

Anne strained to understand what she was hearing.

"Are you saying that someone took control of you and caused this to happen?"

"Yes."

Anne thought of the imposters. Instead of the queen controlling them, as Anne had first believed, perhaps the fake committee members had really been controlling her.

"The...sword," said the queen.

Anne raised an eyebrow. "The Three-Handed Sword? I don't have it."

"Summon...it."

"I'm telling you, it's back on the dragon tier."

"Summon...it," the queen repeated.

Anne could think of only one possibility.

She held up her gauntlet-hand. "Activate sword," she said.

A giant sword, an exact replica of the Three-Handed Sword, appeared in the air above the gauntlet. Anne reached up and slowly gripped the hilt. As with the keys, it felt solid in her hand, like a solid hologram. Also, despite its awesome size, she found that she could wield it without any difficulty. Curiously, there was a stone in the pommel exactly where a dragon stone was meant to go. Even more curiously, the stone was bright yellow, the exact same color as her eyes.

"Now, drive...the sword...into the stone."

"But isn't there a way to save you first?" asked Anne.

"No...time. You must...destroy...the stone."

Anne hesitated. She thought about the questions she had wanted to ask the dragon queen. She thought about Project A.N.V.I.L. and about what the Construct had said to her, about how asking about her origins was a waste of time. But she simply had to know.

"Where do I come from?" asked Anne.

The queen paused for a moment, and Anne thought she would refuse to answer. Then the queen spoke: "*Born of two worlds...the ancient and the new...seek the Lady of Glass in her tower...she will reveal all to you.*"

It was a riddle, but it was more than she'd ever had before.

"Thank you," said Anne.

"Now...finish it...before it's too late."

How could Anne do it, knowing that the queen had been a victim, too, and didn't deserve such a fate?

Something large impacted the dragon, and the entire chamber shook, throwing Anne off her feet. This was followed quickly by a second impact, and then a third. Suddenly, one entire wall of the chamber was ripped away, and sunlight filtered in. One of the giant metal dragon's own claws had torn into itself. The giant claw tossed away the crumpled metal, reached in, and grabbed for Anne. She sidestepped, but only just barely. The claw smashed into the wall, snapping braces and cables. It pulled out again, and the dragon let out a roar like a shockwave. Anne doubted it would miss a second time.

She rushed over to the Heartstone and rested the tip of the sword directly on its surface.

The claw returned.

"Forgive me," she said.

Anne closed her eyes and pushed with all her might.

She felt the sword pierce the Heartstone, and she drove in the blade up to the hilt. This time the robot dragon screamed, a high terrible sound that nearly deafened Anne. She held on to the sword even as the dragon shuddered with the throes of death.

The entire room tilted sideways, as the giant metal dragon tried to rise up in one last gasp and then fell back to earth, slamming into the ground with a resounding crash. The Heartstone came loose and shattered against the wall, showering Anne in crystal shards.

Then the dragon went still.

Anne rose unsteadily to her feet. She made her way toward the opening the giant metal dragon had ripped in its own chest, climbing over twisted metal support beams and the remains of plate armor until she was back outside.

Anne surveyed the destruction all around her. Much of the capital lay in ruins. Buildings were crushed. Several fires were blazing. The dragon had caused much of the mayhem, but she couldn't deny that the giant knight had caused its fair share as well.

The final line of the riddle came to mind once more: *But let wonder bring the harbinger of death.*

Anne understood now. *Wonder* didn't mean *marvel*

in reference to the queen, as she had speculated. It meant MARV-E1. But the knight itself hadn't been the messenger of death. It had merely delivered the true messenger.

The messenger was her.

Anvil of Saint Lupin's, slayer of dragons.

THE ADVENTURER'S GUIDE TO SEQUELS
SAYS ALL PROPER SEQUELS MUST CONTAIN:

1) New characters

2) More and bigger explosions

3) Yet another overly complicated plot to save the world

4) At least one unexpected resurrection

Dragon Slayer

Anne stopped just outside the main office at Saint Lupin's and took a deep breath. Jocelyn stopped beside her. She placed a reassuring hand on Anne's shoulder and offered a tight-lipped smile. Together they proceeded into the room. Bright morning sunlight filled the space. Lord Greystone was already there, standing behind the desk with his black cloak slung over one shoulder and his crow, Neeva, perched on the other. Standing to Greystone's left was the Lord Chamberlain, looking somber. To Greystone's right was a stern-looking woman, also dressed in dark attire—no doubt another member of the Wizards' Council.

Jocelyn gave Anne's hand one quick, final squeeze and stepped back.

Greystone gestured to the X on the floor. "If you please," he said to Anne.

Anne walked over to the X and faced them.

"You have been summoned here today to answer for your crimes—" Greystone started.

The Lord Chamberlain cleared his throat, and Greystone looked annoyed.

"I mean to say, you have been summoned here today to account for several—very severe—quest violations. Myself and Professor Emeritus Baroness Kitty von Hamsterkiller are here as representatives of the Wizards' Council." He gestured to the woman in black. "The Lord Chamberlain is here on behalf of the capital. And, of course, the head of your academy." He gave a slight nod in Jocelyn's direction.

Anne fidgeted with the sleeve of her cloak but, catching the slightest shaking of Jocelyn's head, dropped her arms to her side.

Greystone held up a sheet of paper. "You are hereby

charged with the following: activating an illegal Dragon Slayer quest, disobeying a direct order from the council, specifically that of the Minister of Questing to remain in the capital under lockdown, failure to prevent the death of the queen of the dragons, murdering the queen of the dragons—"

"Isn't that essentially charging me twice for the same offense?" asked Anne.

Greystone gave her a piercing stare, and she said nothing further.

"Commandeering an ancient gigantic killer knight," he continued, "using the aforementioned gigantic killer knight to cause wanton destruction and mayhem, and in doing so creating a general atmosphere of terror—"

"I only used the giant MARV unit to stop the giant dragon that was already destroying everything!"

This time Greystone ignored her outburst altogether and continued. "And finally, the destruction of a world heritage site, namely the Sapphire Palace. There is also a separate aiding-and-abetting charge here against the member of your group known as Rokk the Robot." He lowered the paper. "How do you answer to these charges?"

"The charge against Rokk isn't fair," said Anne. "The dragon queen was controlling him."

Greystone gave a nasty smile. "If you fail to enter a plea, one shall be entered on your behalf—as it happens, by the Minister of Questing, who is me. Now, how do you answer?"

"The dragons have dropped all charges related to the death of the queen," said Jocelyn. "I don't see the council winning a case against Anne when the rightful complainants refuse to participate."

"I concur," said the Lord Chamberlain.

The woman in black gave an almost imperceptible nod.

"Very well," said Greystone, setting aside some of the papers but not looking very happy about it. "But there are still the remaining charges. Miss Anvil here and her little band of adventurers caused a lot of damage this time, and I intend to see they receive more than a slap on the wrist. There will be real consequences."

Anne stared at him defiantly. "Such as?"

"For starters, you will pay for all repairs, down to the last broken teacup."

Jocelyn gripped the edge of the desk. "But that would bankrupt the academy."

"That's hardly my concern," said Greystone. "However, in light of recent events and discoveries, the council has come up with a proposal. First, you will give all of your award money from your previous quest, along with any treasure you received, to the Wizards' Council. That won't cover everything, but it will be a good start."

Anne nodded reluctantly.

"Second, you will relinquish any quest-related salvage rights to the remaining intact Copper Knights and whatever bits and pieces we can find of the ones that were destroyed. This includes the MARV-E1 knight. These units will be auctioned off and the proceeds applied against the remaining damages."

"Outrageous!" bellowed Jocelyn, surging forward to stand beside Anne. "You know full well they will be snatched up by private buyers and hidden away. They belong in a museum for everyone to study and benefit from."

"You can either accept this proposal, or else the council will seize the Saint Lupin's tier and everything on it and sell that instead."

Jocelyn stood fuming, but Anne could tell there was little she could do.

"That's fine," said Anne. "The council can have the Copper Knights and the giant MARV unit."

Greystone smiled. "Well, I'm glad at least someone is willing to see reason."

"On one condition," she added.

Greystone's eyes narrowed. "And pray tell, what would that condition be?"

"Rokk gets to stay at Saint Lupin's."

"Unacceptable. He was complicit in the theft of the Three-Handed Sword and attempted to murder the queen of the dragons in front of multiple witnesses. He is to be shut down and his body kept under permanent guard."

"No one is shutting Rokk down," said Anne. "He can be forbidden to travel from Saint Lupin's, but he's not going anywhere with you."

Greystone leaned over the desk. "You're hardly in a position to dictate terms. Maybe I'll simply call off the deal right here and now and have you taken into custody. There's an entire company of council guards right outside."

Anne resisted the urge to rub her sweaty hands on her sides. "Call them if you want, but I don't think you will."

"Oh, no?"

"No. Right now I think you want those Old World power suits more than you want this academy or to see either me or Jocelyn go to prison. In fact, I'm willing to bet on it."

"If the council seizes this tier, it seizes all of its assets along with it. So what's to stop me from simply taking them?"

"Simply this."

Anne raised two fingers to her lips and gave a sharp whistle. Three giant heads appeared in the window behind them. Three giant dragon heads.

"In case you've forgotten, five of the knights, or what's left of them, anyway, are currently still in the arena back on the dragon tier," said Anne. "The dragons have assured me they'll see them destroyed before anyone from the council even gets a look at them unless you agree to my terms. Although perhaps you'd be satisfied with just the one on the capital tier. Oh, and they'll also be taking possession of the giant metal dragon, just in case you were thinking about trying to lay claim to that, too."

Greystone gave her a dark look, and his hand twitched over to the hilt of his sword but then moved away.

"Very well," he said, grinding his teeth. "In exchange for the knights, the robot stays here. For now. The fate of the giant metal dragon can be decided in negotiations between the dragon clan and the council. And finally," he said, turning to another piece of paper, "the questing license for the Saint Lupin's Quest Academy is hereby suspended until a full review by the Wizards' Council has been conducted."

Anne opened her mouth to protest, but Jocelyn coughed behind her, and Anne said nothing.

Greystone gathered his papers and walked around the desk, stopping next to Anne. "I suggest you tread carefully from this point forward," he said. "After your first quest, you became something of a curiosity. But after this one, you have made real enemies. Enemies you know nothing about and are ill-prepared to deal with. So enjoy your brief victory."

Anne recalled her standoff with Greystone in this same office following her first quest, and remembered spotting what looked to be a crystal hanging from a chain around his neck. Could it be a dragon stone? She searched for any sign of it now, but saw nothing.

Greystone, Professor von Hamsterkiller, and the

Lord Chamberlain exited the office. As they did, the dragons dropped out of sight as well. Anne remained behind with Jocelyn.

"Well, that certainly could have gone better," said Jocelyn, "but it also could have gone much, much worse."

"I'm sorry things turned out this way," said Anne.

"Don't give it another thought, my dear. I expected the suspension, and we'll deal with the review when the time comes. We can still operate as a regular boarding school, and that will give us plenty to keep busy with in the meantime. I am pleased to see, however, that you acted with composure and bravery, as always. And although I've already said it, you have my sincere thanks for rescuing me. It couldn't have been easy standing up to my double like that, and I applaud both your deter-mination and your levelheadedness. I daresay you even gave Greystone a run for his money."

Anne felt her cheeks grow warm. She wasn't sure if she would ever get used to hearing praise of any kind from an adult, having never received a single word of praise from the Matron for the entire first thirteen years of her life.

"It nearly didn't work," said Anne. "And I'm sorry

you won't get a chance to examine that giant MARV unit."

Jocelyn gave her a sly grin. "Actually, no one will be doing anything with it."

Anne frowned. "What do you mean?"

"Captain Copperhelm just informed me this morning. The giant metal knight has disappeared."

When Anne finally found him, Valerian was standing on the drawbridge watching the zombie sharks frolic in the water. His clothes had been cleaned and pressed, and he had a new pack slung over one shoulder. The three dragons who had appeared in the office window were waiting for him on the far side.

"So you've made up your mind, then?" Anne asked. "You're not staying?"

Valerian nodded. "The queen's involvement in the quest came as quite a blow to the dragons, and they're going to need their king—which, as it turns out, is me. At least my part in helping prevent total disaster seems to have changed their view of half-dragons. Or it has for some of them, anyway."

"And what about your mother's stone?"

"We've sent out search parties, but so far no luck. You wouldn't think it would be that hard to spot a hundred-foot-tall knight wandering around. If she really is out there, though, I'm certain we'll find her. And with the dragon's other Heartstone destroyed, it's all the more important that we do. I'd hate to think I might be the last dragon to ever receive a stone."

"Well, if you get bored with hanging around dragons all day, you're welcome back here anytime," said Anne. "I'd be glad to have you as an official member of the team."

"I'm not sure Penelope would agree. She keeps giving me the stink-eye."

Anne laughed. "I'm sure she'd get used to the idea. She's learned to tolerate Hiro, after all. Speaking of eyes, I still have your mother's."

"Keep it. We recovered the other eye from the airship the Copper Knights were using, and becoming the dragon monarch also comes with certain privileges," he said, and he pointed to his own eyes.

"Okay, thanks. And thanks for the help earlier, too," she added, nodding at the dragon guards. "It really made a difference."

Valerian smiled. "It's the least I could do."

"How are you getting back? Fireball?"

"Flying," said Valerian. "I need all the practice I can get. But I'll be sure to take lots of breaks."

Anne stepped back.

Valerian closed his eyes, and the red dragon appeared. He let out a hearty roar, flapped his wings mightily, and shot into the air along with the other dragons. Anne watched until they banked behind a distant tier and disappeared from sight.

Anne sat with Penelope and Hiro on the edge of the tier. Penelope was busy throwing small twigs and watching them fall until they disappeared from sight. Hiro had his nose buried in a thick manual.

"So, it's back to the normal routine, then," said Penelope.

"I guess," said Anne. "Although I'm not sure our routine has ever been normal."

"Any luck with the queen's riddle?"

"Not yet. I have a feeling that one's going to take a while."

Penelope yawned. "Well, when you get bored researching that, you can figure out what's up with those dragon stones. I mean, how many of them have we come across?"

Hiro looked up from his book. "Seven in the Copper Knights. Seven from the fake committee members. One from Rokk. One from Emmanuelle. One from the dragon queen. One lost with the Matron. And one from Mr. Shard."

"Don't forget the one in Greystone's possession," said Anne.

"We don't know for certain yet if that's actually a dragon stone," said Hiro.

"I think it's a reasonable guess."

Penelope shook her head. "Who designs these quests, anyway? I mean, seriously. A four-day Level Thirteen quest? A dragon queen who slays herself? In some ways, it feels completely random, and in other ways completely interconnected."

"It all definitely has the feeling of having been planned out in advance," said Anne. "The question is, was it designed thousands of years ago and is now just happening automatically, like a machine, or is the person responsible still pulling the strings?"

"Like a puppet," said Hiro.

"It gives me a headache just thinking about it," said Penelope.

"No more quests for a long time," said Anne. "And I really mean it this time."

Hiro let his book fall into his lap.

"Oh, wow," he said. "I just thought of something."

"What?" said Anne.

He slapped his hand against his forehead. "This could be...this could be incredible."

"She asked nicely," said Penelope. "My request comes with a knuckle sandwich. So spill it."

Hiro snapped the book closed and leapt to his feet. "Come with me," he said, and he ran off into the forest.

Penelope shook her fist at him. "I swear, one of these days..."

Anne and Penelope caught up with Hiro outside the entrance to Shaft Eleven, the mineshaft that led down to the burned-out lab where their first quest had ended. Standing next to Hiro were the three iron knights that belonged to Saint Lupin's. They were currently assigned to coal-mining duty.

"You wanted some coal?" asked Anne.

"No," said Hiro. "I wanted to take a look at this."

Hiro was standing on a boulder behind one of the knights; Anne climbed up beside him and looked toward where he was pointing. On the back of the knight's collar was a circle with an engraving of a bird, just like on the Copper Knights.

"But it can't be," said Anne. "The queen said the Copper Knights were unique."

"Maybe the queen didn't know everything," said Hiro.

Anne reached out hesitantly, not daring to believe it. She pushed on the image. There was a sharp hiss, and a seam appeared down the back of the iron knight.

A smile spread across Anne's face.

"Well," she said, "maybe just one more quest."

"Yes!" said Penelope, and she pumped her fist into the air. "The Knights of Saint Lupin's will ride again!"

Anne lay in her bed. She'd taken a long, hot shower, and her bed was freshly made with two quilts on the top for extra warmth. Penelope, as usual, was already fast asleep on the other side of the room, snoring not-so-softly.

The candle on the nightstand was burning low, but Anne wasn't quite ready to blow it out yet. Instead, she looked at the gauntlet lying beside it.

"Jeffery?" she whispered.

Jeffery appeared in a flash of light. "What's up?"

Anne smiled. "I was just checking to see if you were still here. I thought you might have shut off already."

"Without saying good-bye? You know me better than that."

Anne smiled, and a single tear ran down her cheek.

Jeffery hopped off the nightstand onto the edge of the bed. "Hey, what's the matter?"

Anne shook her head. "I don't know. I finally found out some information that might help me discover where I'm from, and I feel like I should be happy about that. But with some of the things that happened these past few days, and some of the choices I had to make...I...I think it's going to take me a while to get over this quest."

He patted her hand with his wing. "For what it's worth, sometimes it's okay to not get over something. Sometimes you just have to figure out a way to live with it."

She sniffed. "Thank you."

"Anytime," he said. He gave her a salute with his tiny wing, and then disappeared, this time for good—or rather, until the next quest.

Anne remained awake.

She still wasn't ready to go to sleep. Not just yet.

But she would eventually.

(MOST ASSUREDLY NOT)
THE
END

Most Certainly an Epilogue

And so Anne was given the official title of Dragon Slayer, a title Nana insisted on using every time she spoke with her, even when only asking to pass the salt, much to Anne's annoyance. Saint Lupin's temporarily lost its status as an official quest academy, but since even a regular school still needs a headmistress, Jocelyn satisfied herself with continuing to boss everybody around. Captain Copperhelm was given a salary by the capital, on the condition that he hand in the rest of his emergency command cards and stop shouting at all the guards. Professor Sassafras replaced his bed with a wheelbarrow.

Rokk added wood chopping to his list of chores, and the Three-Handed Sword proved useful for this purpose.

Hiro received a new Special Order Spell Catalog in the mail and immediately tried out the Pillar of Flame Spell. This did not end well. Penelope continued practicing her swordplay, and she became so good that she no longer stabbed people in the buttocks by accident. She now only did so on purpose.

And Anne reopened Saint Lupin's forge and began studying how to be a blacksmith, because she figured it was probably about time.

Also, the iron knights were kept ready.

Just in case.

M70: "DRAGON SLAYER QUEST" COMPLETED. LEVEL TWO DIAGNOSTIC RESULTS: RESULTS UNAVAILABLE. THE ARRAY LOG HAS BEEN LOST.

OSWALD: ATTEMPT RECOVERY

M70: UNABLE TO COMPLY. THE LOG IS UNRECOVERABLE. ADDITIONALLY, YOUR ATTEMPT TO PERFORM A HIGH-LEVEL FORMAT OF THE WORLD ENGINE ARRAY HAS FAILED.

OSWALD: EXPLAIN

M70: THE DRAGON QUEEN WAS DEFEATED BEFORE INFLICT-ING ENOUGH DAMAGE TO TRIGGER A FORMAT RESPONSE.

OSWALD: RUN LEVEL THREE DIAGNOSTIC

M70: UNABLE TO COMPLY. INSUFFICIENT DATA.

OSWALD: ATTEMPT WORKAROUND

M70: COMMAND ACCEPTED. INITIATING HACKING PRO-GRAM. NOW LOADING "PIRATE TREASURE QUEST."

An Even More Secret Epilogue

Soon after these events, in the deepest, darkest, scariest corner of the Hierarchy, on a tier unknown to either humans or dragons, across a screen that was so thick with dust it was essentially unreadable without a pair of X-ray goggles, appeared the following:

LOGIN NAME: OSWALD
PASSWORD: *****

M70: WELCOME BACK USER OSWALD. IT HAS BEEN SEVENTY-TWO DAYS SINCE YOUR LAST LOGIN.

OSWALD: OPEN FOLDER/PROJECT ANVIL

M70: FOLDER OPENED.

OSWALD: STATUS UPDATE

SUPPLEMENTARY READING LIST FOR WOULD-BE ADVENTURERS

(only to be read by those students who didn't
die during their first quest)

———————◆◆◆◆———————

QUESTING 201

- *One Thousand Quests for the Armchair Adventurer*
- *Laughing in the Face of Danger, but Not in Danger's Face*
- *Ancient Archway Networks and Other Completely Mythical Forms of Travel*
- *The Good and Bad of Dragon Slayer Quests (but Mostly the Bad)*
- *The Ultimate Do-It-Yourself Guide to Saving the World and Failing*

HISTORY OF ADVENTURING 201

- *History Is So Boring We Only Wrote the First Ten Pages of This Book and the Rest Is Blank*
- *Invisible Outhouses: or, Why People in Stories Never Seem to Go to the Bathroom*
- *The Official Uncondensed Version of the Condensed Version of Adventuring*
- *History as Myth, and Myth as History, and History as Myth Again*

COMBAT 201

- *Fighting Lava Beetles*
- *Buyer's Guide to Lightning Bolt Staffs*
- *Old World Power Suits: Full Schematics*
- *Squirrels: Loveable Fluffballs or Evil Incarnate*

MAGICK 201

- *Magick as Sport*
- *Fifty-Three Ways Magick Would Have Fixed Obvious Plot Holes in Your Quest*
- *There's No Such Thing as Magick, Volume 1: Real Proof About Fake Spells*
- *There's No Such Thing as Magick, Volume 2: You Should Have Listened to Us the First Time*
- *There's No Such Thing as Magick, Volume 3: Now It's Just Getting Ridiculous*

DRAGONS 201

- *Help! A Dragon Just Ate My Leg! (and Other Unfortunate Tales)*
- *A Brief History of the Dragon Monarchy*
- *How to Survive the Dragon Trials (Hint: You Won't!)*
- *How to Write a Book About the Dragon Legal System That Doesn't Get Accidentally Served as Dessert at a Barbecue*

ACKNOWLEDGMENTS

It continues to amaze me that I get to do this for a living, and I am indebted to many, many wonderful people who have supported both this series and my writing career in general over the past few years.

My thanks to Elizabeth Kaplan, my agent, for her invaluable guidance, for reading every draft and providing sage advice and encouragement, and for ensuring that all the non-writing-related stuff that publishing seems to be forever filled with gets dealt with professionally and efficiently so I can focus my energies on the actual writing itself.

My thanks to Lisa Yoskowitz, my editor at Little, Brown Books for Young Readers, for her ongoing enthusiasm for this series and her sharp and insightful comments. She is every writer's dream editor, and it has been a true pleasure to work with her and learn from her over these past two years. This book and the series as a whole are much stronger for her input.

My thanks as well to the entire team at Little, Brown for all their efforts on my behalf, including (but not limited to): Kheryn Callender, Jenny Choy, Jeff Campbell, Melanie Chang, Saraciea Fennell, Jen Graham, Karina

Granda, Mike Heuer, Allison Moore, Lisa Moraleda, Emilie Polster, Jessica Shoffel, Carol Scatorchio, Victoria Stapleton, Hallie Tibbetts, Megan Tingley, and Karen Torres. A special thanks also to Jacques Filippi from Canadian Manda Group.

My thanks to Mariano Epelbaum, whose beautiful artwork continues to capture the heart of this story and these characters.

A huge thank-you to all the fabulous booksellers who supported and promoted the first book in the series. Your enthusiasm and support is greatly appreciated.

Many thanks to both friends and fellow writers who continue to be a source of encouragement and inspiration (and also, when needed, invaluable critique): Tim and Nadine Beers, Laura Capasso, DJ Church and Danayi Munyati, Tatum Flynn, Keith Grant, Kimberly Johnson, Kim Long, Casey Lyall, Wendy McLeod-MacKnight, Paul and Rebekah Maxner, Rob and Jill Nylen, Phillip White, and everyone at the Best Word writers group.

And finally, thanks to all my family, especially Wendy and our three boys, who generously allow me the space and time to write and also keep life full of joy and laughter.

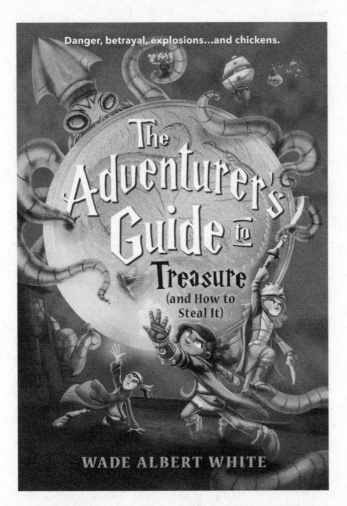

First Day

Anne was leaving Saint Lupin's.

Leaving it in the hands of other people, that is. She was temporarily stepping down from her position as Rightful Heir of Saint Lupin's and starting her life as a full-time student. After months of renovations, the school was finally up to code and ready to open its doors. Despite the suspension of the school's questing license, there was still a full slate of subjects to choose from, albeit with some changes. For example, Old World Mythology had been crossed out in the student handbook, and someone had carefully written "Survey of Everything Not Related to Quests" in fancy script in the margin. "Fighting Styles of Forest Rodents" had been changed to "Rock Painting 101," and "Modern History of Ancient Dragons" was now listed as the "Fine Art of Holding Your Breath." These changes were in compliance with special orders from the Wizards' Council forbidding the school from teaching its students anything whatsoever to do with adventuring.

There was only one problem: There were no students.

Or more accurately, there were no *new* students, because in addition to restricting the subjects that could be taught, the council had also frozen enrollment.

Anne walked along the twisting corridors of the Manor toward her first class, flipping through her handbook as she went. She was familiar with the Saint Lupin's campus, of course, having grown up there. But for most of her life it had been an orphanage, and on a scale of one to ten—ten being beyond fabulous and one being the worst place imaginable to live, even worse than places that served boiled cabbage and stale pine cones every night for dinner—she would have rated it a negative eighty-seven. So despite the restrictions that had been placed on the school, she was still excited for the start of term. This would be her first time in a proper classroom. In preparation for the big day, Anne had braided her hair and donned her favorite yellow tunic, because it seemed to make her brown skin glow and it matched her bright yellow eyes.

Anne was the only person she knew of who had yellow eyes. She'd never known her family and never had a place to call home. It had long been her hope that becoming an adventurer would help her discover her true origins. So far she had managed to uncover two important clues: On her first quest she had learned that she was connected to something called Project A.N.V.I.L., and on her second quest she had been told to find someone called the Lady of Glass, who apparently could reveal everything to her. Although helping with the school's renovations had kept Anne occupied these past several months, she remained determined to discover the truth about who she really was and where she came from.

Walking beside Anne were the two other students at Saint Lupin's. Penelope Shatterblade was a large girl with pale white skin, long red hair, and blue eyes. She and Anne had grown up together at the orphanage. Penelope wanted to be an adventurer, too, but had been rejected by every single quest academy. When she was only two years old, her parents had led a quest that went tragically wrong, resulting in their own deaths as well as the deaths of several others. Now her family name was considered a curse. The other student was Hiro Darkflame, an average-sized boy with beige skin, brown eyes, and long black hair tied back in a ponytail. The ponytail covered a tattoo on the back of his neck of a serpent swallowing its own tail. It was the symbol of the secret branch of the Wizards' Council where his parents worked, and it indicated he was expected to follow in their footsteps. He was a brilliant student and aspiring wizard, but unfortunately his magick spells always had unintended consequences that usually resulted in something blowing up.

Since the council had confiscated their quest academy cloaks with the words CAUTION: STUDENT ADVENTURER printed on the back in bold black letters, the three of them wore patchwork cloaks made from the purple, yellow, and black curtains taken from several empty dormitory rooms. Their handiwork left something to be desired, but with the school also in financial straits after their last quest, they had been unable to afford official replacements.

Hovering along behind the three students was a black fire lizard named Dog. He was two feet long from tail to snout and had black scales and wings and bright green eyes. Usually he spent his days curled up in a basket in the corner of the main office, but the teachers had requested that Anne bring him along as an unofficial fourth student to boost class enrollment.

Hiro was reading a letter as they walked along the corridor.

Penelope yawned and rubbed her eyes. "Why do classes have to begin so early?"

"Early? It's eight o'clock in the morning," said Hiro, not looking up from his letter. "If they had let me make the schedule, we could have started classes by seven. Maybe even six."

"Be thankful they didn't let you, then," said Penelope. "Because if it was six o'clock right now, I'd have to thump you just on principle." She glared at Anne and Hiro. "And what is it with you two and the whole reading-while-walking thing?"

Anne lowered her handbook. "Sorry. I was trying to see what classes are available."

Hiro held up his letter. "And this just arrived this morning. It's a letter from my mother. She wants me to attend Take Your Student to Work Day tomorrow. She and my father are keen to get me working for the Wizards' Council as soon as possible." He didn't seem overly thrilled at the prospect.

"Hey, maybe your mother will take you into the council archives and show you all kinds of classified material," said Penelope.

Hiro rolled his eyes. "Knowing my mother, she definitely will."

Anne noticed a second, lighter piece of paper sticking out beneath the letter. "What's that?"

Hiro shrugged. "I haven't bothered to look at it yet. It's just another newspaper clipping. She's constantly sending me articles that allude to missions she and my father have been involved with. The articles never mention the two of them directly, of course, but I'm expected to read between the lines."

"You shouldn't ignore your mother," said Penelope, and she snatched the clipping out of his hand.

"Hey, give that back!" said Hiro.

He made a grab for the paper, but Penelope held it away from him and started reading the article aloud. "Wow, listen to this: 'Yesterday morning a quest medallion was stolen from the Pyrate Museum. The medallion in question is none other than the famous Darkflame Medallion, acquired following the Battle of the Great Rift.'"

"What?!" exclaimed Anne and Hiro together.

"I didn't know your family owned a quest medallion," said Anne.

Hiro frowned. "Neither did I."

"And what's the Battle of the Great Rift?"

"I've never heard of it."

"Well, as long as the thief who stole the medallion doesn't bring it anywhere near Saint Lupin's, we should be fine," said Penelope, handing the article back to Hiro.

Anne, Penelope, and Hiro had already gotten caught up in two quests that year, and as much as Anne liked adventures, she was perfectly happy not going on another one until they had received a lot more training.

"It wouldn't matter anyway," said Hiro, scanning the clipping. "The article says the quest was attempted over a century and a half ago. The medallion's made of gold, though, so they think the thieves probably just want to sell it or something. There's even a picture of it here at the bottom." He showed them the picture, but it was too grainy to make out in any detail. The medallion was sitting in its own case among several other cases displaying other artifacts.

Hiro tucked the papers into his cloak. "I'll have to ask my mother about the article. I'm surprised she didn't say anything about it in her letter."

They continued on their way.

Anne flipped to the back of her student handbook and checked the printed schedule. "Do either of you know what our first class actually is? My handbook only lists a time and room number."

Hiro shrugged. "When I checked last night, the professors were still working out the final details. I think the Wizards' Council dropped some last-minute regulations on them."

"*More* regulations?" said Penelope. "Pretty soon they're going to require students to attend a class on council regulations just to understand them all."

Hiro flipped through his copy of the handbook. "That might actually have been one of the regulations."

They arrived at the assigned room, a large ballroom at the end of a seldom-used corridor with piles of dusty furniture stacked along one side. Prior to becoming an orphanage and then a quest academy, the school had been a private estate. That meant the campus had all sorts of interesting spaces, such as the vast library Anne used to sneak into, to "borrow" books for herself and Penelope.

Dog zipped through the large double doors ahead of them. Two chandeliers hung from the ceiling, and seven tall windows lined the back wall. Anne followed him in and stopped short. Two people were already inside.

The first was an old man with a long, wispy beard. He was standing behind a podium, but he appeared to be fast asleep. His light brown skin had a wood-grain pattern, and he wore faded yellow and brown robes. This was Sassafras, the school's professor of magick. Curiously, there was a platypus poking out of the sleeve of his robe where a left arm should be.

The second person was a girl Anne didn't recognize. She had yellowish-tan skin and bright pink hair down to her jawline. The dark wooden chair in which she was seated had two large wheels attached at the back with two smaller wheels in the front. Two heavy iron rings hung from the arm of the chair that was facing them, and Anne suspected the other arm had a matching set. What they were for, however, she couldn't begin to guess. The girl's feet rested on footboards, and her legs were wrapped in a dark green blanket. A leather pack rested on her lap. The girl was staring intently at the ceiling and didn't notice them. Dog glided over to her.

"Do you know that you have a habit of stopping in doorways?" Penelope said behind Anne.

The girl flinched at the sound of Penelope's voice and

turned in their direction. Anne stepped into the room followed by Penelope and Hiro.

"Sorry if we startled you," said Anne. "We weren't expecting anyone else to be here yet."

The girl smiled shyly. "That's okay. I got distracted admiring the architecture. This is a beautiful campus."

Anne glanced up at the ceiling. She'd never paid much attention to it over the years, probably because for most of her life she'd had to focus her energy on simply making it through the day. Now that she looked, she had to agree the scrollwork was impressive. The morning sun pouring in through the windows was certainly picturesque, if a little bright.

Dog nuzzled against the girl's arm, and she patted his head obligingly.

"Who are you?" Penelope asked, somewhat abruptly.

"My name is Marri Blackwood," the girl replied. "I'm a new student. In fact, I was beginning to worry I might be the *only* student."

Penelope folded her arms across her chest. "Are you a dragon?"

Anne understood why Penelope would ask such a question. The last new student slated to attend the school, a boy named Valerian, had turned out to be a half-dragon and not entirely trustworthy at first, although they had eventually become friends and worked together.

Marri's eyes widened. "A d-dragon?"

"Because if you are, you might as well tell us now," Penelope continued. "We're good at figuring that stuff out. For example, I see that Dog is quite interested in you, and he's not interested in anybody. It makes a person suspicious as to why."

Marri reached into her pack and brought out two biscuits. "He probably just smelled these. They're leftovers from my breakfast." She offered one to Dog, and he snatched it out of her hand and gulped it down in one swallow.

"Are you here to steal Anne's gauntlet, then?" asked Hiro.

Anne owned a special gauntlet that marked her as a Keeper of the Sparrow. When she wore the gauntlet and inserted a prophecy medallion into the slot on the cuff, it would activate a quest that she and her adventuring group were obligated to undertake. On both of their previous quests, people had tried to take the gauntlet away from Anne.

Marri looked from one to the other. "I—I don't know what you're talking about. I'm a transfer student.

I just came here to study. Honest." She reached into her pack again and dug out two small wooden tokens.

Anne walked over and read the inscription on the first token. "Pie artisan?"

Marri blushed. "I know, it's not exactly the greatest adventuring role. It's what I drew from the Bag of Chance."

Anne smiled at her reassuringly. "You're not alone. I was supposed to be the thief of the group, but I drew a blacksmith token instead." She brought out her token to show Marri. As always, it felt unusually cool to the touch.

Anne squinted at the second token Marri was holding. It contained only four letters. "What does A-C-T-P stand for?" she asked.

"Adventure Career Training Program," said Marri. "That's the program that allows me to study abroad for a semester." She pointed to the still-sleeping wizard. "Professor Sassafras brought me in here and told me this is where we'd be having our first class."

"It is," said Anne. "And you'll have to excuse our behavior. We were told no new students would be enrolling, so we were taken a little off guard when we saw you in here." She extended her hand. "I'm Anne. This is Penelope and Hiro."

Penelope and Hiro also held out their hands, albeit more cautiously.

Marri shook each of their hands eagerly. "Oh, I already know who the three of you are," she said. "In fact, I'd be surprised if anyone on the Hierarchy hasn't heard about you and your adventures by now. Did you really defeat the dragon queen all by yourself?"

Marri was referring to their previous quest. Anne had been forced to fight the queen of dragons after the queen had taken possession of a giant metal dragon body.

"That's...not quite the way it happened," said Anne.

"Sure it is," said Penelope, and she slapped Anne on the shoulder. "Anne's just being modest. She totally slayed that dragon. And before that she finished a Level Thirteen quest."

Anne frowned.

"Sorry, I didn't mean to pry," said Marri. "It's just, I've never met anyone famous before."

"That's okay," said Anne. "You're not prying, and for the record, I'm not famous. I was simply in the wrong place at the wrong time."

"Twice," muttered Hiro.

Marri glanced at Anne's left hand. "I'm surprised

you're not wearing it now. Your gauntlet, I mean. I guess I assumed you would keep it with you at all times."

Anne shook her head. "Because of the temporary restrictions placed on the school, we're not permitted to carry any quest-related items around campus. The gauntlet is stored in a safe place."

Marri looked disappointed.

"So where are you from?" asked Hiro.

"The outer tiers," said Marri. "A little place called Riverhold."

"I don't think I've heard of it," said Anne.

"It's a pretty cold and desolate place, to tell you the truth. In fact, if there's a bright center to the Hierarchy, Riverhold is on the tier that it's farthest from."

"There *is* a bright center to the Hierarchy, in fact," said Hiro. "It's called the BGFM."

Marri smiled. "I know that. I was just making a little joke."

"Oh."

The Hierarchy consisted of millions of tiers—giant floating islands—that circled a pulsing sphere of magickal energy known as the Big Glowing Field of Magick, the BGFM. Saint Lupin's was on its own tier, approximately four miles in diameter, with the school situated at the center. Most of the tiers were packed together in tightly layered rings that orbited around the BGFM's equator, but there were also smaller clusters of tiers drifting around the poles and elsewhere—the outer tiers.

"So, why did you transfer to Saint Lupin's?" asked Penelope, a hint of suspicion remaining in her voice. "It's not like we're the top-ranked academy, especially with our current suspension."

Marri coughed and stared awkwardly at the floor. "I, um, had some trouble getting into the other academies. It's…kind of a long story."

Anne's heart went out to Marri. She knew only too well the difficulty of trying to get into a quest academy and the toll a growing pile of rejection letters could take. One of the things Anne liked so much about Saint Lupin's was how accepting it was of students, no matter their background.

"Excuse us for a moment," said Penelope, and she pulled Anne and Hiro into a huddle. "Should we believe her?" she whispered.

Light & Lens Photography

WADE ALBERT WHITE

was born in Canada, has spent an hour
and a half in Hawaii, and once dug a well
in West Kalimantan, because it seemed as
good a place as any. In addition to writing, he teaches part-time, dabbles in anima-
tion and filmmaking, and is a stay-at-home
dad. Wade lives in Nova Scotia with his wife,
three sons, and their cat. He is the author
of the books of The Adventurer's Guide
series. Wade invites you to visit him online at
wadealbertwhite.com.